# Tranquility  Falls

Center Point
Large Print

Also by Davis Bunn and available from
Center Point Large Print:

*The Domino Effect*
*Firefly Cove*
*Moondust Lake*
*Outbreak*
*Unscripted*

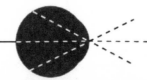

**This Large Print Book carries the
Seal of Approval of N.A.V.H.**

# DAVIS BUNN

# Tranquility Falls

CENTER POINT LARGE PRINT
THORNDIKE, MAINE

This Center Point Large Print edition
is published in the year 2020 by arrangement with
Kensington Publishing Corp.

The text of this Large Print edition is unabridged.
In other aspects, this book may vary
from the original edition.
Printed in the United States of America
on permanent paper.
Set in 16-point Times New Roman type.

ISBN: 978-1-64358-619-9

The Library of Congress has cataloged this record under
Library of Congress Control Number: 2020932640

# CHAPTER 1

Daniel sat in his usual place at the back of the classroom. The church basement was frigid, which suited newcomers sweating off a hard night or facing the thought of another sober day. Daniel rarely made more than two AA meetings a week. But this one, today of all days, he never missed. He considered it an annual ritual, starting this day here, marking another year clean and sober. Such small triumphs were a huge part of his new world.

Maintaining his normal calm was harder today. Added to the prospect of what lay ahead was the text Daniel had just received from his sister. He had not heard from Lisa in over a year. Her message simply read that she was arriving in a half hour and they had to meet. Immediately. Which left Daniel worried that Lisa wanted to join him for this annual ritual. The prospect had him sweating as hard as the newcomers.

When the meeting broke up, a woman seated around the curve of chairs made a beeline straight for him. It didn't happen so often anymore. Four years out of the limelight was an eternity in the world of television stardom. Daniel watched her approach and mentally retreated into his safe little shell. No matter what she said or how she came on to him, he would stay shielded.

Only this time his friend and former sponsor was there to block the lady's arrival. "You're new, aren't you?" Travis was African American, six years older than Daniel's thirty-five, and a former linebacker with the LA Rams. When his knee went out, Travis had discovered the glory of combining prescription painkillers with sour mash. He'd been clean for nine years and counting. "Can I help you with something?"

"I just want to speak with—"

"We don't do that here." Travis held up a hand wide as a shovel. "Anonymous means exactly what it says on the sign out front."

But addicts were not people who were big on restraint. Obsessive behavior was part of their personality. The woman tried to shoulder past him. She might as well have tried to move the church off its foundation. "I'm not going to *bother* him."

"That's right, you're not." Gentle as he could, Travis spun her about. "Coffee and doughnuts are to your right, and the exit's to your left. Those are your only choices."

"But—"

"You have yourself a good and sober day, now." When he was certain the woman was well

6

and truly gone, Travis turned around and asked, "You okay?"

"Never better." Which was at least partly the truth. "You?"

"I'm not the one looking at another visit to the Ninth Step." He referred to the ninth stage of AA sobriety, making peace with past mistakes and the people who littered that dark road. Travis gave him a moment to respond, then asked, "You ready to head on out?"

Today would mark the fourth time Travis had made the journey. Daniel replied, "You don't need to come. Goldie's waiting in the car." Goldie, his dog, had been found in the local rescue shelter, the name stamped on a tattered collar. Kimberly, his late fiancée, had gone with a friend who was looking for a pet. But Kimberly was the one who had come home with Goldie. Four weeks later, Kimberly was gone.

"Dog or no dog, I'm not letting you do this on your own." As they started toward the exit, Travis said, "There's this lady, she works for Miramar Township. I'm telling you, man, the lady is a definite ten. Ricki wants to get you two together." Ricki was Travis's wife, and a mover and shaker in the Miramar community. "The lady's been divorced for seven years, almost as lonely as you."

"Today's not a good time."

But Travis blocked that easily enough. "Ricki's

outside waiting. You'll need to tell her that yourself. If you dare."

When Daniel stepped through the church doors, Ricki stood by his pickup, chatting happily with one of the church staffers. Goldie had managed to slip through the truck's partially opened window and sat contentedly by Ricki's feet. Daniel said, "Handle this blind date thing for me, I'll owe you big-time."

Travis grinned in response. "Not a chance in the whole wide world."

"Isn't that what sponsors do? Handle?"

"Best you not suggest to Ricki that her wanting to hook you up with a friend threatens your walk down the straight and narrow. Ricki might see that as a good reason to go ballistic."

As soon as she spotted Daniel, she hugged the woman and hurried over. "Did Travis tell you about my friend?"

"Today's not a good—"

"I'm telling you the same thing I did my man when he tried that line on me this morning." Ricki was a statuesque beauty in her late thirties. She was tall and sloe-eyed and had run hurdles and relay for the US Olympic team. When Travis had been at his weakest, Ricki had stood by him and given him a reason to crawl out of that dark cave. "It's time you woke up."

Travis stepped around to stand beside his wife.

8

He made Ricki look as small as a porcelain ballerina. "Might as well go with it, my man. Treat it like a trip to the dentist."

Ricki looked up at her husband. "Did those words actually come out of your mouth?"

But Travis wasn't done. "Fighting just don't do a thing but prolong the misery."

"Oh, you." Ricki gripped her husband's arm and swung it back and forth. It was like tugging on a tree trunk. "I'm telling you what's the truth. It's time you returned to life."

"Girl, do you even hear yourself?" Travis tried to reclaim his arm, but Ricki refused to let go. "The man is about to go visit the grave of his one true love, and you're hooking him up with another lady."

"That's exactly what I'm doing." Ricki kept swinging her man's arm.

"Look at him. The man is not interested."

"That's because Daniel hasn't met her yet."

Travis shook his head. "Like a dog with a bone."

"Only because I'm right, and you two know it." She glared at Daniel. "You just wait 'til Chloe hears how you're acting."

Chloe was their teenage daughter. She was strong and beautiful, like her parents, and considered Miramar to be the most boring place on the planet. Forcing her to live there was all the justification Chloe needed for being perpetually sullen. Daniel said, "I have to go."

"You're coming over for dinner tonight," Ricki said. "That's not an invitation, it's an order."

Up until that moment, Goldie had been tracking the conversation as though she understood every word. Labradoodles were known as the smartest breed going, though they were not officially a breed at all. Daniel was amazed at the number of people who felt it was their duty to stop him on the street and lecture him about his dog, like the two of them couldn't possibly survive without some additional fact or criticism. It was usually an older person, somebody who had been born cranky, who'd spent years waiting for the chance to poke him in the chest and tell him how fortunate he was, or what a travesty of a dog Goldie was, something. All he could say for certain was, Goldie had seen him through some very rough times and in the process had become his best friend.

Goldie chose that moment to swivel about, inspect the empty street, and give a soft whoof.

Daniel had long come to trust the instincts of his almost silent dog. He was about to ask what it was when he heard it too.

So did Ricki. "What is that?"

Travis smiled at Daniel. "Sounds to me like the bad old days."

Then the silver-gray rocket appeared at the road's far end, downshifted, and blasted around the corner, doing maybe eighty miles an hour but handling the curve like it was planted on rails.

"Yep," Travis said. "All the trouble that money can buy."

The Ferrari GTC Tourer had cost a cool quarter mil. It possessed a five-liter twin turbo that produced twice the horsepower of an Escalade but weighed about as much as Daniel's right front tire. Thankfully, its acceleration was matched by four ceramic brakes as large as serving platters. Lisa sprang from the car the instant it halted. His sister's energy had always amazed Daniel. She raced through each day with lightning speed, chattering a million miles a minute, sparking the world with her runway smile. The light in her eyes was positively magnetic. She had been drawing male moths to her flame since before she could walk. Their mother had liked to tell people what a trial it had been taking the infant Lisa to the supermarket, how strangers would follow them around, wanting to touch or hold or coo over the incredible baby with the magnetic glow. Daniel was more like their father, a placid and scholarly gentleman who had been great with numbers. Lisa was more like . . .

No one, really.

Their mother had called Lisa her changeling, and had not always meant it in a positive manner. Lisa had learned early on how to shape her energy and her beauty to fit the moment. She'd started modeling at fourteen. Nowadays she lived by the principle that the world could be molded to suit her mood. Daniel thought she played at life like an electric butterfly, flittering from one experience to the next. Her one constant was Marvin, a Jewish entertainment lawyer who endured Lisa's mercurial ways with stolid good cheer. Marvin loved Lisa enough to accept that she would never change. She in turn remained with Marvin. Their friends said it was as close to a perfect marriage as LA allowed.

There were two distinct downsides to Lisa, two elements that marred the oh-so-perfect image she showed the world.

One was her rage. It did not surface very often, but when it did, Lisa treated the world to a scorched-earth policy.

The other issue was Nicole, their daughter. Mother and daughter had a relationship that could best be described as molten. Daniel's niece basically had nothing whatsoever in common with her mother. Nicole was by no means unattractive. She was simply not in Lisa's league. Nicole was placid and reserved and watchful. The people who populated Lisa's world tended to dismiss Nicole with an empty smile. Nicole, in turn, thought they were Hollywood dodos and not worth the space they occupied.

Daniel had not seen his niece or her mother in four years, since the day Lisa had banned him from ever communicating with her or her family. Another sample of his sister in a rage.

When Lisa sprang from the car, the word that came to Daniel's mind was *incandescent*. She did not speak. Nor did she actually look at anyone directly until Goldie greeted her with a cautious whoof. Then Lisa wheeled about and glared at the dog with such intensity, Goldie backed up between Daniel's legs and cowered.

Which gave Nicole time to get out of the car, race around, and hide behind Daniel and his dog.

Lisa proceeded to open the Ferrari's minuscule trunk and dump an amazing amount of clothes and gear on the sidewalk by his feet. It was like watching a clown act at the circus, twelve jesters tumbling out of a car the size of a tuna can. Clothes and teen cosmetics and laptop and phone and shoes and schoolbooks and two satchels and more clothes.

Finally, Lisa slammed the trunk shut and stormed over to Daniel. He could feel Nicole take a two-fisted grip on the back of his shirt and hated how she crouched in genuine terror. From her *mother*.

Electric friction turned Lisa's white-gold hair into a witch's hat. "You owe me."

Daniel nodded. That much was certainly true. "Lisa, you're scaring your daughter."

His sister gave off a cackle that Daniel thought

came straight from the *Night of the Valkyries*. "She's lucky she's not *dead*."

Without another word, his sister wheeled about and headed back for the car.

"Wait. Where are you going?"

She paused long enough to shoot another laser-guided bomb, this one directed at her daughter. "To try and save my marriage."

No one moved until the Ferrari vanished from sight. Lisa's rage was that strong.

# CHAPTER 2

As Lisa's car whined into the far distance, Daniel heard the sound of quiet snuffling. He turned around and saw Nicole struggling to hide her sobs.

Daniel was still searching for the right response when Ricki wrapped her arms around the girl and said, "We got you, honey."

"It wasn't my fault," Nicole said.

"Of course not. And even if it was, your mama has no right—"

"All I did was have a gene test."

Travis asked Daniel, "Say what?"

The day flashed into clarity, like a broken lens knitting itself back together. Daniel said, "Nicole has insisted for years that Marvin isn't her dad."

The two of them, Travis and Ricki, would have made a comic pair if the moment had not been so serious. Two strong and intelligent people reduced to standing there in slack-faced shock, their mouths twin round O's.

"I called the hotline of that website," Nicole said.

"Ancestry.com," Daniel said.

"No. The other one. Twenty-Three and Me. They sent me the sample kits." She turned slightly, not exactly a shrug, but enough for Ricki to release her. "I knew I was right. And now I have proof."

Travis studied the sky, the pavement, the parking lot. Daniel said, "So you told them, and now you're—"

"Why don't you two just get on down the road," Ricki fastened a hand on Nicole's shoulder, her tone sharp. "Let us get on with living."

"I just said—"

"I know what you were saying, and I know what you were thinking, and I don't know which is worse." Ricki fastened a hand on Nicole's shoulder and steered her around. "When was the last time you had something to eat, child?"

"I don't know." The sniffles returned. "Yesterday, I guess."

"You like pancakes? Of course you do. You just come with me." Ricki glared at the two men. "Don't y'all have someplace better to be?"

Daniel watched them walk away. "When did I become the bad guy in all this?"

Travis was already gathering a load of Nicole's gear. "Sometimes you just got to accept that all the world's problems are your fault. Come on, let's get ourselves gone."

On the three previous anniversaries, Travis had insisted on driving them in his Escalade. Daniel's

16

F150 twin cab had more than enough room, even for Travis. But Daniel's former AA sponsor liked to be in control for this particular jaunt. His aim was to get Daniel there and back, safe and sober. Let his pal know Daniel didn't face this alone. Even if he thought Daniel was just adding to the list that no longer existed. The one that was headed Reasons to Go Get Wasted.

But today Ricki had their SUV and was off doing whatever it took to convince Nicole that she had not single-handedly tossed a grenade into her mother's version of happy-ever-after.

As soon as Daniel pulled into the cemetery's main lot, Goldie poked her head between them, gave a single whoof, then started scratching at the rear door. Which was amazing. They only came here once each year. And Goldie had only been six months old when the accident had claimed Daniel's fiancée. But every year it was the same. As soon as the cemetery came into view, Goldie was frantic to get out there. He cut the motor and watched Goldie fit her entire body through five inches of open window.

Goldie leapt from the car and shot down the path rimmed by Monterey cypress. But Daniel did not move. Not yet. Travis had a spiel he used to start every lecture about staying clean and sober. It began with how guilt would kill a guy faster than a Glock.

Only today was different.

Travis cleared his throat, tapped his fingers nervously against the side window, and said, "About what we were just talking about."

Daniel assumed he meant Nicole, which seemed an odd thing to bring up now. But Daniel's attention remained mostly elsewhere. The wind was up, blowing off the ocean strong enough for the tree limbs to wave like beckoning hands.

Travis went on, "Maybe it's time for you to wake up, like the lady said."

That turned him around. "You really think this is the place and time for us to be having that conversation?"

Travis shrugged. "To tell the truth, I'm thinking maybe Ricki doesn't have it wrong. What if it's time to get back into the big world?"

Daniel studied his friend. The man who had stared down the world's most fearsome offensive linesmen actually looked worried. "Tell me what's going on, Travis."

He sighed. "Ricki's friend is concerned there might be money missing from the city's accounts." Travis had been born in Nashville and raised there until his massive build and his speed brought him to the attention of university scouts. His native down-home roots tended to come out when he was stressed. Like now. "She and Ricki have been worrying over this for two, maybe three months now."

Ricki had served two terms on the city council. That was back before Chloe, their daughter, turned into a full-time occupation. "Why don't they take it to the police?"

"This is where things get complicated."

"What were they before?"

"The lady claims the way things are structured, it looks like she's been the one with her fingers in the till." Travis swiped his face with one massive hand. "Ricki got worried enough, she tried to bring in an outside accountant and got shut down."

"Who could do that?"

"The mayor. Her office, anyway. Said it was none of Ricki's business, and everything was fine, like that." Travis gave him a look that came as close to fear as Daniel had ever seen. "We're talking over seven million dollars. This is bound to come to light. Ricki is up nights, worrying the real thieves have set up her friend to take the fall."

Daniel was tempted to open his door and start down the path. But he remained where he was, staring out the front windscreen. If he didn't shut this down now, Travis would start in on him again when he returned from the grave site. When he was too weak to resist.

The emerald lawn to either side of the central lane was dotted with headstones and regret. Daniel knew exactly what Travis had not said.

That his past life had made him the perfect guy to dive into the hidden numbers and find out what was going on. But that man had died in the accident, along with his fiancée. Daniel was a different person now. He lived a simple life. He stayed clean. He took one day at a time. No matter what Travis might say once he returned to the truck, Daniel's answer would not change. Those days were over and done for good.

# CHAPTER 3

Stella's day began by breaking the contract she thought she had signed with fate. This one day it was guaranteed to rain. Even during California's three-year drought, it had rained each time this horrible anniversary crept into view. Seven years and counting, she had been able to set her calendar by the fact that a deluge would greet her that particular morning.

This year should have been no different. It had rained steadily for two weeks. Last night, the weatherman had offered dire warnings of floods, mudslides, lightning, hail, everything but an invasion of locusts. Which was why Stella had slept as well as she had. She knew it was silly. She could tell herself that she was acting like a superstitious ninny all the other days of the year. But this morning, she needed rain and the simple assurance that this one thing would go her way.

Only she woke to a blade of sunlight slicing through her bedroom window.

Amber, her eleven-year-old daughter, bounded into the room and shouted, "It's sunny!"

Stella rolled over. "They said it was going to rain."

"It's not raining now!"

"Bad storm, that's what the weatherman said." She settled the pillow on top of her head. "Stay inside. Lock your doors. Don't even think of going anywhere."

Amber plucked the pillow away. "Which is why we have to go *now!*"

Stella squinted against the light. Her daughter was impossibly excited. "Honey—"

Amber responded with an exact duplicate of her late grandmother's favorite reaction. Amber's arm cocked at a ninety-degree angle, the hand tilted so far back it almost faced the ceiling. Her voice turned sharp. "Don't you even *think* of giving me lip."

Which was good for a smile. Any day but today. "Go turn on the coffee. That's a dear."

They drove through brilliant sunlight, as if the day was determined to challenge her right to be sad.

"There it is, Mommy. On the right."

"I know, dear." But truth be told, Stella would have driven right past it if Amber had not spoken. She parked in front of the florist, cut the motor, and took a hard breath. One of many.

But as she reached for the door, Amber announced, "I want to do it, Mommy."

"What, alone?"

She nodded. "Please?"

Truth be told, Stella had no interest in going inside, enduring the florist's shared sorrow. They had been friends since forever, and the florist knew everything there was worth knowing about today. Stella reached in her purse and pulled a bill from her wallet. "You know what to buy?"

"Of course, Mommy. I'm not a child."

That was hardly a reason to get teary-eyed. But still. Stella could not quite focus on her daughter as she scampered down the sidewalk.

Now that she was alone, Stella felt her mind settle into a discordant drone. Eventually, Amber emerged from the shop, holding the bouquet with both hands. The Peruvian lilies formed a pastel rainbow as she hurried back. They had been her late daughter's favorite flower. For the six long weeks of basically living inside Jenny's hospital room, buying these flowers had been a daily event. Now every time she saw them, she was drawn straight back to the moment she had laid the bouquet on her daughter's casket.

The florist was a slender man in his late fifties. He followed Amber from the shop and called something to Stella, the words lost to the buzzing in her head. Stella leaned and pushed open Amber's door. She heard herself say, "Those are lovely."

"Freddie let me choose them myself."

Stella waited while her daughter fastened her-

23

self into the child seat, exchanged waves with Freddie, and drove away. Around them, Miramar sparkled like a town-sized jewel. The day's colors were impossibly brilliant. Coral and jade and emerald and . . .

Amber asked, "Did Daddy leave because of me?"

Stella found herself shocked out of her mental drone. All the anniversaries of Jenny's death followed the same leaden path. Amber asked about the sister she remembered mostly from photographs and bedtime chats. She focused her questions on the early days, those lighthearted months before Jenny's illness was diagnosed. Back when Stella was mother to two amazingly beautiful twin daughters. Amber liked to hear stories from that time. Like how she and her sister spent hours together, long before either of them had learned to talk, chattering and laughing and singing. Like they had shared a secret language. Like they understood precisely what the other said. Like their infancy was reason for hilarity. Like the good times would last forever.

Not once in seven anniversaries had Amber asked about her absent father. "What, darling?"

The look Amber gave her silenced the buzz entirely. Her daughter was rarely sad or down. Now she seemed to be both. Her liquid gaze held an ancient's burden. "Something Daddy told me last time he called."

Stella felt the old wrath rekindle from the ashes. "What did Ben say, honey?"

"I asked him why he didn't come see me. He said he looked at me and saw the one who would never grow up."

Her ex was too low a life form to murder, tempting as it was. Stella took another of the day's hard breaths and replied with a calm assurance that amazed her. "Your father left because he felt our family was too full of sorrow. He said he could not go on with us. I disagree totally. I think we would have become whole again much more swiftly if we had stayed together. I think our love would have healed us. But Ben didn't agree, and so he left. But he loves you very much, sweetheart. That is what you must always remember."

Amber was satisfied enough to turn toward the window and hum softly. Stella waited a few moments, until she was certain her daughter was not watching, and swiftly wiped her face. She continued the dialogue in her head, saying the things she would never repeat to Amber. After Jenny's death, during the hours when Ben's wife and remaining daughter most needed his strength and support and comfort and love, he wrapped himself in a gray mantle of drunken self-pity and retreated into a dark abyss of his own making.

When Ben finally declared that he was leaving, Stella had responded with, "I thought you already had."

# CHAPTER 4

The Miramar cemetery rested on a lonely bluff north of town. On the clearest days, like now, the cliffside walk became a place to stroll and commune with all those beyond reach. To the south, Miramar Bay greeted the shimmering Pacific. Stella parked facing the cemetery and the day. In front of her stretched three rows of ancient cypress. A strong wind blew off the ocean, spicing the air with a force that seemed determined to lift her spirits. The swaying trees cut sharp-edged shadows, as if seeking to unfetter the graves and lift their company into the racing clouds.

Stella was still working on what else she should say about her ex-husband, when Amber exclaimed, "Look at that, Mommy!"

A golden head poked through the window of a large pickup parked two rows up. The dog barked once and struggled through the partially opened window. Finally, the animal leapt out and bounded down the cemetery's central lane. When it reached the path running parallel to the cliff, it scampered straight toward Jenny's grave.

Her daughter moved almost as fast as the dog.

She unclipped herself from the child seat, opened her door, and raced away.

Stella stuck her head out the window and called, "Amber, wait for me!"

Daniel walked the central path alone. He watched a woman run ahead of him and had to assume it was the young girl's mother. The one who had followed Goldie into the cemetery. An impatient breeze turned the trees into a nervous green veil. Daniel tried to tell himself there was no need to feel so apprehensive. But the years could never erase the burden of unease as he approached Kimberly's grave. And guilt, of course. Deservedly so. As he rounded the corner, his heart pounded like it was determined to burst from his chest.

As with every visit, Goldie lay on her belly upon the grave. Daniel had no idea how the dog could remain so connected to a woman she had known for just six short weeks. He assumed it was some form of synergy, Goldie taking on as much of Daniel's remorse as a dog possibly could, doing what Daniel secretly did in his heart—prostrating himself over the ashes of all that might have been.

Only today a young girl knelt beside the dog.

She stroked Goldie's pelt, so fascinated she did not even glance up as Daniel squatted on the dog's other side. He was very conscious of

27

the mother who hovered just behind the girl, watching the scene with genuine unease.

She was a lovely child, with copper-blond hair and a spray of pale freckles. Then she lifted her gaze, and Daniel peered into eyes more gray than blue, like morning light seen through an ocean mist.

"She's so beautiful," the girl said. "Is she yours?"

Three minutes later, Daniel accompanied the mother and daughter across the cemetery. Or rather, he followed his dog. Goldie had firmly attached herself to Amber's side. Which was astonishing. Goldie was not unfriendly. She simply took her time, not so much hostile as cautious and watchful. Sometimes for months.

Not today.

Goldie did not so much walk as gambol while the girl chatted softly and stroked her pelt whenever she came within reach, like two old friends strolling through the park, rather than following the cliffside path from one grave to another.

The woman spoke for the first time. "Well, isn't this awkward."

"I was thinking the very same thing."

"Were you?" She smiled, or tried to. "I'm Stella. And the jumping bean up ahead there is Amber."

"Daniel. I'd say it's a pleasure to meet you both. And it is. Except . . ."

"For how we're here to mark the anniversary of my other child's death." Stella softly slapped her fingers against her lips. "I can't believe I said that. I never speak about it."

He nodded. That was certainly something he could understand. "How long . . . ?"

"Seven years." She pointed at the child rushing on ahead. "Jenny was Amber's twin sister."

"I am so very sorry for your loss."

She must have caught an element of his own shared remorse, for she asked, "And you're here because . . ."

"My fiancée died four years ago today."

"Oh, my."

They stopped before a grave. The headstone was a simple wedge of dark granite, the child's name embossed in copper. DEAREST JENNY.

Beneath this, instead of dates, were the words TOO SOON.

Goldie planted herself on the grass, just as she always did on Kimberly's grave. Daniel watched as Amber knelt beside the dog and spoke softly, stroking her pelt and pointing at the gravestone. He knew Stella was fighting for control and did the only thing that seemed right at the time, which was to settle his hand upon her shoulder.

Amber looked up and exclaimed, "Mommy, we left the flowers in the car!"

It seemed the most natural thing in the world. Walking over and offering the child the bouquet he had neglected to leave with Kimberly. "Why don't you use mine?"

# CHAPTER 5

It was mid-afternoon before Ricki called to say she was bringing Nicole over. After returning from the cemetery, Daniel did a bachelor's job of cleaning the house and preparing the home's guest room. The second bedroom had not been used in four years. Daniel's only relatives were all back on the East Coast, and they were not close. He no longer had contact with any of his LA crowd. In the beginning, Daniel had maintained a clean break from the man he had been before. It was the only way he could do what he most wanted—staying clean and sober. Now it was hard to say what was habit and what was still necessary. Which was one reason Ricki's invitation felt so threatening. Meeting a woman meant testing his boundaries. The prospect terrified him.

Goldie gave another of her soft whoofs a few minutes before Ricki pulled into the drive. When he hesitated to open his front door, Goldie looked up and tapped the wood with one paw.

As Nicole rose slowly from the car, Goldie rushed over and nuzzled the girl's hand. Another astonishment. Today his normally shy dog was three for three, making friends with Amber and Stella and now welcoming Daniel's first house-guest in four years.

Daniel was uncertain how to welcome his niece. He had no experience with children of any age. He had not seen Nicole since his sister had expelled him from their lives, which had happened a week after Kimberly's funeral.

Nicole stood by the SUV and studied everything with an uncertain air. Ricki moved around the vehicle, draped a hand over Nicole's shoulders, and led her up the walk. As they approached, Daniel saw the tracks of recent tears on Nicole's cheeks.

He came close to hating his sister at that moment. But all he said was, "Welcome to your new home."

Ricki showed Nicole to the guest room while Daniel unloaded the pickup's rear hold. Seeing the young woman's belongings tossed in a heap inside the vehicle brought up the sort of burn he had not known since leaving LA. Life in Miramar had kept him sheltered from the casual brutality of ambitious city people. He swallowed down on the anger at how Lisa had scolded her own daughter. Ricki came out and helped him carry in the second load. "She's hiding in the bath-room."

"As good a place as any," Daniel said.

"You're bringing her to my place for an early dinner tonight."

Daniel walked Ricki back outside and accepted both her hug and her command to show up in an hour and a half. When he reentered the house, he found that Nicole had taken up a station by the living room's front window. The afternoon wind had died, and a sunset fog was rolling in. Basically, all Nicole could see was her own reflection. Daniel wondered if she even saw that much.

He stepped up behind her. "Can I make you a cappuccino?"

"Mom doesn't let me . . ." She stopped speaking because Daniel settled a hand upon her shoulder.

"I don't know how to say it any clearer than this," Daniel said. "Your mother is not here."

He stood there, feeling as uncertain as he had in years. He could see the new tears in her reflection and feel the tight tremors from her young frame. It would have been nice to embrace her, try and heal the wounds caused by all the wrongness in this world. Instead, he simply stood and held her shoulder and gave her time.

When she spoke, Nicole's voice was constricted to a near-whisper. "A coffee would be nice."

When the money had started rolling in, Daniel had gone for the best of everything. And in LA, that covered a lot of ground. He got to know the Beverly Drive wineshop owners by their first names. He had accounts with three of the city's top men's clothiers. Toward the end, he was recognized as a trendsetter. The press junkies who tracked stars would call out his name, wanting to know what was hot that night and where the elite were gathering. He ate, he drove, he partied . . .

All that was behind him now. Except for coffee, the one addiction he still allowed himself. Most of the AA crowd either junked out on sugar or smoked a couple of packs per day. The term they used to describe themselves was *highly dependent*. They needed something, a crutch of some kind. Daniel didn't disagree with them. He just despised the effect it had on their daily lives and their health and their outlook and . . .

As someone in rehab had put it, you gotta find pals where you can, since they done stole your *best* friend.

Daniel's machine of choice was an Expobar Onyx Pro. He opened the vacuum-sealed glass container and measured out two scoops of Caffé Prima Roma beans. While he ground them, he made sure the water distiller was on, then grabbed the fresh unpasteurized milk from the fridge and filled the metal pitcher. He steamed the milk while the coffee brewed, tamping the pitcher twice in order to thicken the foam. When he set the two mugs on the counter and began pouring in the milk, he realized Nicole had silently slipped over and stationed herself where she could watch. "You take sugar?"

"No, thanks." She accepted the cup, took a sip. "This is nice."

"Would you like to take a look around?"

Daniel let her set the pace. He was uncertain how to speak with this stranger. It had been four years since their last contact, and in the interim, Nicole had become a young woman. So he remained silent and simply followed her down the main corridor, pausing with her as she inspected the family room, now fitted out as a gym, and on into the master suite.

Kimberly's parents had built this home. They had died within six months of one another, leaving their only child an orphan at twenty-three. The place had become his and Kimberly's haven from the LA craziness, the place where they returned when things got totally out of control. Daniel seldom tracked back to those bad old days anymore. The memories led to regret, and regret to desire, and desire to . . .

Nicole walked back through the living room, took a left where the front wall met a trio of broad stairs, and entered what previously had been the den.

"Whoa."

"This is my office."

She took another step. "You *work* here?"

Having her become fully engaged, even for

a moment, left him breathing easier. "Right. Travis and Ricki's daughter suspects I have a hundred online games that I play when no one's watching."

"This is insane." She walked over and stood behind his desk. "I didn't know they even made monitors this big."

The room ran almost the entire length of the house. The front wall was floor-to-ceiling glass doors. Beyond the glass was the stone veranda holding an outdoor table and outdoor chairs. Everything else—the lawn and the retaining wall and the bluff and the sea—was lost to the floating mist.

Daniel's desk was a custom job, big as a dining table with a half-moon divot cut from the center. He pulled out the ergonomic chair and said, "Have a seat."

Nicole now faced six fifty-five-inch curved OLED monitors, a row of four with two more stacked on top. The electronic array dominated everything. "What *is* this?"

"Live feeds to the global markets." He pointed to each in turn. "Right now it's Singapore, Tokyo, Hong Kong, and Shanghai; they're all active. See those red lines?"

"This is so totally rad."

"Those are recorded losses. The markets are in steep decline. There have been problems with the Chinese economy and political situation, and now it's coming to a boil. Here." He used the mouse to shift markets. "Okay, Rio is shut, ditto for London and Paris. But there are still off-book trades that happen twenty-four-seven. See how there are red ribbons appearing? This is the Far East decline hitting the after-hour trades."

There was a soft electronic refrain from *Night of the Valkyries*. "That's my alert of bad news on the wire. Want to listen in?"

"Sure."

He shifted the left-hand monitor to show her. "This is Kara Chen. She's business editor for the biggest independent channel in Singapore."

Because the volume was cut off, a stream of words ran along the bottom of the screen. The news was genuinely bad. But Daniel had evacuated the Far East markets the previous week. So for him it was just confirmation of having gotten it right. Again.

Nicole said, "She's a total hottie."

"Among financial analysts, Kara Chen is known as the Queen of Antarctica."

"So . . . you and Miss Chinese Hottie . . ."

"No way." But Nicole had a small smile illuminated by the screens, the first he had seen. So Daniel added, "Actually, before Kimberly, I did try. Once."

Nicole swung her chair around enough for him to see her smile full on. "She shot you down? Really?"

Daniel dragged down the collar of his sweat-shirt. "See the scar?"

Nicole shifted back around. "Her loss."

"Use the mouse. See the symbols at the top-right corner of each screen? Those are your alternative settings." Daniel took a step back and watched her shift around the globe. Television news-casters, trending stocks, economic graphs—Nicole bounced from Japan to Cairo to Sao Paolo to Australia. "I could set you up a system of your own on the room's other side, I've got tons of . . ."

Nicole's good humor vanished into a crimping of her features. Tight as rage.

Daniel asked, "Did I say something wrong?"

Her voice had gone small again. "Am I staying here?"

Daniel took his time, giving his answer the care and thought it deserved. "There are two answers to that. First, you are welcome to stay here as long as you like."

"For real?"

"Yes. I will try to be straight with you always. Starting now."

Nicole swiveled partway around. "This is where I get the line, right?"

"Excuse me?"

"As long as I behave. As long as I do what you say. Something."

Daniel settled on the three narrow steps that

ran the length of the room, separating the living room from this glassed-in parlor. It meant Daniel was positioned slightly lower than Nicole. He watched her young features tighten in a determined effort to maintain control. "No, Nicole. I've wrecked too many days to try and tell you how to behave."

She fashioned a silent *Wow.*

"Okay, ready for the second part?"

"I guess . . . yeah."

"Your mom's temper is the stuff of legends."

"Or nightmares."

"Correct. So our best bet is to lay low and give it time."

"As mad as she was, that could take years."

Daniel thought so too. He had seen his sister walk away from several lifelong relationships—including their own—without a backward glance.

But all he said was, "One day at a time, okay?"

Nicole turned her attention back to where the Shanghai exchange was in free fall. "Works for me."

# CHAPTER 6

On the drive over, Daniel described the day's mystery. The trip to the cemetery, Goldie, and the dog's response to the little girl.

"I don't get it," Nicole said. "This girl, what's her name?"

"Amber. Her mother is Stella."

"So this Amber, she's at the cemetery to visit her dead sister . . ."

"Twin sister. Right."

"On the anniversary of her death, which was, like years ago."

"They were four. I guess she's around ten or eleven now."

"And she falls in love with your *dog?*" Nicole gave a mock shudder. "Creep me out."

"And then she and Goldie go dancing over to her sister's grave." Daniel liked this easy camaraderie. A lot. "And she introduces my dog to her sister's headstone."

"This is the start of a major horror show. Do they go back for some blood ritual at midnight?"

"I'll ask her next time we meet," Daniel

replied. "Which will probably be three hundred and sixty-four days from now."

"Do things like this happen to you all the time?"

"Actually, my life here in Miramar is very quiet." He glanced over. "I'm afraid you're going to find it very boring."

Their entire afternoon had been like this, ever since that first difficult conversation. Easy. Normal. No further mention of Nicole's mother or why she was here. With him. Or how long she was staying.

Nicole said, "Can I ask you something?"

"Of course."

"Why didn't you ever come down to see me? I mean, I got all these presents and cards, but you never called . . ."

"Actually, I did call. But your mother told me to stop."

"Mom wouldn't let you talk to me? Why?"

As he showered and dressed for dinner, Daniel had decided he was going to be straight with his niece. The simple fact was, he had zero experience with teens. So he was going to treat her as if Nicole was, for all intents and purposes, an adult. And he was going to hold to honesty, as hard as that might be.

Like now.

They were less than a mile from Travis and Ricki's home, and this was not something he was going to cover in their driveway. So he pulled over to the side of the road and parked.

Instantly, Nicole resumed the same semi-crouched and fearful demeanor she had shown in front of her mother. Which hurt Daniel. "I will be straight with you about everything you want to know. I just need to be sure. You really want to hear this?"

To her credit, she did not give a knee-jerk response. Daniel could see her take his words in deep. "I need to know."

"Okay. Your mother and I had an argument."

"It must have been some fight."

"It was. Before today, the last time I saw Lisa was the night I moved to Miramar."

She tasted the air, hesitated, then decided to ask, "What did you fight about?"

"I told her I was leaving town. That night. I hadn't said anything to her before then. She . . ."

"Flipped out."

Daniel nodded. "Basically, she showed me the same fury she gave you this morning."

"But *why?*"

"Your mom thought I was nuts, blaming myself for my fiancée's death. I was asleep at the time. Passed out, actually. Which happened a lot back then. It was the only reason Kimberly was driving. She was a fraction more sober than me."

Nicole needed a moment to sort through all he had said, and what it meant. "Whoa."

"Kimberly was your mom's best friend. Lisa introduced us. Kimberly lost her parents when she was in college. Lisa, your mom, basically adopted Kimberly as her sister. She was going to give Kimberly away . . ." Daniel waved that aside. "I should have handled things better. But I knew Lisa was going to be upset. So I put it off until the very last minute, and she . . ."

"Exploded."

"She set the dogs to howling in San Diego." He tried for a smile. "Bad joke."

"Then you left."

"I felt like I didn't have a choice. Not if I was going to stay sober. LA had its claws in too deep." Daniel found it necessary to reflect momentarily on how easy it was to talk with this young woman. Like they were restarting a conversation that had never been interrupted. "Miramar had always held a special place for me, ever since my first visit. Plus, up here, living in the home that was supposed to be our retreat from the world was a daily reminder of why I needed to stay straight."

"I remember how much fun you were." Nicole studied him. "You laughed at everything I said. Mom and Marvin, they never laugh. Not, you know, with me. The most I ever get is this polite, ha-ha."

"You call your father Marvin?" He stopped. "That didn't come out right. I meant—"

43

"I know what you mean." Nicole took a hard breath. "I started around the time I became certain he wasn't . . . you know. He put it down to me being a difficult teenager. Mom just freaked out." She went silent, then added quietly, "And now I know why."

Daniel could not defend his sister. But he could be honest. "The year before it all fell apart, whenever I was off-air, my state was generally pretty wasted. I don't actually remember the last time you and I spoke face-to-face."

She watched him, somber now. "You took me to the zoo. You don't remember?"

Daniel felt about two inches tall. "No."

"It was the best day of my life." She gave that a long pause. "When you stopped calling or stopping by, I thought, you know, I'd done something wrong and you were so mad at me you never came back."

"Nicole, I'm so sorry. I don't know how I can ever make that up to you."

"You're here." She struggled and managed to hold onto control. "On my worst day."

"You're welcome to stay as long as you like." He amended, "As long as you need."

"Thanks. Maybe that's Mom and Marvin's problem. They don't get stoned enough to find me funny. Bad joke." She tried for a smile and almost succeeded. "So . . . you're sober now?"

"Yes. I have been since I arrived in Miramar."

He pointed into the dusk. "Travis is my AA mentor."

Nicole turned and stared at the dark beyond the windshield. "This is heavy."

Daniel nodded. "It's a lot to hit you with."

"I'm glad you did."

"Really?"

"Yes, Daniel. Can I call you that?"

"Of course. It's my name." He started the car. "Hungry?"

# CHAPTER 7

Daniel pulled up in front of Travis and Ricki's home. As he cut the motor and rose from the car, Nicole slipped around the car and took his hand.

She didn't speak. She didn't need to. The air was cooling, and the dusk was windless, and Daniel could smell her hair's floral scent from a recent shampoo. This particular walk could take forever, as far as he was concerned.

Then Travis opened the front door, and instantly Daniel knew something was seriously wrong.

Daniel lifted his free hand, stopping Travis from joining them. He said to Nicole, "I need to explain something. Travis and Ricki have been having a lot of trouble lately with Chloe. And the situation is getting worse by the day."

"Should we leave?"

"I can take you home if you want." Daniel liked how she silently mouthed the word *home,* as if she was coming to terms with the fact that he really meant she was welcome. "But I need to stay here. Having others around keeps things, well . . ."

"Smoother than they might otherwise be," Nicole said. "I know how that is."

"Chloe won her first beauty contest four years ago, just before she turned twelve. Last year she was runner-up in Miss Junior California."

Nicole studied Travis standing there, filling the doorway. "So they're pushy parents being ambitious against their daughter's will?"

"Just the opposite. They never . . ." Daniel waved that aside. Another time. "Eight months ago, Chloe got a modeling gig in Santa Cruz. Small-time stuff, a local distributor of teen clothes made in Mexico. She pretended to be her mom, called the school, claimed she was sick. Took the bus up four days in a row."

"So . . . when did they find out?"

"Last week. The company called to say they wanted Chloe to model their new line of swimwear."

"Wow."

"Chloe is grounded until she's thirty-five. But that's not the problem. She wants to go into modeling full-time. Now. Today."

"So . . . fireworks."

Daniel nodded. "Maybe I should take you back."

"Are you kidding?" Nicole did her best to fashion a smile. "I'll feel right at home."

"Let me know if you change your mind."

The two of them started forward, still hand in

hand, up to where Travis stood, his broad features creased with a worried frown. Travis greeted them with: "We got us a situation here."

"I've explained the issue with Chloe."

"Yeah, well, if only that was all we had on our plate." Travis pushed the door open. "Ricki went ahead and invited her friend."

"The lady from the town council?"

"She's not on the council. She keeps the town's books." He halted Daniel's protest with a palm the size of a catcher's mitt. "Ricki did not ask my opinion on the matter."

Nicole asked, "What's wrong?"

"Aw, Ricki's been trying to hook my pal up since forever. Look at the guy. A firing squad couldn't get this man any tighter."

Travis's daughter stepped up beside her father. "Daniel, you better come in or else Daddy will poison us all. Hi, you must be Nicole. Welcome to the worst place on earth."

"Chloe . . ."

"You said to behave. This is me behaving." She said to Nicole, "My parents decided to raise me in the town where cadavers go to be buried. What's your excuse?"

Nicole didn't bat an eyelid. "I'm not exactly sure. My mom was screaming so loud on the way up, I couldn't actually catch what she was saying."

"Like, I know exactly how that is." She pushed the door wider. "Come on inside."

When the two girls departed, Travis said, "Her name is Stella. She's here with her daughter, Amber."

"Wait . . . what?"

"They're nice, Daniel. And Stella is one sweet-looking lady."

"I don't believe this."

Travis gripped his arm and pulled. Being chained to a bulldozer would have made for an easier struggle. "Come on, buddy."

Ricki stepped up beside her man. "What are you two doing out here?"

"Daniel is just digesting the news about Stella."

"I've had about all I'm going to take from you." Ricki took hold of Daniel's other arm. "Inside, mister. Now."

# CHAPTER 8

Travis was possibly the worst cook Daniel had ever met. An assortment of perfect ingredients became charcoal mush in his hands. Most of the time it did not matter, since Ricki treated the kitchen as her exclusive domain. But much to his family's dismay, Travis loved his grill. Which was where Daniel came in. Any time Travis got the itch to fire up the Weber, an emergency alert went out for Daniel to drop everything and hurry over. On the rare occasions when Travis grilled alone, Ricki and Chloe ate out.

The Weber was set up at the garden's far end. It had been shifted there from the rear veranda after Travis had set a corner of the roof on fire.

Daniel was lighting the charcoal when Ricki's friend walked over. As he feared, it was none other than the woman from the cemetery. "Good evening, Stella."

"Surprise." She looked equally uncomfortable. "If it helps, I didn't know you were coming until ten minutes ago. When Ricki told me your name, I half-hoped there were two Daniels."

"No such luck."

She tested a smile. "She described you, and I replied that I had an urgent need to be somewhere else. Ricki basically barred the door with her body."

Daniel found himself liking the woman. "Ricki is a wonderful person. But she tends to insert herself where she's not wanted. Forcefully."

Anywhere but LA, Stella Dalton would be classed as a remarkably beautiful woman. Raven hair fell in abundant waves over bare shoulders. Her arms and wrists were strong in the manner of a professional tennis player, her long legs ending in sandals with little coral flowers over the toes. Her dress had a matching design, as did her amber necklace. Her eyes were either blue or violet, Daniel couldn't tell in the dusk. She was strong, and she was resilient, and the hollow void at the center of her gaze spoke to him.

She watched him fan the coals. "Well, it's nice to meet you. Again."

"Likewise."

Stella's daughter then raced up and demanded, "Where's Goldie?"

"Not here."

Stella said, "Be polite and say good evening, Mr. Riffkin."

"Daniel," he corrected.

Amber sketched a wave. "Why didn't you bring your dog?"

"Chloe has a cat named Shah. A long-hair mix, white with a touch of cinnamon and the bluest eyes you've ever seen."

Stella said, "She sounds beautiful."

The fire was going well now, so he shut the top to let it burn down. "Shah is a he, and he is a lover and a fighter."

Chloe and Nicole walked up, both carrying plates, one of steaks and the other of vegetables. Chloe said, "About once a week, we get a neighbor who comes by with either a box of little part-white kitties or a cat who's been torn to shreds. You should see Daddy play the innocent."

Amber said, "Cool."

Daniel said, "Nicole, this is Stella and her daughter, Amber. We met earlier today."

His niece almost dropped the plate. "Wait. What?"

Amber said, "So Goldie and Shah, they don't get along?"

"The one time Daniel brought her over, Shah basically decided she wanted to have Goldie for breakfast," Chloe said.

"Goldie said no thanks and set off for Long Beach," Daniel said. "I chased her for a week."

Nicole said, "This is *the* Stella and Amber?"

Amber asked, "Where's your kittie now?"

"Under my bed," Chloe replied. "Shah doesn't like visitors. He isn't happy unless he's the center of attention."

Stella pointed with her wineglass at Nicole and asked Daniel, "Your niece knows?"

Chloe asked, "What am I missing here?"

Nicole said, "You won't believe it."

"Try me," Chloe said.

Stella said, "I take that as a big affirmative."

Amber asked, "What is everybody talking about?"

# CHAPTER 9

They dined outdoors in the lovely September night, the coastal wind gentled by the valley walls separating their neighborhood from Miramar. They sat around a soapstone table on cast-iron legs that Ricki had found at a junk shop and lovingly restored. The dinner was a success because of Amber. At eleven years old, she was small for her age, a happy child who watched everything with a wide-eyed eagerness that Daniel found touching.

Chloe was one of the most stunningly beautiful young women Daniel had ever met, this from a former inhabitant of a city that drew beauty like moths to a flame. Chloe had her father's height and her mother's sharp features. At nearly sixteen, she topped six feet. But where both her parents had the strength and solidity of professional athletes, Chloe possessed a winsome grace that was all her very own.

And something more.

Ever since the first time they met, Daniel wondered if there was some island strain to her bloodline. Not Caribbean. Polynesian or Maori or Fijian. Daniel had spent time out there in his late teens and early twenties, island hopping and working as a bartender or waiter or whatever. He loved the water-bound world and had promised he would someday return. Chloe possessed an internal fire that reminded him of the natives, especially those not yet tamed by the modern world. High cheekbones tilted her almond-shaped eyes, which possessed a dark golden tint, like a volcano at midnight.

When Chloe started in on her normal tirade of being imprisoned in Miramar, Amber came back with, "I don't understand you."

"You're young," Chloe said. "Give it time."

"Chloe," Ricki said, suddenly tired.

"What."

"Give it a rest. For once. Please."

Amber asked, "Where do you want to go?"

"Los Angeles. Tomorrow."

Nicole spoke for the first time since they had seated themselves. "Don't get your hopes up."

"What's that supposed to mean?"

Nicole directed her words at her plate. "LA is a great place for people who want to be somebody else. The truth gets ground down to dust. Telling lies is fine, as long as you make people believe you."

Chloe crossed her arms and huffed, "Being somebody else is fine by me."

Nicole kept her gaze on her plate and did not respond.

"But I don't *understand.*" Amber's gaze stayed steady on Chloe. "Miramar is *great.*"

"Thank you, honey," Ricki said. "You're welcome here any time."

Chloe glared across the table at Nicole. "I don't understand either. You left LA for *Miramar?*"

Seeing his niece go small and sad, like she did at that moment, made Daniel's chest ache. "I lived in LA for years. I'd say Nicole has the place down cold."

"Cold is right," Travis said.

Amber asked Daniel, "You like Miramar, don't you?"

"I love it. This place is home."

"Not for me." Chloe's face pinched up tight. "LA would suit me just fine."

"Finish school," Travis said. "Get your grades up so UCLA will take you. Then we'll see."

"I am *not* spending three more years caged in Miramar!"

"That's enough, girl!"

*"No!"* She sprang, cat-like, up and away from her table so fast she frightened Amber. "I've *had it* with *you* and *this place!*"

Ricki stabbed the air between them. "Go to your room!"

But Chloe was already moving. "I *hate* you! And I'm *running away!*"

# CHAPTER 10

Routines defined Daniel's life. They maintained the boundaries that kept him safe. Yet the next morning, for the first time in years, Daniel overslept.

When he opened his eyes and glanced at the bedside clock, Daniel actually did not believe the numbers. He could not remember the last time he had slept until ten-thirty. Certainly not since becoming sober. But after the previous day's events, he had tossed and turned for hours. Finally, at one in the morning, he had stepped outside and spent over an hour seated by the rear hedge, staring at the night, listening to the sea below.

Now Daniel rose and dressed and entered the main house to discover Nicole seated on a counter stool. An empty cereal bowl rested beside her phone. His greeting was halted by the sight of her form, made small by whatever she read on her screen.

Goldie lay stretched out by the stool. Normally when Daniel appeared in the morning, she danced. The only time his dog appeared morose was when Daniel refused to let her go out with him on his rare nights away. Whenever he forgot and left the bedroom door open, Daniel woke up wearing a Labradoodle helmet. But this morning, as Daniel approached the kitchen, the only parts of Goldie that moved were her eyes.

Daniel had no idea what to do or say. He wanted to reach out and hold Nicole, offer the hurting girl a share of his own strength. But it seemed like a great yawning gap existed between them, far too wide for his arms to reach across. So he retreated into the next part of his morning routine. "Would you like a coffee?"

She gave a fractional nod, still not having looked at him.

Daniel ground coffee and poured milk into the heating pitcher. He brought out two mugs and set them on the metal counter and tapped in the coffee and twisted the handles and punched the buttons. He steamed the milk as the coffee dripped through. He did his best to give Nicole space, even when he saw a tear slide down her cheek. He had never felt so much a stranger to his niece as then.

He tamped the pitcher on the stone countertop, then used the flat wooden ladle to push it into the mug. "I usually take my first cup in the garden. Would you like to join me?"

In response, Nicole slid off her stool and followed him across the living room.

The fog had returned with the dawn. This often happened in the early spring, when the winter winds breathed their last. Mornings like this, it was hard to believe the summer heat would ever arrive, as if the world told fables no one believed anymore. Daniel had always loved how the central coast was truly an in-between land. On days when the arid winds blew off California's high desert, Miramar was linked by sunlight and easterly fires to Southern California. Temperatures could soar fifty degrees between dawn and ten o'clock.

Today was different. A San Francisco-style light drifted in gentle waves with the mist, a feather-like whisper of a world that remained just out of reach. Homes lining the first hills were high enough to look down on the fog, and they cost twice as much as here. Most people disliked how their view was dependent upon the wind. But Daniel had always loved the way the mist held him here, tight as a lover's embrace. He hit the switch and lit the gas firepit, then led Nicole through the glass-fronted office and into the backyard.

Metal chairs made a half ring around the fire-pit. Daniel placed his cup on the firepit's stone rim and went back for two sets of cushions. He couldn't leave them out at night because they'd be drenched by dawn. As he settled two into Nicole's chair, the dog came out and nuzzled her way under Nicole's free hand, which was another astonishment. Goldie hated how the mist clung to her pelt. Daniel had always considered her a true California dog, happiest when the sun blazed and the ocean winds blew. Daniel asked, "Would you like a blanket?"

"No, thank you." It was the first time she had spoken that morning. When she was seated, Goldie wedged her head under Nicole's legs and just lay there on the grass. Normally on such wet days she had to be prodded outside to pee.

Nicole drank her coffee in small tentative sips. All the while, she kept a tight grip on her phone. It buzzed twice while she drank. Both times, whatever it was she read caused her face to crimp up tight.

Daniel waited until she set her cup on the firepit's rim to ask, "Do you want to talk about it?"

She gestured to the mist-clad morning with the hand holding her phone. "Marvin keeps texting me."

"What does he say?"

"He wants to talk. He says he's not mad. I guess Mom's mad enough for both of them."

"What do you want to have happen?"

Nicole took a long time to respond. The firepit's glow put out so much heat the mist was almost comforting, as if time itself held no sway in this small space. Finally, she said, "I don't know."

"Well, when you decide, if you want to talk about it, I'm here. If you don't, that's okay too."

Nicole's silence left Daniel feeling as though everything he'd said was wrong. He sat there a while longer, then decided he wasn't helping. He rose to his feet and said, "I'm going to make myself some breakfast. Do you want anything? Another coffee?"

"Maybe later."

Daniel padded across the lawn, leaving wet footprints in his wake. As he entered the office, he glanced back. Nicole had drawn her knees up to her chin and cradled her phone with both hands. She stared into the mist. Daniel hated his sense of helplessness. But he was also intensely glad he could be there for her. He carried these balanced and conflicting emotions back into the kitchen. It felt like a cold breeze of past events had bitten its way into his present life, which he found both very good and very frightening indeed.

He made himself a bowl of granola and berries and ate it standing by the front window. He then brewed another coffee and carried it to his office. But as he turned on his monitors, he was struck by a sudden idea.

Daniel returned to the house and walked down the hallway to the big closet that was probably intended to hold linens. Instead, he used it to store all his office files. He pulled out three monitors and a base unit he kept around in case of an emergency, carried these into the office, then went to the garage for his crate of extra cables. It felt good doing something for Nicole. Trying to make her feel that she was welcome, that he wanted her around, that she could consider this her refuge for as long . . .

"Daniel?"

He emerged from beneath the desk. "Yes?"

Nicole held out her phone. "Will you call him for me?"

# CHAPTER 11

Daniel waited almost an hour before placing the call. He continued to wire up Nicole's station and talked as he worked. He discovered Nicole was much more comfortable speaking when he was not focused directly on her, as though the weight of his gaze and his attention was too heavy. So long as he remained under the long table, fiddling with wires, she relaxed. When he was finished, he pulled over his own office chair, seated himself, and began checking the connections. All the while, they talked in quiet snatches. Daniel would ask a question, and she would think, then reply in a soft voice. But she was comfortable now. Sad, of course. The reason all this was happening remained a burden and a wound. She took the same position in the second office chair as she had by the firepit, knees pulled up so her chin could rest on them, staring at the brightening day. But there was a new ease to her now. As if she was trusting him to make the next step. For her. Daniel found himself filled with an exquisite sense of rightness as he left the office. He washed off the dust and returned to ask, "Ready?"

She nodded. "What have I got to lose, right?"

"A joke. I like it."

"A bad one."

"Hey. You still get an A for effort." He took her phone and connected it to his computer. This allowed him to set up a conference structure with two sets of headphones. Nicole could listen in, and speak if she wanted, but only to him. Daniel's headset contained a microphone as well. "Test, test."

"I'm scared."

"Me too, a little."

"You're not. You're as cold as ice."

"It's a façade. Developed after years in front of the camera, pretending I knew what I was talking about." He held up the phone. And waited.

"Thank you, Uncle Daniel."

"Let's drop the uncle, okay? It's just Daniel between friends." He hit REDIAL. "Here we go."

Marvin answered with, "Nicole, honey?"

"It's Daniel."

A pause, then, "How is Nicole?"

Daniel swiveled his chair around so he faced Nicole. "Surprisingly good, all things considered. And Lisa, how's she doing?"

"Angry. Hurting. Venting steam. You know Lisa."

Daniel kept his gaze on Nicole, trying to read

on that troubled young face what he should say. "How are you guys?"

"We're coping. Or at least we're trying to."

"Nicole will be very happy to hear that."

There was a silence long enough for Nicole to wipe her face twice. Then Marvin asked, "Can I speak to her?"

Daniel had taken all this time both to prepare Nicole and to prep his response. Because this was where it all came together. Getting the next thing right. He suspected Nicole knew this. And it was one big reason why he was the one having this conversation. "Are you sure you want to?"

"What is that supposed to mean?"

"Are you willing to do what it would take? Because this isn't about having a chat, is it, Marv? You want to make peace."

Daniel had learned this particular method of conversation since coming to Miramar. California had a new homegrown industry, thanks to the opioid epidemic. Even the smallest town now had counselors specializing in addiction and recovery. There were a lot of people like Daniel, who had no interest in the public spectacle aspect of rehab centers. They were intensely private people, and yet they knew that this habitual seclusion was part of the problem. So they sought help, but did so within an environment of solitude. Addiction therapists assured these patients a higher degree of confidentiality and discretion. But they also

65

probed. And the best, like Daniel's therapist, did so by redirecting comments and questions so that it was the patient who asked, and not them. Uncovering the hidden issue in the process. Just like Daniel did now.

The LA attorney took a long moment before responding, "What are you suggesting?"

"Two things. That you come up and speak with Nicole in person."

Marvin did not respond. But Daniel had learned the pressure of remaining quiet, even when he was watching his niece leak tears. He waited.

Finally, Marvin said, "I'm faced with two dilemmas. I want to make peace with my daughter. . . . Does she still consider me her father?"

Daniel watched Nicole nod. "She absolutely does, Marvin. But on her terms. Which means in total honesty."

"Having you say that . . . it brings so many things about Nicole into proper focus."

Daniel knew what was coming next, but he wanted it out in the open. "You said there were two dilemmas."

"Lisa would absolutely freak out."

"I understand."

"She would see it as treachery of the first order."

"But she doesn't have to know, Marvin. I won't tell her. Nicole won't either."

"Nicole put you up to this?"

"Wrong question, Marvin. She didn't put me up to anything. She asked for my help."

"You're right. That was not the right way . . . I'm still stressing over everything." He was silent a long moment, then said, "This whole affair is a heartbreak of the first order. I'm coping. I want to find some way to make it work with Lisa." His voice almost broke. "And I want my daughter back."

That was what Daniel had wanted his niece to hear. "So come up and make peace. We'll tell Lisa when the time is right. Together." When Marvin did not respond, Daniel went on, "And I sit in. Until Nicole says I should go."

"Is that really necessary?"

"Nicole thinks so. And for the moment, hers is the only voice that matters." Daniel gave that a beat, then went on, "Clarity and control, Marvin."

"I don't understand."

"The question nobody appears to be asking is, Why did Nicole do this in the first place?"

"She suspected what I didn't want to see." Marvin's voice cracked wide open over the words. "Hang on a second."

There was the sound of footsteps across a wooden floor and of a door opening, and words spoken that Daniel could not make out. Then the door shut and the footsteps returned. "I needed to reschedule something. Go ahead, Daniel."

"It seems to me that at least part of what Nicole has been after is freedom from Lisa running her life. And, even more important, *defining* her life."

Marvin went quiet.

"Nicole is growing up. She's chosen a different reality than the one Lisa designed for her. You need to address this head-on. And that has to be done in person."

Marvin sighed. "You're probably right. Tell Nicole—"

"Excuse me, Marvin. Try that again."

Another sigh, then, "*Ask* her if I can come up tomorrow afternoon."

# CHAPTER 12

As Daniel cut the connection, he was filled with a unique sensation, one he had never known before. It was utterly illogical, completely without reason. And yet . . .

Two images arrived at once. The first was a childhood memory, something he had not thought about in years. When he was six years old, his parents had taken him and three-year-old Lisa to Washington, DC. It was their last family vacation before his parents divorced. That year the cherry blossoms had come early, and on the afternoon of their arrival, they had walked alongside the National Mall's Reflecting Pool. They were joined by thousands and thousands of other people. Overhead had been one tree after another, all of them looking as though they had managed to capture the clouds. Suddenly a great rush of wind had come out of a clear blue sky. To young Daniel it had seemed as though the entire city had frozen solid. All the people and all the cars he could see just stopped. And they watched with upturned faces as it rained pink and white petals. And then everyone cried aloud with joy.

Daniel's childhood home had never been a happy place. Even at six years of age, he had known that something inside their home was broken in a way that could not be fixed. There had been none of the anger or shouting that he had observed in other families. Just a melting away, a recognition of what had existed for a long time. After the separation, his parents had not become happy, nor had they healed. Instead, they had merely settled into lives that suited them better, morose to the end, emotionally distant from their children and everyone else. But perhaps as close to finding peace as they were able.

Daniel had not thought of that afternoon in years. It was the only thing he remembered from the Washington trip—the way even his gloomy parents had lit up with unbridled joy. Their faces had been so transformed, Daniel had found himself watching them more than the blossoms. He recalled how, in that one brief instant, as they shed their pasts and their shadows, they looked like Lisa. His three-year-old sister sat in her stroller with arms and feet outstretched, shrieking with joy as she tried to catch the petals. Just like Daniel's parents.

The other impression that struck him as he cut the phone connection was not about the past at all. Instead, he had the sense of being free.

Daniel felt as though he had broken chains he had been unable to see, much less identify. All the therapy, the four years of small living, all brought together in a single moment of release.

He leaned back in his chair, thinking of who he had once been, back before he had become trapped in a fog of his own making. Before his life began and ended inside LA's electric high.

He knew what it meant. That he might indeed be ready to move on. To open the door to his life and his world. To chart a course that took him beyond the safe confines he had needed for recovery.

He was still grappling with this when his land-line phone rang. Nicole took the phone from its holder by the coffee machine and walked over. The screen read, STELLA. Seeing her name offered a surprisingly strong lift. "Good morning."

The woman sounded slightly breathless. And something else. Excited, perhaps. Or scared. "I have something you need to see."

# CHAPTER 13

Just have one look, Stella asked, pleading, her tone softly desperate.

Daniel should have recognized the words as a siren's call, filled with deadly dangers. He should have turned away from rocks as sharp as dark teeth, should have stayed out of the currents seeking to swallow him whole.

But just then, Daniel was too full of what happened after Nicole handed him the phone. She wrapped her arms around his neck. She stood, while he remained seated. His chair creaked softly as the strength of her arms tilted him right and then left, then back again, fractional shifts that caused his chair to click like a metronome. He counted off those fragile seconds when he was filled with the wonder of having gotten this one thing very right.

When Nicole released him and stepped back, the two of them shared a gentle smile, as if they knew a secret too precious for words. Nicole said, "All of a sudden, I'm hungry."

"Hang on a second, Stella." He asked Nicole, "Do you want some eggs?"

"Can I make them?"

"Of course." Daniel rose and began pulling out plates and implements. He watched Nicole open the refrigerator and inspect his wares. And suddenly he was staring at a fully grown woman.

All the while, Stella waited for him to lift the receiver and say, "I apologize. Nicole and I are still finding our way."

"Ricki told me a little. It's wonderful what you're doing for that girl." But Stella's words were rushed, as if she was impatient to move on to the reason for her call. "Would you please just take one look at some documents?"

"I'm not sure I can do anything."

"Ricki says you trained as a forensic accountant."

"That was years ago." Daniel watched his niece wash a bundle of chives. When she looked a silent question, he pointed to the cabinet holding the chopping boards. She found a sharp knife all on her own. And the cheese grater. Daniel found it a marvel. Nicole's mother treated the kitchen as enemy terrain. As far as he knew, Marvin had never made anything more complex than oatmeal.

Stella was saying, "I've downloaded the files that scare me. It's taken almost three weeks. Every time I had a valid reason to go into questionable accounts, I made a duplicate save."

Daniel walked the phone across the front foyer

and opened the door, taking Stella's tension out where it would not disturb the home's fragile joy. "You're being watched?"

"I don't know. You must think I'm paranoid. And maybe I am. Maybe everything is just fine. I keep telling myself to ignore it all."

Daniel found himself captured by the woman's nerves. But he did not mind. In fact, it felt as though a hidden component of his being was nudged awake, the slumber of years cast aside. "Where are you now?"

"I walk across the street for a coffee more or less the same time every morning. I've become defined by habits like this one. Just in case, you know . . ."

"So there's nothing to alert any watchers," Daniel said. He had dealt with any number of whistle-blowers during his on-air years. Watching them clutch at him like he offered the only lifeline within reach. Their gnawing fear worked on him every time. Just like now. "That's smart, Stella."

"I could be wrong. I hope I am."

"In that case, you will have a reason to sleep better tonight."

Her voice rose a full octave. "You'll help me?"

"I will look at your files. Yes. Hang on one second more."

Daniel walked back inside and found Nicole whisking eggs and cream and chives and cheese in his mixing bowl. He said, "Stella wants to stop by later."

"Will she bring Amber?"

Daniel passed on the question, then added, "Bring your daughter and your appetite and the files. Nothing else. What time do you get off work?"

# CHAPTER 14

They spent the day getting used to doing normal things together. Daniel spent a couple of hours going through the motions of inspecting the markets and preparing his daily analysis. He was paid a retainer by two investment funds, one out of San Francisco and another based across Upper New York Bay from Wall Street. The markets remained teetering on the edge, stable only because nobody knew which way to jump.

Daniel was known for offering solid intel on developing trends. He did not hedge his predictions, which meant he was often wrong. But these two companies liked balancing his unvarnished attitude against their in-house analysts, who often were so concerned over their jobs, they dithered. Most Wall Street analysts couched their reports in what Daniel used to call economic foliage. While he'd been on the air, he had developed a number of signature terms to describe everything he despised about the industry, one he consistently accused of being weighted against the little guy. Which was one reason why he had remained popular, even when he was often wrong. Because he was never afraid to confess on-air that he had missed the mark, that his analysis had led him and the people who followed him down a dark road at midnight. Even so, the ones who stuck with him made a consistent return on their investments. And as Daniel liked to say, success in this business came down to rolling with the punches, rising from the mat, and climbing back in the ring.

It was almost lunchtime when they left the house and drove into Miramar. The first Thursday of every month, the parking lot fronting the town hall hosted a small farmers' market, basically an offshoot of the much larger one in Paso Robles. Daniel bought them veggie burritos and fresh-brewed iced tea from his favorite stall and let Nicole decide on the evening's menu as they walked the aisles. They talked in brief snatches. Daniel asked her where she'd learned to cook, and Nicole turned momentarily sad as she replied, "From books." But before his wrong question could build into regret, she reached over and took his hand, silently saying that the morning's good move still dominated their day.

Ricki called just as they were heading back to Daniel's ride. Lack of sleep and a high stress level deepened her voice and ironed it flat. "Where are you now?"

"The market. You need something?"

"I need my daughter to straighten out

before . . ." She coughed, or sighed, or perhaps even sobbed. "Never you mind that. I've spoken with the school superintendent. We're friends from the council. She wants you to stop by with Nicole so the child can get registered for school."

Daniel kept his voice as neutral as possible. "We're not clear on how long—"

"I know all that, and so does she. But the child needs to be registered. Then the LA system can be notified of a temporary change of address, and she won't be listed as truant with the police."

"I hadn't thought of that." Daniel ached over how his closest friends had come by this wisdom. "Thank you, Ricki."

"You're welcome." She was silent a moment, then added, "It's a shame not of all life's problems are this easy to solve."

When they arrived home, Daniel piled mesquite charcoal on the grill next to the firepit. Once it was lit, he went inside to find Nicole working on a salad. He unwrapped and washed the filets of turkey breast, then split four German sausages lengthwise. Nicole watched him as he scored the turkey and inserted sage twigs. He said, "I'm thinking we should invite Chloe. She needs some time away from her family."

Nicole replied, "She's nice when she's not mad. Which is basically all the time."

"Is that a yes?"

Nicole just stared at him.

"What?"

"You're asking me?"

"Yes, Nicole. I'm asking. This is your home . . ." He stopped because she walked over and gave him a one-arm hug.

When she released him, Nicole said, "It'd probably be better if I called."

"There's no probably about that."

She picked up his phone from the counter. "Is Chloe's number in here?"

Daniel scrolled through his address list, handed back the phone, then carried the wooden carving board out back. He checked on the coals, then stood there by the rear hedge, staring out over the sea. He could hear Nicole's voice from inside the house. It surprised him, how little he seemed to mind having all these people invade his space. He had come to see solitude as a vital piece of the story titled How to Stay Sober and Grounded, by Daniel Riffkin. The principles were carved in stone, or so he thought.

He was still standing there when yet another young girl's voice asked, "Why does Goldie bark at butterflies?"

He turned to discover Amber and Stella standing by the firepit. He had been so involved in his not-so-solitary thoughts that he had not even heard them enter. "Goldie thinks they come out to play with her. She gets mad because they won't let her catch them."

Amber clapped her hands. "This is the best dog ever!"

Goldie responded with a happy bark, and the two of them began an elaborate game of tag involving a ball, the butterflies, and a solitary hummingbird who probably thought it had entered a free-fire zone. Stella watched her daughter with a distracted air, then held out a memory stick. "I feel like this thing is burning a hole in my pocket."

As the sun set, the wind breathed a chilly note off the Pacific. Daniel lit the firepit and shifted the table over so the heat would keep them sheltered while they ate. Amber sparked the gathering with an elfin magic, drawing smiles from everyone, even her mother. Goldie bounded joyfully back and forth between Nicole and the younger girl, as excited as Daniel had ever seen her.

The only stain darkening the sunset was Chloe. The beautiful young woman lurked around the edges, mostly staring out at the ocean. Her face looked bruised from the ongoing situation at home. Daniel had no intention of speaking with her that night, not unless Chloe made the approach. What he wanted was for her to experience a place where she could feel safe even while carrying whatever baggage she felt unable to set down. Accepted. Among friends.

But whatever Daniel wanted her to see was not getting through. As he opened the grill's lid and tested the pieces of turkey breast he was cooking, Chloe came up alongside him and demanded, "Why am I here?"

He took his time responding. Another gift from his early days in therapy, when the sweats and the grief and the anger were a battle he fought every hour of every day. "Do you want to help?"

"Is that all you are going to tell me?"

"You can help if you want, or you can stand there and watch. Whatever makes you feel most comfortable." Daniel decided the turkey needed another couple of minutes. He transferred the sausages to the warming plate. "I will tell you whatever you want to know. I always have."

She stood there a moment, then gave him a sullen response. "So tell."

"When I was at my absolute lowest point, your father was there for me. And your mother. They helped me see that life did not begin and end with the crisis I faced at the time. If I can, I hope to show you the same thing."

"The only reason I have a crisis at all is because they won't let me be me." Chloe gave him a moment to object, then added, "They're punishing me because of what they did wrong."

Daniel hated being placed in a position where

anything he said might be heard as criticism of his closest friends. "I understand."

"I'm not them. I am my own person. I can handle things better than they did. I want . . ." She wrapped her arms around her middle. "They're crushing my dreams, and they don't care."

Daniel reached for the mixing bowl holding asparagus marinating in lemon juice and olive oil. He used his fingers to place the vegetables on the grill, then opened the smoker and set the turkey on the carving board. "If they didn't care, it wouldn't be so hard on everyone."

"Whatever."

"Would you please take this to the table, and tell everyone to find a seat?" But when she reached for the plate, he said, "I am here for you. Do you understand what I'm saying?"

Her sullen fury sparked a honeyed fire in those almond-shaped eyes. "Then get me a ticket out of this place."

Had it not been for Amber, Chloe's attitude would have overshadowed the meal. The young girl showed a delight in everything—dining under the stars, the firepit's warmth, the sea breeze, the meal. Goldie spent the entire meal with her golden head resting on Amber's thigh, watching every bite the young girl took with solemn expectation.

The firelight and the candles helped form a

flickering barrier between the three girls and where he sat next to Stella at the table's opposite end. The food's aroma was spiced by Stella's fragrance, a heady mix of oriental spices and something close to home, he thought perhaps honeysuckle. He watched her thoughtfully inspect one forkful after another and said, "Please tell me you're not vegetarian or vegan or something."

"Not while my little carnivore is in the house." She set down her fork. "I'm sorry."

"For what?"

"I actually don't know what to say to you."

"Because . . ."

"You make me feel so much at ease. It's crazy. We only just met, all I've done tonight is dump a load of worry in your lap, and already I feel so . . ."

Daniel pushed his plate to one side and leaned in close. "Tell me."

She stopped avoiding his gaze. "Relaxed. Lighter. Happy." She breathed softly. "I haven't used that word in a long time."

Daniel was caught by a sudden recollection. Back when he was living the high life, up in the stratosphere of LA society, he received so many formal invitations he stacked them like playing cards. He had always liked the ones that included the phrase *the pleasure of your company*. That was exactly how he felt now. Daniel felt a sudden urge to share how these few short hours in her company had ignited a spark in him at the level of his heart. It was something so foreign, he was not sure he could even name it. But if he tried, if he said what he was thinking, Daniel was fairly certain Stella would gather up her daughter and flee. So all he said was, "Can I make a suggestion?"

She hesitated, the candles painting beautiful designs over her features. "Go ahead."

He chose his words carefully. "Just for this one night, pretend we've been friends for years."

His words melted something in her gaze. At least, he hoped it was so. But while she was still testing her response, Nicole spoke up from the table's far end. "Uncle Daniel?"

He was sorry to release himself from her gaze. But at the same time, he felt a moment's pause wasn't altogether a bad thing. "I told you. Between us, just Daniel."

She nodded. "Why doesn't Mom ever talk about her past?"

He liked this intensely, how the newcomer to his home felt comfortable enough to open up in front of others. People who, until the previous night, had been total strangers. Daniel replied, "What has she told you?"

"Almost nothing." She adopted Lisa's singsong crispness. "We were poor, and it was awful, and I don't want to talk about it anymore."

Daniel took a contemplative bite. "I don't remember it that way. Being awful."

Stella asked, "Where are you from?"

"Born and raised in LA. Glendale to start—my dad worked for Boeing—then after the divorce we moved to the Valley, about two miles from the Universal gates. Mom worked as a secretary and bookkeeper. Dad was always late with his payments, then he disappeared entirely. Lisa hated everything about the Valley. She called it 'the cage.' "

Daniel turned to the night. It was easier to talk about their life when he wasn't gazing back into three sets of eyes. Four now, as even Chloe was watching him. "Then Mom was hired as the PA to a movie mogul's wife."

Chloe asked, "Which one?"

Nicole said, "Harvey Overton. I know that much."

Stella said, "Wow. Overton Studios. Even I've heard of him."

Daniel went on, "After two years of Mom being on call twenty-four seven, Vanessa Overton insisted we move into a small cottage at the back of their Bel Air estate. It had previously been used by the gardeners, and when we moved in, it stank of machine oil. But for us it was heaven."

Perhaps it was merely a shift of the candles' flames, four of them stationed along the table's center. Or perhaps it was his own relief at being able to fully turn away from Chloe's shadowed mood. Accept that he had done his best, and move on. Return to the more pressing matter of making his fragile niece feel safe enough here to explore forbidden reaches and perhaps even spread her wings for the first time. Daniel went on, "Lisa was twelve when we moved in."

Nicole said quietly, "Mom said she was eleven."

"Maybe. What's more important is, your mother was already something to behold."

Stella asked, "Beautiful?"

"Oh, no. LA is full of beauty. Lisa was something else entirely. It was like looking at an open flame. She was a shimmering beacon that could draw looks from miles away."

The candles turned Nicole's features into something twisted, like she saw her own absence of such unique beauty in the flickering light. "Sounds like Mom."

Daniel said, "Lisa attached herself to the mogul's wife. Vanessa gradually began treating Lisa like her young protégé."

Amber asked, "Did her mommy mind?"

"Maybe. But she didn't say anything. Lisa had never been happy. Life to her was a battlefield." Daniel saw the way Chloe jerked at the words, like someone had stabbed her in the back. He felt the young woman's pain anew. "Vanessa changed all that. Lisa just blossomed. At thirteen,

86

sis was taking classes in dance and etiquette and cosmetics and fashion. All compliments of the Overtons. At fourteen, she was launched into the world of modeling. At fifteen, she was taken by the Anne Ford Agency. She had her first *Vogue* cover at sixteen."

"The youngest ever," Nicole said, watching the flame dance. "She has a blowup of that photograph on the wall next to her vanity."

"That's right," Daniel said. "I forgot about that picture."

"Hard to miss," Nicole said. "What was she like? Then, I mean."

"I know what you mean." He spoke to her, and to Chloe, and to the tears on one face and the aching, burning desire on the other. "She would walk into a room, and every light would track her." He had seen it happen enough, the envy and hatred from most women, and the burning desire she ignited in almost every man. Daniel had loved his sister and admired her. But there was something about that fierce determination, and the draw she created at will, that made him feel like an outcast from his own family. His mother felt that too, he knew. She was proud of her daughter's accomplishments and accepted that Lisa was leaving her behind. And she was fearful, of course. They were all afraid of what might happen to their brilliant flame of a child.

Daniel watched Chloe sigh hard enough to

blow out the nearest candle. And he wished he knew what he had to do.

As they were clearing up, Stella followed him into the kitchen. "What you said out there . . . It touched me like few things do."

Daniel took his time, lining up his plates in the dishwasher like little porcelain soldiers. "I feel like everything I said was wrong."

"I know you do. And that's why I'm here. To tell you that it was very beautiful."

There was something new to her gaze, an openness that kindled another spark at heart level.

She liked his silence enough to smile and say, "Thank you for a lovely evening."

# CHAPTER 15

Daniel woke at six, his normal hour. The house was silent as he entered the kitchen. Even so, he could still sense lingering traces of the women who had been there the previous night. A faint hint of Stella's fragrance, and something more. Stella's tightly suppressed fears. Chloe's bitter enmity. Amber's effervescence. And strongest of all, Nicole's tremulous regret and remarkable determination. Daniel was tempted to walk back and place a hand on the closed door of her bedroom, to see if he could detect her mood through the wood.

He slipped on a jacket and took his first cup of coffee in the rear garden. The sky was overcast, and he thought he could smell coming rain. The previous winter had brought some heavy storms. Mudslides had caused havoc farther south in the Santa Barbara hills. The cliffs around Lompoc had also been hard hit. But Miramar had been mostly spared. Four times Daniel had volunteered to serve with groups cutting out the hilltop brush, reducing the risk of wildfire ravaging their area. It was the first time he had become involved in a regional activity. His group had been drawn mostly from professionals, lawyers and teachers and two accountants and their families. Daniel had heard from the volunteers that other groups contained some truly wild men, clans from the inland hills who normally had nothing to do with the more affluent seaside towns. The state's fire service had ended the season with a pot roast supper for all the volunteers, where Daniel had met several of the bearded folk, with their electric eyes and their raw-throated roars. They reminded him of the life he had left behind, only with more hair.

He made a second coffee and took his mug into the glass-fronted office. He gave the markets a perfunctory check, then opened his laptop and slipped Stella's drive into the slot. He used the device for all personal activity and e-mail and general Internet searches. His office system was monitored hourly by professional online security. This was definitely an investigation he needed to keep off-line.

Daniel scanned the files by name, then drew up the earliest, going not by the file's internal date but rather the point at which Stella had saved it onto the memory stick. He figured she would have started with the one that was most worrisome. Ninety seconds later, he was lost in the intricacies of a numerical maze.

He had possessed this ability for as long as

he could remember. As a child, he had begged his mother for magazines filled with number puzzles. For Daniel, their move into the Bel Air gardener's cabin had meant a bedroom of his own and access to a private pool. He could swim as long and hard as he liked, so long as he was out by eight-thirty, when the movie mogul emerged for his morning paddle. Swimming had become his haven growing up. He had joined the municipal league as a young teen, then swum for the city, and this had led to a partial scholarship to UCLA. He had twice competed in the nationals and might have made the Olympic team if he had been willing to give up on his other passion. The one that had brought him here.

Daniel had been tempted to major in higher mathematics. But the company of single-minded geeks had not interested him, just as he had no desire to take a rifle-shot approach to life as a jock. So he had majored in business. The result was a new first love.

In truth, he fell in love twice. The first was with economic trends, analyzing the constant flow of numbers generated by the American economy and predicting which way people would jump.

The second passion arrived unexpectedly during his first year in the graduate business program, when a professor introduced Daniel to forensic accounting.

In the wildest days of LA's electric highs,

Daniel had often looked back to those moments of discovery and wondered what his life might have looked like. If he had not allowed himself to be lured down the road to ruin. If he had stayed locked in his comfort zone, unraveling mysteries people assumed were hidden in their balance sheets. Revealing truths and righting wrongs. On many sleepless nights, coming down from his latest thrill ride, staring out over the treetops and his glistening pool, Daniel had pondered that stabbing mystery. How things had gone so wrong. Wishing he could take it all back and return to those first heady days of finding a task that he was great at, something it almost felt like he was born to do.

Just like now.

Three hours later, the two of them were seated in the coffee shop closest to the town hall. Daniel had offered to meet Stella alone, and he had promised to return in time for Marvin's arrival. But Nicole insisted on coming, and Daniel found himself enjoying the young woman's company. Even today, with all the shadows looming just out of sight.

The very first time Daniel had come to Miramar, he had wanted to call the place home. There was a singular vibe to the entire central coast. But as far as Daniel was concerned, Miramar was the jewel in the crown.

He considered Miramar to be a way station on the route to California's new millennium. He had never thought of it as a throwback to some distant time, when women wore modest two-piece bathing suits and the Beach Boys promised a life that began and ended in the sun. Miramar was very much anchored in the here and now. And yet it also stubbornly defined *which* here and *which* now.

Until arriving in Miramar, Daniel had secretly assumed he would never find a place he liked enough, identified with so intensely, that he would want to call it home. He had met any number of people like that in Los Angeles. That high-octane world attracted the sort who were only half alive. They thought that, because they were beautiful enough, or rich enough, or temporarily held sufficient power, they could overlook the fact that a core component of their being was missing. Daniel had always assumed he was fated to remain one of them. It was why he had found no need to resist the lure of sex and drugs. Rock and roll had never done it for him. But the on-air stage and the lights, well, that was something else entirely.

Nicole broke into his thoughts by asking, "How long do we need to wait?"

Daniel could see she was borderline terrified. Which was another reason why he had thought it was good for her to come along. There was nothing he could do about their meeting with Marvin that afternoon, except remind Nicole with his presence that she was not going into it alone. He replied, "Yesterday Stella called me as she was walking to a coffee shop. She said she came here every day. The next one is three blocks farther away."

"Meaning, you don't know when she's coming."

"If you like, go for a walk, get something at the other place, and I'll text you when we're done here."

"You really think she's in trouble?"

Daniel nodded. "That's why we're sitting here. Why I didn't call and ask to meet."

She pulled out her phone, checked her screen, and said, "Marvin again. He'll be here at two."

Daniel said the same thing he'd told her when he'd emerged from his office and found her hunched over her coffee mug, staring at the dregs with eyes shaded by another broken night. "I will be there for you. If you like, I will carry the conversation."

"I don't know what I want."

"Then I'll start, and you jump in whenever you're ready."

"Or jump out the window, more like."

"Another joke. I like that."

She sighed. Stuffed the phone back in her pocket, dismissing Marvin and the coming confrontation. "So what is it you mentioned, that thing with the numbers?"

"Forensic accounting. That was where I got my start. On the good days, I could play detective with a balance sheet."

She lifted her gaze, showed him the determined young woman lurking behind the purplish half-moons bruising her eyes. "No. I mean, what is it really."

He liked that, how she felt comfortable enough to demand a clear look at a reality beyond her own crisis. "The actual definition of forensic is 'suitable for use in a court of law.' Studying forensic accounting starts with learning the laws that govern bookkeeping, corporate taxation, board governance, and so on."

This was the point where Daniel watched most people's eyes glaze over. Instead, Nicole leaned her elbows on the table, like she had finally found something interesting enough to focus on. Even today. "Did you go to court?"

"A couple of times. I was very junior. But yeah, I went. And testified in three cases."

"How was it?"

Daniel pushed his cup aside and leaned in as well. "It was great."

"Really?"

"Terrific. The senior forensics expert in our firm liked to say that discovering the bad guys and learning what they did was only half the battle. A great forensics expert was somebody who could make it live for the jury."

"Did you?"

He nodded. "That's how I got my big TV break."

"Get out."

"The board of a major San Diego manufacturer suspected their executives of malfeasance. That's a fancy word to describe a senior figure using their powers to steal."

"Which they did."

"Big-time."

"And you discovered it?"

"I was part of a team of eight." But she just sat there, watching him, the light back in her gaze now. So he added, "Yeah. Okay. I made the discovery."

"Cool."

"The day of the trial, the senior guy was out sick. He appointed me as spokesman. So I did my schtick on the stand, and the four executives were convicted. And then I was invited onto the local business hour. The producers saw something they liked, so they started asking me back. I was brought in half a dozen more times to talk about stuff. Then they offered me a Friday afternoon gig."

"Were you excited?"

"I was scared out of my tiny mind," Daniel replied. "But yeah. I was excited, too." Daniel smiled at the memory. "All the other on-air talent were so on top of things. So authoritative. They wouldn't give me the time of day. I was just this newbie, in to fill an empty chair. I'd get bounced out soon enough."

"You showed them, though, didn't you?"

He nodded. "The producers who had hired me were the ones who decided what topics were going to get covered. I talked to them. Showed them things the other analysts had missed. Explained how I wanted to cover the issues. They gave me some rope, and then waited to see if I'd hang myself."

"The other talent must have hated you."

"All but one. This lady—the first ever they'd given a lead position to on the business side— she was a former Wall Street analyst, the smartest person I'd ever met. She didn't like me, but she didn't try and shut me out."

"She gave you a chance to prove yourself," Nicole said. She was totally into it now, the café somewhere out there beyond her zone of attention.

"I did what I'd been trained to do. One in-depth study each week. Sometimes it came from the producer, a couple of times from the on-air lady. Mostly, though, I found cases myself. Companies who defied the trends. Or had potential the market had not yet picked up on. Or were overpriced and potentially headed for a big decline in stock valuation." He smiled at the memory. "That got me in a lot of hot water. One company threatened to take us to court after their stock tanked."

"What happened?"

"The network took me," Daniel replied.

"What does that mean?"

"They started adding my Friday spot to their national roundup. Ratings climbed, so they added a Monday slot for me on *Good Morning America*." Daniel found himself flooded with memories of the heady thrill of those first weeks. "It seemed like overnight everything changed."

Nicole's response surprised him. She leaned back, drawn away by something only she could see. "Limos became just another way to get to work."

He felt the severed connection like a wounded nerve. "Something like that."

She started to ask another question. Hesitated. Then the need to know finally won out. "Was that when you started . . ."

"Using." Daniel forced himself to remain as he was. Leaning forward. Pretending it was all still very cool. "I had always enjoyed the occasional high. But yeah. That was the turning point."

Nicole was quiet for a long moment, steeling herself for the question Daniel knew was behind it all. Finally, she asked, "Did Mom . . ."

"No. Lisa never used anything. She was always totally clean, though I guess you could say she was addicted to juice bars." When Nicole did not respond to his feeble joke, he answered the next question without forcing her to ask. "She might have known I was using. She had to suspect. But Lisa saw what Lisa wanted to see."

Her voice was scarcely a whisper. "Sounds familiar."

"If your mother had known anything for certain, she would never have introduced me to Kimberly."

Nicole opened her mouth to ask something else, something that revealed the wound at the center of her day. But the words remained a mystery, for at that moment another voice said, "Daniel, what are you doing here?"

# CHAPTER 16

Even in her nervous and fearful state, Stella Dalton was alluring. Daniel stared at a woman who endured her sorrow like another might a bad scar or a missing limb. But neither her absent daughter nor her divorce defined her. Daniel wondered what kind of person could do that—endure all she had and still live a full life. Build a haven for her other daughter. Nurture a child like Amber, who, despite her effervescent joy, was no doubt a challenge and a handful.

As Daniel stood in line for Stella's latte, he glanced back occasionally and watched her talk with Nicole. Stella was a lovely woman, perhaps a year or so younger than his own thirty-five years. But he couldn't be certain. Nor did it really matter. She wore little or no makeup, just a touch of lip gloss. Her hair was black with reddish streaks; Daniel was certain the mixed color was the result of the sun and not something from a bottle. She wore it just a touch beyond shoulder length. When she smiled at something Nicole said, her features knitted into well-defined lines. Daniel liked that immensely, how this lovely woman had held on to such a heartfelt smile. As he returned to the table, he found himself wanting to tell her all these things, how nice it was to be in the company of a woman who was not just appealing but reflected a life he genuinely admired. But the quiet good cheer Stella had shown to Nicole vanished as he set down her cup and seated himself. Just then, all she had room for was what he had come to say.

Daniel launched straight in. "You were right to be worried."

All the air escaped from Stella. All the tension and the fire gone in one long silent breath. She managed to shape two words, "You're sure?"

"As sure as I can be at this point." Daniel caught sight of Nicole. Her eyes were so wide they appeared almost completely round, as though this glimpse into the world of adults granted her yet another reason to be afraid. Daniel worried that he had made a mistake, agreeing to her request to come along. But it was too late for that now. "I haven't found a smoking gun. There's no file headed 'Stolen Funds.' But the signs are all there."

"You think or you know?"

"I am ninety percent certain."

"But if there's nothing concrete, I mean, you can't be really certain . . ."

"I've been here before, Stella. Something

improper is happening inside your organization."

Stella glanced at Nicole, but something in her gaze left Daniel fairly certain she did not see the younger woman at all. Just then all Stella had room for was the looming threat. "Tell me what you think you know."

"The people behind this are definitely pros. This is not some small-town shifting of funds from one account to another. They've done their best to hide their trail."

"I'm sorry, Daniel. But I'm not hearing . . ."

He held up a hand and nodded at the same time. "You want facts. I understand. What must have alerted you was a regular pattern of mistakes, correct?"

Stella released another sigh. He supposed it was the kind of noise a patient would make when the doctor starts applying medical terminology to her worst fear. "Over and over and over."

"See, that's not real. That's not something you would ever expect to see unless—"

"Unless it's not a mistake at all."

"Right. I checked thoroughly. Twice. The earliest quarters you sent me, everything was fine."

"That's why I included them. So you could see what I considered normal."

"Then the errors begin. Almost immediately, your records start to form a recognizable pattern. Account balances shift around too often. Pension fund losses are too great. A complete idiot playing roulette would do better than the town's investments. It all adds up to a steady siphoning off of savings."

Stella wet her lips. Her eyes were filled with the dread of whatever she was going to ask, which Daniel assumed would be about next steps. He could see the woman's fear was infecting Nicole, and he had no idea what to say to make it better. Because Stella was right to be afraid. Whoever was behind this had carefully established a pattern that could be blamed on her.

Then Daniel spotted a new figure poised just beyond the café's side window. He had no idea how long the newcomer had been standing there. But only one thing came to his suddenly frantic mind. Daniel leaned across the table and said, "Quick now. Smile and kiss me."

# CHAPTER 17

To Stella's credit, she did just that.

Her movements were so fluid, Daniel wondered if she had perhaps been thinking of it herself. Wishing it would happen. Then the kiss enveloped him, and everything else was shoved aside.

It had been over a year since he had kissed anyone. And that had been a polite punctuation to end an awkward first date, another woman Ricki had set him up with. The last time he had been on any sort of date at all.

This was something else entirely. Stella's kiss carried a remarkable flavor, a womanly mixture of coffee and a spice that reminded him of cinnamon. The warm fullness of her lips, her scent . . . Daniel was genuinely sorry when she pulled away.

Daniel caught a brief glimpse of something there in her gaze. More than just surprise over the move. At least, he hoped so.

Then another woman demanded, "What do we have here?"

• • •

Daniel had met the mayor of Miramar on any number of occasions. Catherine Lundberg was a born politician, or so she liked to claim. The sort of person who lived and breathed for the public eye. Daniel had known any number of such people in the film and television worlds. They shared a common set of gut instincts, an ability to gauge every event from the standpoint of how it made them look—not to the world at large, but to the people who mattered. Daniel neither liked nor disliked them. They were merely a common thread running through every power structure he had encountered.

As he pulled away from Stella's kiss, the mayor sidled up to their table, planted her hands on her hips, and demanded cheerily, "Aren't you going to introduce me?"

"I'm Daniel," he said, regretting the need to turn away from that mesmerizing gaze. "Caught in the act."

Daniel was worried about Nicole's response. If she had been unsettled by their kiss, if she was pushed away from the heart of things, then he was going to have to change course. Because she was the most important issue just now. But when he glanced over, Nicole was smiling. She met his eye and said, "All right."

Daniel smiled back. "Surprise."

Stella said, "Won't you join us?"

"Not if I'm disturbing." Catherine pulled a chair over and asked Nicole, "Have we met?"

"Nicole is my niece, up visiting from Los Angeles. Nicole, this is Catherine Lundberg, the town mayor."

"Our little town must be quite a change from Los Angeles."

"I'll say."

Catherine said to Stella, "I don't recall your mentioning a man in your life."

"It's all happening so fast."

"Well, I for one could not be happier."

Daniel rose to his feet. "What can I get you?"

"Perhaps a small latte."

Nicole stood with him. "I'll help." She followed him to the counter. "Quick thinking there."

"It was the only thing that came to mind."

Nicole kept her back to the table. "Is she the town baddie?"

"Too early to tell. What will you have?"

"One of those melty-cheesie things."

"You got it." Daniel paid. Then as they walked over to the pick-up counter, he said, "The problem is, I don't have any idea what comes next."

Nicole showed a delight that repositioned the creases of sorrow and worry on her face into something that was almost beautiful. "Are we talking about the lady or the other thing?"

"The other. Definitely."

"Hey. It looked to me like you were enjoying yourself there."

Daniel could not risk denying it, not with her eyes sparking with something akin to joy. "I have to admit it rocked my boat."

"She's nice. I like her. And her daughter is great." Nicole started to speak, then compressed her lips into an almost-tight line.

"You might as well go ahead and say it."

"No, no, I couldn't possibly." Nicole twisted back and forth, arguing with herself. "Well, okay. I'd say she wouldn't object to a second dose."

"Really?"

"If you like, I could slip her a note at lunch break."

"Thank you ever so very not at all."

She accepted her sandwich, then said, "Hey, we do what we can."

# Chapter 18

When they returned to the table, Catherine was talking in excited tones, leaning against the table, her hands moving in animated motions. Stella was the same as always, at least on the surface, listening intently, her body and face and hands still. She glanced up as Daniel set the coffees down in front of the two women. Her gaze was a bit more fractured than before, permitting him a brief glance at the fear that he hoped only he could see. He had met any number of people like Catherine Lundberg, playing for the lights even when they faced an audience of one. Almost always they had totally forgotten who they were. When the lights went off and the audience went away, they faded into shadows themselves. Daniel watched Catherine talk about nothing of importance with empty enthusiasm. He figured a stiff breeze would blow that woman to Oregon.

It was not the first time that he had read an individual totally wrong.

Twenty minutes later, they left the coffee shop in order to go meet Marvin. Moving from one high-octane situation to another. As they departed, Daniel asked Stella if they were still on for that evening. Casual and comfortable, as though the two of them were a semi-permanent item. And then sealing the conversation with a farewell kiss.

Daniel could still feel her lips as he drove them home.

He felt something else as well, something that had triggered yet another memory. Something that frightened him in ways he had not felt since the lonely midnight hours following his arrival in Miramar.

Adrenaline.

All this was a minor taste of what he had previously known. Being in conversation with a possible criminal, readying himself to step inside her universe and unravel the mystery of stolen funds. Leaving there to take his niece to meet the man whose world she had effectively demolished. They were small potatoes, compared to what he had once known.

But still.

He tasted the back of his throat, wondering if the old hunger was about to strike. But all he felt just then was . . .

Affection.

Nicole was making herself small again, on the far side of the seat against the passenger door. Daniel reached out and touched her hand. "I'm here for you."

She looked at him. "You know what I was thinking?"

"Tell me."

"I've been in Miramar less than two days. And already I have more friends than I left behind." She tapped her fingernails on the side window. "I know a lot of people in LA. But it always felt like, I don't know."

Daniel replaced his hand on the wheel. He knew. All too well. "You drift around the outskirts of other people's lives."

"Too right."

"LA can be a very lonely place," Daniel said. "Especially in a crowd of friends."

"I see how you are here. And how they are with you." Nicole reached over and touched his arm. "Someday I'm going to find a way to tell you what all this means."

The good feeling remained between them until Daniel pulled down the narrow cliffside lane. The road was only wide enough for one car, which meant anyone coming the other direction had to pull into one of the drives. NO PARKING signs ran like sentries down both sides. Daniel's was one of four houses lining the final cul-de-sac. Beyond that, the ocean shifted inward, like a great bite had been taken from the land in eons past. Daniel and his three neighbors occupied a headland shaped like the grass-covered bow of a ship. Daniel rounded the final bend, and there waiting in his drive was Marvin's car.

Nicole's breath drew in sharply. "He's early."

And like that, the good feeling between them was gone.

# CHAPTER 19

Nicole rose slowly and just stood there waiting as Daniel rounded the front of the truck. He closed her door, as softly as he could. And waited, wanting her to know it was okay. Whatever she decided to do, including turning and fleeing down the road they had just driven.

She breathed in and out, then slipped in close enough to nestle her arm on his. She did not actually take hold. Rather, Daniel cupped her hand, which rested in his as they walked forward. Her fingers trembled like the wings of a captured bird.

Marvin started to step forward, then hesitated. He tried for a smile. "Hello, darling."

Nicole huffed in the same manner she had used after Lisa's departure. As if a sob was just too big an effort.

Marvin was dressed in a starched striped dress shirt and the trousers to a suit. Daniel had rarely seen the man in casual wear, even around the house. He was not unattractive, and his money and power lent him a subtle polish. He was a couple of inches shorter than Daniel's six-two and perfectly groomed. The last swatches of his hair were trimmed into a silver-black wreath. Twice Daniel had observed the man in court, watched him take hold of the jury with true star power. But the man was rendered mute now, his smile as unsteady as the grip he kept on his open door.

Daniel was about to insert himself into this silent emotional storm when his phone rang. "Excuse me. I forgot to cut it . . ."

Then he saw who it was.

Daniel said, "I have to take this."

He did not turn away. He could not let Nicole face this alone, not even for an instant. So he used his free hand to make the connection and spoke facing Marvin. "Ricki, now isn't a good—"

"Chloe didn't come home last night." Ricki was wound so tight her voice came out like a teakettle's hiss.

"Did you check with the police?"

Both Nicole and Marvin focused on him as Ricki said, "There's no report of anything. And they can't treat her as a missing person until twenty-four hours have passed."

"Where are you now?"

"At her school. She's not . . . Daniel, I can't find Travis. He left after breakfast and . . . I'm afraid he's gone over the edge. Please, please, can you help me . . ."

"I'm on it." Daniel cut the connection and told them, "Something's come up."

113

● ● ●

The only point where Nicole objected was when Daniel tried to get her and Marvin to stay, wait at home, do anything except come along. Because the outcome Daniel dreaded most was being successful. Finding his friend. And having to deal with the aftermath.

Nicole's response was surprising enough to cut through his panic. "You might need me."

"Nicole, there's no telling what state he's in." Daniel struggled to find words that suited a teenage listener. "Chloe has always been his weak point. Knowing Travis, if he does go over the edge, he'll go hard."

"Maybe it's not too late." She halted any further discussion by heading for Daniel's truck. As she opened the passenger door, she called back, "Marvin, are you coming?"

They started in the eastern valleys because that was Travis's favorite escape route. Whenever things got bad, that was where he went. Travis carried a toolbox filled with free weights and exercise cables and workout gear. He stopped in one of the state parks, hooked his gear up to a picnic table or a small eucalyptus, and fought down the bad things with a routine that could last hours. Daniel searched there first, even though Ricki had already made the rounds before heading to Chloe's school. When they came up empty, Daniel began the real hunt.

Daniel had no idea what Marvin thought of that frantic search. Two and a half hours of racing through the surrounding county, popping in and out of the bars and hideaways Daniel had successfully avoided for four years. Nicole sat in the passenger seat, doing a Google search for the next place. All the while, Marvin sat in back, rocking through each high-speed turn, saying almost nothing. This after leaving his law practice and driving four hours north, only to be shunted to one side. Everything he carried with him was left unspoken.

Marvin finally broke his silence when they stopped at a no-name roadside burger joint. "Why aren't we looking in town?"

Daniel stared at the order window, wondering whether his stomach would keep anything down. "Travis wouldn't want to be found. His ideal bar would be in a cave."

Nicole, on the other hand, was as animated as he'd ever seen her. "Marvin's right. What if he *wants* to be found?"

Daniel stared at her. "I'm still getting used to the fact that you're a lot older than your years."

"Welcome to my world," Marvin said.

The three shared a smile. The first. Daniel asked, "Anybody hungry?"

"I'm too nervous," Nicole said.

"I don't remember seeing greasy burger with fries on my diet list," Marvin replied.

As Daniel pulled from the lot, his phone rang. He fished it from his pocket, saw it was an unlisted number, and handed it to Nicole. "Mind handling this?"

She answered, listened, spoke a few words, listened some more, then lowered the phone and said, "He claims he's Connor Larkin."

Marvin leaned forward. "The movie star?"

Daniel said, "He's married to a local lady. She runs a restaurant in town. Castaways."

"Cool." Nicole lifted the phone, spoke again, then cut the connection. "Connor says to tell you that Travis showed up at their place about an hour ago. He needs a friend."

# CHAPTER 20

When they arrived, the lunch hour was over, and Castaways was empty except for the dark-skinned giant seated at the bar. A half-full coffee mug was the only thing on the polished wooden surface. Afternoon light spilled through the floor-to-ceiling bay windows that formed the restaurant's western wall. The bar curved like a polished wooden wave around a central station that held a wall of glittering bottles. Every now and then, Travis lifted his gaze from the mug's black depths and stared at the liquid temptation on display. He frowned as he did so. As if the sole decision he needed to make was precisely where he was going to start his descent.

Daniel settled onto the stool to Travis's right. He had not called Ricki, nor did he intend to until Travis made up his mind. Daniel also had not spoken. He waited patiently for Travis to start talking. If necessary, he would remain there all day. He had said as much to Nicole before entering the restaurant, explaining how he needed Travis to be the one to step voluntarily from the cliff's edge. Otherwise, his friend would simply find another lonely place from which to jump.

Through the mirror behind the bottles, Daniel watched Nicole and Marvin follow Connor Larkin from the kitchen. All three of them carried plates and glasses. The movie star was dressed in a USC School of Cinematic Arts sweatshirt with the sleeves cut off, ragged denim shorts, and sandals. If Connor had anywhere more important to be, he did not show it. He directed them to a table by the receptionist's station. He spoke words too softly for Daniel to hear. Nicole laughed for the first time Daniel had heard since her arrival in Miramar.

Travis shifted on the stool. "All the times I've said the words to other fools, you'd think the message would have sunk into this thick skull of mine."

Daniel nodded to his reflection, glad the man had finally spoken. He said, "You can't control anyone else's actions. You can't take the blame. And you can't use it as an excuse for falling down."

"Glad to know you've been listening."

"All the time."

"I just wish I knew what to do." Travis's hands were large enough to completely swallow the mug. "All this while, I thought I'd done a good job bringing that young lady into a happy place."

Daniel said it because somebody needed to. "Between brothers, I need to tell you, Chloe is already gone."

Travis appeared to stop breathing.

"Your time of protecting her is over. The fact that she's underage and not ready doesn't matter. This is the world we live in. She is not going to wait, much as she should. If you tighten your grip, she'll find whatever exit is closest."

Travis lifted his mug, sipped, grimaced at the cold black brew. "This is going to shatter Ricki."

"Not necessarily." Daniel sketched out the idea that he'd been formulating since receiving Ricki's call. Throughout their countywide drive, Daniel had been putting together his pitch, trying to frame this in a way that would make the idea seem acceptable to Chloe's parents. But as he spoke to the immobile man seated beside him, all Daniel heard were the holes. The flaws. The multitude of ways the whole thing could go awry.

Travis neither spoke nor moved when he finished. Daniel waited with him, giving the friend and father a chance to digest.

Finally, Travis said, "You talked this over with anybody?"

"Of course not."

"This could work."

"I'm glad you think so."

"You want to go ask the people in question if they'd help my little girl?"

"Of course." Daniel pulled the phone from his pocket. "As soon as you call your wife."

# CHAPTER 21

Daniel followed Travis's Escalade from Miramar's main street to Chloe's school. He did not need to ask Nicole or Marvin how it was going. His niece spent the entire journey turned in her seat, her chin settled on the seat back, watching Marvin. The LA attorney was in his element now, speaking to his erstwhile daughter with the same quiet force he used to convince juries. "I hate to say this. But I understand why you did what you did."

"I didn't want to hurt anybody."

"I know."

"Especially you."

Marvin reached out and touched her arm. "I know."

"But I needed . . ."

"You needed clarity. You needed to set your own course." Marvin withdrew his hand. "And I should have seen this a long time before now."

"Mom is so . . ."

If Marvin had any difficulty with Nicole's unfinished sentences, he did not show it. "Lisa is a wonderful person. And I love her very much."

"Still now?"

"Yes, honey. I won't lie to you. This has hurt. A lot. And it's going to take time for us to recover."

"I'm so sorry."

Marvin started to respond. Daniel watched the man absorb Nicole's distress like stones tossed into a lake, with all the conflicting ripples. A sigh, a slight shake of his head, then Marvin said, "I've known since before we were married that Lisa has her own way of seeing life. And sometimes the perspective she wants to claim is real is, well . . ."

"A lie."

"I prefer the word 'myth.' We all do it at some level. Pretend something is real because it suits us. But Lisa takes this to a totally new level. It is her survival mechanism—at least, that's how I've chosen to see it. But it's just so . . ."

Daniel stopped at the light with the school up ahead. Ricki was standing in the forecourt, her arms wrapped tight around her middle. He heard Nicole say, "Tell me. Please."

"You know about her and Daniel's past?"

"A little. Only because Daniel told me."

"Darling, her early years remain an open wound. I know that much. I don't know how Daniel survived intact—"

"I didn't," Daniel said, speaking for the first time since they left the restaurant. "So please don't hold me up as some paragon of right living. Because I'm not. And I never have been."

That drew them both around. The tears Nicole had been almost ready to shed were blinked away. She said, "I think you're great."

"I second that," Marvin said.

"Thanks, but . . ." Daniel decided there was nothing to be gained by telling them how wrong they were. He pulled into the parking space next to Travis and watched as the big man rose from the SUV, walked over, and embraced his wife. Then he asked Nicole, "Will you be okay here without me?"

"Definitely." Nicole touched him with the same tentative gesture Marvin had used. "Thanks."

Daniel got out of his pickup and walked over to where Travis held his wife. Ricki had always struck him as a champion, a woman who had risen from hardscrabble beginnings and triumphed, both on the field and off. She had become the first African American female to serve as a spokesperson for Nike. She had remained a rock through her husband's descent into the cave of addiction to painkillers and booze, and had been there to welcome him back to clarity and clean living. She had a deep laugh and the strongest embrace Daniel had ever experienced. And yet she stood there in her husband's arms, trembling like a leaf, so fragile it was only his strength that kept her upright.

Travis said, "Let's go home."

"I don't even know why I came here." Her tear-streaked face shone ruddy in the afternoon light. "The school already called me to ask why Chloe hadn't shown up."

"We've got good friends who are going to help us now." Travis slowly steered her around, giving her a chance to object, to struggle, to remain planted in futile desperation in front of the school. "Let's go get you settled."

"I've been standing here, trying to remember the last time I heard my baby girl laugh." Ricki allowed her husband to start toward the Escalade.

"Maybe she'll be there waiting for us at home," Travis said. "You can ask her that very thing."

"I wish I knew what to do."

"You're doing it, sweetheart. You're letting people be there with you and for you." Travis shot Daniel a look over his wife's head. "It's something I needed to remember myself."

Daniel watched them pull from the space, returned his friend's wave, then went back to studying the terrain. He figured he'd stand there until the recess bell, watch all the young people come piling out, then ask around. See if anyone could give him a list of places where he should start looking. He glanced back at his car in time to see Nicole open her door. She rose to her feet, sketched him a tiny wave, then opened the rear door and climbed in beside Marvin.

Which was when he spotted the sandwich shop.

Across the street and half a block down, it was a typical sort of student dive. Big windows, tables spilling through the open double doors and crowding the sidewalk. The perfect place to hang out and be seen. Daniel walked over and checked inside. But with school still in session, all save one of the tables were empty.

He started back toward the school's entrance when a soft voice called from behind him, "Are they gone?"

# CHAPTER 22

Daniel did not take nearly as much time outlining his idea to Chloe as he otherwise would have liked. He felt pressured by leaving Nicole in the pickup with Marvin. It had seemed like everything was okay, but he had promised to be there every step of the journey. Even with her saying it was fine for him to come over here, despite the fact that he could see them, his absence felt like a slightly fractured vow. So he sketched out what he had in mind far too swiftly, watching Chloe's eyes go round in the process. Then he asked, "What do you think?"

"What difference does it make what I think?" She gave him a petulant response, the angry teen venting at the only person within reach. "My parental types will never go for this."

He did not raise his voice. He showed no anger because he didn't feel any. "Chloe, I love you like you were family. But I swear you can be your own worst enemy."

"What, you don't think I'm right—"

"Of course you are. At least from your perspective. But that is a sixteen-year-old's attitude."

125

Chloe wrapped her arms around her middle. An exact replica of her mother. "What do you want me to say?"

"For this to work, you need to grow up, focus, and answer the question."

Her grip tightened. "I want it so much it hurts."

"That's my girl." Daniel put his arm around her shoulder, pretending the girl's tension did not reverberate in his own gut. "Let's go see if we can make it happen."

# CHAPTER 23

Daniel called to say he was running half an hour late. Which was a good thing, because Stella had yet to decide what she was going to wear.

She had left work early in order to prepare her daughter's dinner. She had ended up telling the Miramar town hall office staff the truth. That she was going out on a date. Which had drawn the mayor from her quarters, so that she could announce to everyone that Stella had a beau. A famous one at that. Who, she could report as a firsthand witness, was a great kisser.

Stella picked up Amber from the neighbor who operated a happy afternoon way station for several young children of working single parents. She drove home, made Amber's meal, went upstairs, and stood staring at her closet for fifteen minutes before admitting defeat. She had no idea what she was doing. Or why she had agreed to go on this date in the first place. It was impossible to tell herself this was merely part of the act, or that it all came down to Daniel helping her with this problem issue.

Because the truth was, she could still feel his lips.

Stronger still was how she stood there looking at all the clothes she had not worn in ages, and what she saw most clearly was the look in his eyes.

He had drawn back slowly from the kiss and looked at her. Really looked. The way lovers did. A smile had tightened the edges of his eyes. The grin had not needed to reach his lips. The spark in his gaze was enough. She had seen a sorrow as old as time itself. And a wisdom. Or so it felt to her then, standing immobile in the middle of her closet, seeing not clothes but what the moment represented.

She might have stood there for hours. Except Amber skipped her way into the bedroom and announced, "Daniel's going to be even later than he thought."

That drew her around. "Why am I hearing this from you?"

"Nicole texted me." Amber did a sort of pirouette and fell on the bed, still holding out her phone. "He's really sorry. But he's doing something for Chloe. She ran away."

Stella stepped out of the closet. "Why is Daniel giving you a running commentary on the daughter of a friend?"

"He's not. Nicole is."

"Same question."

"She's great, Mommy. I like her."

"That's no answer." She stepped over. "Give me your phone."

Stella expected an argument. Amber was as private as any preteen when it came to what she discussed with her friends. But this time she simply rose to her knees, handed over the device, and said, "They found Chloe. Daniel's still working on an idea he had to make things better."

Which was exactly what she read, as she scrolled through a dozen back-and-forth texts spanning the past few hours. "I'm not sure how I feel about you two being in such close contact."

"Why, Mommy?" Amber began bouncing on the bed. "She's really, really nice."

Stella had a hundred reasons, but none of them actually sounded good enough to express. Because the truth was, it had very little to do with Nicole and everything to do with Daniel. Stella declared, "I'm going for a run. Did you finish your dinner?"

"I don't like spinach."

"Amber . . ."

"Okay, Mommy."

She dressed in shorts and jogging top and running shoes, bound her hair back as tightly as she wished she could control her thoughts and emotions, and left the house.

Stella had run her way through any number of hard-edged late afternoons. The regular pattern of steps, the steady breathing, the trail, the sunlight, the passing joggers—all helped immensely in making sense of whatever problem she carried. Just like now. By the time she turned around and started back, she had reached the only conclusion that made sense.

She was going to end things the moment he showed up.

She would just have to weather this emotional tempest by herself. There was a chance, a real one, that Daniel would arrive, and he would have had a bad day, and he would introduce another horrid crisis into their lives. She heard his honest description of who he once had been for what it really was—a warning of things to come.

By the time she left the trail and started down her road, she had convinced herself that she was better off alone.

Which was when she arrived at the end of her driveway. And found Daniel seated on the front step. Laughing at something Amber was saying, the two of them as easy and intimate as lifelong friends.

She had been determined before. Now she was terrified.

# CHAPTER 24

When Stella came jogging around the curve in their road, Amber was saying, "I'm trying to decide if Goldie would look good in a sailor's suit. You know, like they show on the videos. With the little hat and everything."

But one look into Stella's eyes and Daniel felt the happy moment drain away. Not even Amber's lilting charm could erase his certainty over what was coming next. He rose to his feet. Stella's unspoken message needed to be heard standing up.

Tension tilted Stella's body slightly to the left. Her arms were clasped along her middle and twisted so the thumbs pointed back at her thigh. "Can I speak with you a moment?"

Amber announced happily, "We were talking about Goldie. Can I have a puppy?"

"Go inside, please." Stella stood there, tight as a drawn bow, staring at some vacant point beyond Daniel's shoulder. As soon as the door clicked shut, she said, "This isn't going to work."

Daniel did not pretend to misunderstand. He stood there, and he took it in silence.

"I should never have agreed to go out with you. It's just . . ." She released her grip and wiped her face with an unsteady hand. "Now isn't a good time."

Daniel had a hundred things he wanted to say. How this was the first date he'd actually been looking forward to in four years. How her daughter had already captured his heart. But Stella continued her thousand-yard stare, her body charged with all the arguments she was just waiting to fire in his direction. So he simply said, "I'll be going, then."

He walked back to his pickup and started the engine and pulled from the drive, all without looking directly at the woman who still stood there on her walk, staring at the empty space by her front drive.

His stoic strength only lasted until he reached the stop sign at the end of her road.

The old familiar friends rose from their four-year slumber. The bitter acrid taste filled his throat. The desperate burning, the yearning as strong as fury.

He stared at the two alien hands clenching the wheel. All he had to do was head back to one of the places he'd entered that very same day. One of them surely had his favorite single malt. He could taste the first smoky swallow. Travis wasn't there to argue away the fraught moment. There was no reason not to give in. What was the point of holding back? What reason could possibly be good enough to keep him sober?

When Daniel entered his home, he had no recollection of driving back. Nor could he say precisely why he was still straight.

Nicole was seated at the counter, her laptop open to one side, making room for a plate with the remnants of a sandwich, along with a coffee mug. She must have seen something in his expression, because she instantly turned fearful. "I thought it'd be okay if I got something to eat."

"It's fine. Where's Marvin?"

"He left almost an hour ago. He said to tell you he'd be in touch." She hesitated, then asked, "What's the matter?"

*So much,* was the answer. Though it made no sense at all. One part of him said it was ridiculous to get so bent out of shape by a woman's rejection. But he was aware enough to know it wasn't just that. It was how his entire world was being redesigned. "Where is Chloe?"

Her head rose above the sofa's back. "Right here."

Daniel had not known what was going to happen next until that very moment. "I want you to come with me."

Her face turned pinched, angry. "I'm not going home. Don't you dare try and make me."

"We're just going for a drive. There's something you need to see." Daniel waved the hand holding the keys at the door. "Let's go."

Nicole slid off her stool. "Can I come too?"

Daniel skirted Miramar's downtown, though it meant taking the longer route. Chloe reverted to the sullen teen. But even scrunched against the passenger door, arms crossed and knees drawn up, her face a mask and her eyes blank, she remained a truly beautiful young woman. Daniel did his best to ignore her. But what he thought was, Ricki and Travis were probably right to worry. Given half a chance, LA would not even leave the bones.

He took it slow, watching the clock, wanting to time it just right. Every now and then he was hit by tremors as strong as the aftershocks that followed a major quake. The hunger had left him now, leaving behind a hollow ache, an empty space at the core of his being.

The territory south of Miramar Bay was dominated by a headland that had been turned into a city park. There was a little open-fronted chapel he liked to use as a turnaround point on long runs. Benches rimming the park's seafront filled up on the weekends, when families liked to picnic and lovers shared a bottle of wine and children were constantly called back from the fence lining the overhang. But on a chilly weekday like this, the place was empty save for a few people walking the paths. Daniel parked in the lower-level lot and announced, "From here we go on foot."

He could have driven a good deal closer, but he was hoping the climb would still his jerky muscles and bring Chloe to a point where she might actually hear what he had to say. By the time they crested the rise, all three of them were breathing heavily.

Daniel pointed them onto a bench, placing Chloe between himself and Nicole. He had no idea whether it was a good thing to have Nicole along for this. But she had asked, and he was not ready to tell her no. Their bench was positioned directly over the mid-level parking area, divided into three sections by stands of Aleppo pines, bent and twisted by the constant winds blowing off the Pacific. He pointed to the far segment. "There's a silver Dodge SUV parked beneath the trees, see it?"

Chloe said, "Not too well."

"His position is intentional." He shifted slightly to face Chloe. "I need to know if you're ready for what is about to happen."

She crossed her arms. "I already told you that."

Daniel nodded slowly, taking his time. "Take a good look at that Dodge."

"I already told you I can't see it very well."

His own recent near-trauma left him completely immune to her tense anger. "There's a man seated

135

inside. His name is Clark. His wife has lupus. Do you know what that is?"

Chloe replied with a tight head shake.

"It's a terrible disease. There's no cure. She is dying. But very slowly. It could take years." Daniel gave that a beat to sink in, then went on, "They have a daughter with Down syndrome. Financially, Clark is hanging on by his fingernails. He's within a few inches of losing his house. Which means his daughter would go into foster care and his wife would spend the rest of her days in a state-run nursing home. If she's lucky."

Nicole said softly, "That's so sad."

"Clark joined AA the same week as me. We were friends. Sort of. But the pressure of an awful life just got too much. So now he comes here. Every night after he gets off his terrible job. Which he hates. But he has to keep going so he can pay all their bills." Daniel pointed down the ridge. "He comes here. And he drinks until the pain goes away. Then he goes home. To his wife and his daughter."

He stopped, giving Chloe a chance to object. But he had her now. He could see the spark of something in her eyes. Curiosity. Sorrow. Something that was drawing her out of her tight little shell.

He said, "There's a term we use in AA for people like Clark. We say, he's not ready to get sober. It means exactly what it says. So I'm asking you again, Chloe, are you ready?"

"Why are you talking to me like this?" Chloe cried out loud enough to attract the attention of nearby cliff walkers. "I already told you. I'm not my parents! What else do you want me to say?"

"Your anger will only take you so far. If I'm able, I'm going to help bring your dreams a little closer. If you walk forward with nothing but rage, people will take advantage of that. Being successful at your game—"

"It's not a *game!*"

"Being successful only makes the chances of falling off the rails come more easily. Do you think your father *wanted* to stay wasted? Do you think that's why he spent years fighting and struggling to become a pro football player?"

She swiped her face. "He got hurt."

"And you'll get hurt too. I'm sorry. It's a hard thing to face when you want something this badly. But it's true. You *will* get hurt." Daniel pointed down the rise. "I'm not saying it will be what your father faced. Or me. Or Clark. But the risks are real. The threat is there."

"What do you want me to say?" she repeated. Only this time it was in her mother's voice. Low. Deep.

"That you can listen beyond your rage. I'm not saying, don't be angry. If that's what fuels your rise, so be it. I don't agree with it, but I can't tell you what to feel or how to climb your own mountain. What I *am* saying is this. It's not enough."

The wind rushed through the trees sheltering the silver SUV, pulling the branches apart just as the man behind the wheel lifted a paper bag. And drank. Chloe shivered. "Okay."

It wasn't much, as responses went. But as far as Daniel was concerned, it was enough. "Let's get out of this wind."

As they were walking back to his pickup, Nicole took a soft hold of his hand and pulled Daniel back. When Chloe walked on ahead, Nicole asked, "You help him, don't you?"

"What are you talking about?"

"Clark. Only that's not his name, is it. You promise to be anonymous, isn't that right?" There was no questioning in her voice. Just a quiet certainty. "You help him. And I bet he doesn't know it's you."

They took the main road that snaked just inland from the shoreline. Chloe remained scrunched up against the opposite door, but Daniel did not sense the same tension she had carried on the way out. Nicole stared out her window, wrapped in her own little isolation bubble. But every now and then, Daniel thought he heard her hum a couple of notes. Like she was carrying on a musical dialogue with some song inside her head.

When they arrived home, Daniel unlocked the door and asked Chloe, "Do you want to stay here tonight?"

"Can I?"

"Will you call your parents?"

"It won't do any good." She glanced at him and shrugged. "Okay."

As Nicole started to pass him, he asked, "Is there anything I need to know about what you and Marvin talked about?"

"Probably. But can it wait?"

"Of course."

"So . . . I can stay?"

"As long as you like." He felt awkward speaking the words, but just the same, he wanted it out. "I like having you here with me, Nicole."

"Give it time," she said. "The charm rubs off quick."

"I doubt that very much."

She bobbed back and forth, heel to toe, as though readying herself for a leap off a high dive. Then she lifted up on her toes and kissed him on the cheek. "This day just keeps getting better."

# CHAPTER 25

Under other circumstances, Stella would probably have considered the conversation that followed Daniel's departure mildly hilarious. As it was, however, she found herself completely on the defensive.

Dealing with her daughter, who lobbed one verbal bomb after another, in the form of all of Stella's own arguments. In other words, eleven-year-old Amber was dressing her mother down.

"I cannot believe you would behave so badly."

"That's enough, young lady."

"No, it's not enough!" Amber stabbed her arm at the kitchen phone. "Now you will call Daniel and you will *apologize.*"

"I will do no such thing!"

"Don't you talk back to me!" Amber stomped her foot. "If you weren't being so *childish,* you'd already be on the phone!"

Stella felt herself stabbed by a great deal more than her daughter's ire. "Amber, honey, I did that for you."

"Oh, *please.* I *like* him. Doesn't that mean *anything* to you?"

"Of course it does . . . Sweetheart, the last thing we need is a man wrecking the life we've built for ourselves."

"That is the most ridiculous nonsense I have ever heard come out of your mouth!" Another little item Stella had often said to her growing child. Right down to the inflection points. Lobbed right back at her. "Daniel won't wreck *anything*."

What kept Stella from shouting back was how her daughter was so very close to tears. Only her fury kept Amber from sobbing. Which was another astonishment. Her daughter never became angry. Upset, of course. But she could not recall the last time her daughter had lost her temper. "All right. Then it's all about me."

"Of course it is!"

"I can't let another needy man work his way into our lives. I just can't." There. She had said it. Revealing her innermost fears. To a child. Because she had to.

Amber was having none of it. "Don't you *get* it? *You* need *him*."

"Sweetheart, that is absolutely the farthest thing—"

"No! I'm not saying another word until you *call him!*" She stomped her way across the foyer and started up the stairs.

"Amber, come back here."

"You know I'm right, Mommy!"

"Amber!"

*"No!"* She did her best to drum each foot through the step. "I am sick and tired of picking up after you!"

Which made no sense at all. And should have been good for a smile, had it not been for the door that slammed at the top of the stairs or the hollow ache the exchange left in the place where Stella's heart normally resided. Her trembling, vulnerable, frightened heart.

She crossed the kitchen on leaden limbs. Picked up the phone. And dialed the number from memory.

When Ricki answered, Stella said, "I need help."

Her best friend responded with a lengthy sigh. "Girl, that makes two of us."

"I've just had the worst argument of my life with my daughter."

Ricki went silent. Then, "Is that a joke?"

"Do I sound like I'm joking?"

"I have no idea what a joke sounds like these days."

"Maybe I should call back when you're actually on the phone with me."

"Okay, now that sounded like a joke. Am I right?"

"Half. No, less. A quarter right."

A big sigh, strong as a soft cough. "Go ahead. Give me something else to worry about."

"Ricki, what has happened?"

"No, no, you called me. Lay it on me, girl. Then we'll see if you're up for my version of the happy home."

But when Stella started talking about Amber, she had to accept the fact that none of it would make sense unless she first relayed the *other* issue. And relating what she had said to Daniel felt like talons raking across her heart.

When she went quiet, Ricki said, "Okay, so we're actually talking about two things. There's Daniel, and then there's you."

"You're forgetting the reason I called."

"I'm not forgetting a thing here."

"So you're saying that Amber is right."

"I wish you could hear yourself. That young lady is a jewel. And she loves you. And you two will work it out. There. Are we done talking about your daughter?"

"I don't get you at all."

"What you need to understand is, my husband is sober because of that man. And my daughter has a roof over her head tonight because Daniel has given her a home. And most likely a lot more besides."

Stella heard how much those last words cost her. "What is going on over there?"

"You just listen to what I'm saying. Daniel is a good man."

"That's not the point—"

"Hear me out. What you haven't said, and what

I know has got you scared silly, is what he told you this afternoon."

Stella went silent.

"You're terrified that the man is going to stop helping you. After he confirmed that you and I are right to be worried about somebody stealing the town's money. Not to mention possibly setting you up to be the fall guy. Or lady. Whatever."

Stella opened her mouth, but no sound came out.

"And I'm telling you that nothing's changed."

She managed, "You spoke with him?"

"Of course not. Don't talk silly. I just heard about it from you, remember? What I'm saying is this. Daniel will help you out because that's who he is." Ricki gave her a chance to respond, then went on, "Daniel has no earthly idea just how good a man he's become. These years he's spent holed up in Miramar, it's like, what do you call that thing when the butterfly comes out of its cocoon?"

"I have no idea what you're talking about."

"Girl, you can just go sell that down the street. You know *exactly* what I'm saying. All Daniel sees is who he was. And the damage he caused. He can't see who he's become." Ricki paused, then added, "I was hoping you'd be the one to show him. But never mind that. Whether or not you decide to let him into your heart has nothing to do with him helping you through this crisis. That's just who the man is."

"Ricki . . ."

There was a click on the line, then Ricki said, "Honey, I've got to go. My daughter's calling. We'll talk."

Stella stood holding the silent phone. She said to the night gathering outside her window, "The word is *metamorphosis*."

# CHAPTER 26

Daniel woke an hour or so before dawn, drenched in sweat. The dream had been one of those repetitive flashes he had often experienced during the bad old days. He had been standing at his favorite bar, the polished surface gleaming in the candles and chandeliers. He was surrounded by all the beautiful people, and they watched him, and they laughed. And there before him on the bar was not a drink. Instead, he faced a little cage, like a cat-carrier, with a hinged door on the front. Daniel was laughing with all the others, having a grand old time, as he reached out and unlatched the door. Then the laughter and the beautiful people vanished, and he faced a rattler. As long as a train of death, as long as all the lines of coke he'd done. It slithered across the bar, its mouth open and fangs dripping golden venom in the candlelight. Daniel wanted to run, scream, anything but stand there and watch death's approach. But he was held in place by all the bad moves. Helpless to do more than watch as the snake lunged.

He rose from the bed and stripped off his

sodden clothes and dressed in running gear. As he left his bedroom, he was halted in the darkened hallway, trapped as securely as if he was still held by the dream.

To his right, Nicole slept secure behind the closed door of his guest room, the first person in four years to use the space. To his left was another door, this one leading to what had been his office before he had glassed in the rear patio. Now it was mostly used as an in-house gym. Daniel had shifted all that equipment to the side wall and fashioned a pallet. Chloe slept there now. She shared Nicole's bathroom. But neither girl had complained.

Daniel stood in the hallway and listened to the predawn hush. He was surrounded by just how close he had come to demolishing the trust he had built with those two wonderful young ladies. The prospect of all the damage he might have wreaked left him sick to his stomach.

He padded across the living room and let himself out the front door. He forced himself to stretch, warming up gradually, even though his entire body jerked with the electric need to let go, to run as hard as he possibly could, to flee the hungry ghosts.

Daniel came home just as the sun crested the eastern hills. He showered and dressed, then woke the two girls. By the time they emerged, he had prepared a breakfast of coffee and hot milk and poached eggs and toast made from a whole grain loaf. Neither girl spoke a word as they ate.

Forty-five minutes before school was to start, he gathered them into his pickup and drove straight to Chloe's home. She did not protest when Daniel pulled into her drive. Nor did she make a move to leave his ride.

Daniel cut off the engine and said, "Might as well get it over with."

Chloe did not respond.

"It's not going to get any easier."

She asked in a too-small voice, "Do I have to stay here tonight?"

"This is your home. You love them, and they love you." When she remained stationary, he added, "If you really want to stay at my place, it's okay."

Chloe still did not move. "What you said last night, it's really, really happening?"

"There's a lot that still needs to be put in place. But the first steps have been taken . . ." Daniel stopped because she opened her door and started down the walk. At that same moment, Ricki opened the front door and came rushing out to meet her.

Daniel watched mother and daughter embrace, then turned to Nicole and said, "I haven't had a chance to ask how you feel about all this."

"It's okay. She doesn't say hardly anything."

She continued to watch as Ricki released Chloe and led her up the walk and into the house. "It's kind of like having a beautiful live-in ghost."

Daniel swiveled back around and faced forward. "Maybe she'll decide to come home."

"Doubtful."

Daniel nodded. He thought so too.

"You really think you can do what you said?"

"All I can do is set things in motion. After that, it's all up to her."

Nicole leaned forward so her face was lined up with his. Together they watched the silent house. "Still. That's a lot."

"It's a start."

"Tell me again what's happening this weekend."

Daniel didn't mind in the least repeating what he had told them the previous night. "Today is Friday. This afternoon she'll meet the photographer."

"The wedding lady. From your group."

"AA. Right. Weddings are how Veronica makes her living now. But she used to be a major player in the LA fashion scene." Daniel pointed with his chin at the front door. "She'll have a talk with Chloe. See if there's a chance the camera will like her."

"Mom talks about that a lot," Nicole said. "How the camera decides."

"It really comes down to that. Whether Chloe's looks and her charisma translate onto the screen.

Or page." Daniel shook his head. He was taking so many chances. And with such a young life. "If Veronica thinks Chloe has what it takes, she'll help design both the shoot and the wardrobe. Which will probably require some serious shopping."

Nicole was close enough for Daniel to smell the floral shampoo she had used that morning. "Did you see Chloe light up at that news flash?"

"Everybody on our street was momentarily blinded." He leaned toward his door to bring Nicole into his field of vision. "You can go with them, if you want. My treat."

"Puh-leese. Do I really look like I'm all that interested in clothes and fashion?" She kept her gaze firmly on the front door. "Which was a constant theme in our happy home, by the way. What then?"

"Veronica doesn't have a booking for this weekend. She's going to do a two-day shoot." Daniel turned back to the house. "Then we'll see."

# CHAPTER 27

Stella entered the town hall half an hour late. Her normally ebullient daughter had spent the entire morning wrapped in sadness and silence. There was no repetition of the previous day's argument, not even when Stella snapped at her. Amber simply wasn't there. On the drive to her school, Stella had tried to break through, apologize, remind Amber how much she was loved, how these problems came up in adult relationships . . . As she parked in the employee spaces behind the town hall, Stella could not actually remember what she had said. Not that any of it had actually made a difference.

Miramar's old town hearkened back to California's gold-rush era. Back then, hardy Italian immigrants had defied the Pacific currents and hunted the shores off Miramar for abalone. The shells made many families rich. Some of them moved inland and farmed the rich bottomlands of the verdant central coast valleys. They started some of America's first vineyards, producing a rich red wine that was swept up by locals and rarely made it any farther than San Francisco.

Others became caught up in the hunt for underground riches and emigrated a second time, to the Wild West towns around Sacramento. Still others remained there in Miramar, put down roots, and became movers and shakers in the local community.

Miramar's old town was fashioned from cedar and redwood and cypress, and was set firmly upon foundations of local granite. The city and county offices formed the rear portion of what was formerly a dance hall and gambling saloon. When she'd started working as the town's bookkeeper, Stella had heard all sorts of wild tales about the place. Jesse James and Bat Masterson and Wyatt Earp all supposedly played roles in Miramar's early days. If even a fraction of the stories were true, her office walls still held bullets from historic duels.

The building was fronted by a wide veranda with a cedar-planked floor and a multitude of rockers. A great deal of the town's business was still conducted there. As a result, Stella had a nodding acquaintance with most of the people who shaped Miramar's future.

Stella shared the main office with the county records keeper, the lady responsible for all building permits and her assistant, and the mayor's secretary. The secretary also served as the office receptionist. Their office was separated from the main foyer by a counter that held two computer terminals and phones, one of which connected directly to the police station around the corner.

Most of the building—formerly the saloon and dance hall—was an open-plan space used for any number of city and county events. Back in the nineties, the city had revamped the entire structure and torn out the upper floor, so the hall now looked straight up thirty feet to polished cedar rafters.

The fear that someone in a position of power had sought to drain off funds from her safe haven was another reason she entered the office that morning feeling bruised.

Adele, the head of building permits, took one look at her and said, "Don't tell me you've got the flu."

"I'm fine."

"You don't look fine. You look about as fine as sardines on burnt toast." Adele was a tiny African American with sculpted features. Both her voice and her opinions were far too big for her ballerina build. "Don't you go giving me some nasty bug. I've got too much on my plate to get sick with the never-get-overs."

As soon as Stella saw the mayor step from her office, she knew how she needed to respond. "I had a fight with my boyfriend."

Adele pushed back from her desk. "You've got a man in your life?"

153

Stella nodded to the mayor and slipped behind her desk. Just another day at the office. "Not anymore."

Adele looked at the mayor. "Did you know about him?"

"Not until yesterday."

"Girl, why am I just hearing about this now?"

"I wanted to wait until I was sure."

Catherine's smile did not touch her eyes. It seldom did. "He was certainly a looker."

"I thought so too."

Adele showed a genuine irritation. "How long has this been going on?"

"A while." Stella watched herself go through the motions of starting her daily routine. Turning on her computer, bringing up the daily calendar, checking her messages. "Long enough to know it was wrong."

Catherine said, "Somebody that good-looking and famous and still single, he's bound to be broken goods."

Stella found it easy to nod. Like she totally agreed with everything she was hearing. "He told me he'd changed."

Catherine sniffed. "Well."

"He's been sober for four years."

Adele said, "Will somebody please tell me what I'm missing?"

"His name is Daniel Riffkin," Catherine replied.

"Formerly a big TV star. What was his show called?"

"*Market Roundup.* On NBC." Stella felt as though she was observing someone else play at whatever this game was. "That was years ago."

Catherine surprised her then. "What did he think of your little girl?"

Stella pretended to give it serious thought. "I honestly don't know. Amber adored him."

Catherine pondered that for a moment, then asked, "Is she part of why he was interested in you?"

"To tell the truth, I have no idea what that man is after."

Adele huffed. "I believe I've sung that particular song myself."

Catherine nodded slowly. "Do you need to take some time off?"

"Thanks. But I'm probably better off here." Stella waited until the mayor returned to her office, then pretended to get to work. But staring out of her computer screen was the face of her broken-hearted daughter.


Daniel dropped the two girls at their school. He waited until Nicole and Chloe entered the building, like any other hovering parent, wanting to make sure they actually got to where they were supposed to be going. He then drove around the block and parked his truck. He entered the main office and asked to see the principal.

Karen Darby was physically a small, delicate woman, but she carried herself with an iron-hard attitude. She rose long enough to shake his hand, pointed him into the chair opposite her desk, and said, "You were standing outside my school yesterday."

"I was, yes."

"You picked up a young lady who had played truant."

Daniel knew nothing less than the full truth would work with this lady. "And dropped her off this morning."

"Her mother and I are friends. Ricki explained the situation. How are you involved?"

"Chloe stayed at my house last night."

"Was that wise?"

Daniel found himself liking her very much. "I may be able to help resolve the situation."

"Unwrap that a little further." She listened intently as Daniel explained what he had in mind. When he was done, she rose and crossed over to the side windows. Karen Darby was scarcely as tall standing as Daniel was seated. Even so, she carried a giant's intensity. She examined the empty street in front of her school. Thinking.

Finally, she said, "Of course I've known of Chloe's desires. Perhaps a big-city school might have assisted her more than we could here in Miramar."

156

"What she needs can't be found in any standard curriculum."

"How can you be so certain of that?"

"My sister is an Anne Ford model."

"Interesting." Darby continued to examine the empty vista beyond her window. "Will your sister play a role in this?"

"She might. But we won't know enough to ask her until Chloe jumps through the hoops this weekend."

"And if she doesn't? What then?" Darby turned around and nailed him with her gaze. "Will you extinguish this young woman's lifelong hopes? Is that part of your game plan?"

"Right now, I can't see much further than the next two days. What I most want her to see is that there is an adult who cares enough to try and help her." When she responded with a narrowed squint, Daniel pressed, "There are no guarantees in this game. A thousand fail for every one who succeeds. Ten thousand. But I think Chloe has a shot."

"How good a chance?"

"We'll know more on Sunday."

"And if your photographer friend gives her approval, what then?"

Daniel took a huge breath. Tried to force out the words. That he would take Chloe to LA and introduce her around. But the next step was too big, the ledge too high, the drop too dark. All he said was, "One step at a time."

Darby walked back behind her desk and seated herself. "Keep me posted."

Daniel took that as his dismissal. As he rose to his feet, he said, "If things do move forward next week, I'd like to take Nicole with me. She needs—"

"You may call me Sunday evening. We'll discuss the coming week at that time." Darby slid a card across the table. "My cell phone number is at the bottom. Good day, Mr. Riffkin."

Daniel returned home and took Goldie for a long walk. The dog kept glancing back, searching every passing car, clearly wondering where her two new housemates might be hiding.

He spent an hour and a half surveying the markets and preparing his next client report. Try as he might, though, he could not bring his full attention to the work at hand. Every time he looked up from the screens, thoughts of Stella were there to confront him. Telling himself he could not have done anything to change the situation did not help.

Just after eleven, the photographer called to say her afternoon appointment had canceled and they could start a day earlier. Normally Daniel didn't even hear the phone when he was deep in market data. But today it was a welcome break. As the noon hour passed, Goldie came over and settled her head upon his thigh. She had not done this since forever. She gave him the sad look only a dog could.

Goldie followed him into the kitchen, where Daniel warmed up leftovers he wasn't sure he actually wanted. As he ate, Goldie remained poised by his side, which was what she usually did, but she kept casting glances at the front door, which was definitely new. Daniel stroked the soft golden pelt and said, "I know, girl. I miss her too."

They probably weren't talking about the same woman. But still.

After lunch, Daniel returned to his glass-fronted office, only this time he refocused on the data supplied by Stella. He could do nothing about the empty space where a new feminine presence should have been inserting itself. But Stella's problem was real. The longer he pushed, the deeper he went, the more certain he became.

Goldie's whoof alerted him to a change in the air.

The doorbell rang, then the front door unlocked and Ricki called, "You decent?"

"Not only that, I'm glad you're here. I could use a break." He entered the kitchen to find her unloading two sacks of sealed plastic containers. "What on earth?"

"It's amazing how much I can get done when I'm not stressed out over another argument with my daughter." She pointed to each carton in turn. "Chloe's favorite foods. Tabouleh, falafel, lamb kebabs in this one, beef in the other. Fresh chopped salad with mint and coriander, hummus . . . I'm forgetting something."

"Ricki, this is a feast."

"And yogurt with chopped cucumber and spinach." She continued to tap the last container. "How is she?"

"Coping. How are you?"

"About the same. Travis will probably want to thank you some time further down the road. Right now . . . You understand?"

"Of course."

She showed him overbright eyes. "Just so you know, you've just become my personal favorite hero. I can't begin to thank you for helping us deal with Chloe and helping Chloe deal with her dreams."

"Ricki . . . we're a long way from knowing anything for certain."

"But still. You're doing what we should have put in motion a good while back. Only we were too frightened by all the things that don't matter at all to that child."

"They don't yet, but they will."

"Still, she needs to make her own choices."

Daniel nodded. "I think so."

"And you'll be there to help her."

The prospect of returning to LA loomed as dark as a cave. "If she'll let me."

She started to say something more, then stopped herself. "Change the subject?"

"Sure thing."

"You're going to help Stella." It was not a question. "Even though she did what she shouldn't have."

"She had her reasons to stop us from becoming any closer."

Ricki shook her head. "None of that lady's reasons are good enough. And you both deserve better."

Daniel had no idea how to respond, so he said, "Yes, I'll help."

"Will you tell me what you're thinking?"

He spent almost half an hour laying it out for the woman. Watching her back away from the tangle of emotions she had brought with her. When he was done, Ricki said solemnly, "It's a good plan, Daniel."

"Thanks. That means a lot."

"So, you're certain there's something going on."

"Better than ninety percent."

"Is the mayor involved?" When he remained silent, she hissed softly. "She is. I knew it in my bones. I could wring that woman's neck."

"I need to go pick up the girls."

Ricki opened his fridge, shifted things around, and started fitting in her containers. "Tell me something. If you were me, what would you do?"

He knew the conversation had shifted back to their daughter. "Veronica is going to want to go through Chloe's clothes, choose a selection for the shoot. Be there at the front door. Welcome them like it's the most natural thing in the world."

"Daniel . . ."

"Make them coffee. Offer to show Veronica your closet as well." He could not help but smile at her expression. "Sorry you asked?"

"Maybe a little." Ricki hugged him tightly. "There needs to be a new word. One that packs in the kind of thanks you deserve."

# Chapter 28

Stella sat in front of Amber's school, wanting everything to be okay with her daughter. That Amber would pop out like she normally did, a bright flash of joy surrounding her as she searched for Stella's car. The look she gave, the happy wave, the excited chatter on the way home, all the things that made the empty days worth enduring.

Stella stared at the school's silent front doors and thought about what Ricki had said. About Daniel only seeing who he had been, not who he had become. Ricki had accepted Stella's opposition to a relationship without argument. Which suggested . . . what, exactly?

Stella nodded to the empty front lawn. Ricki knew who Stella had become. A woman intent on never allowing a man to hurt her again, disturb her safe little existence, threaten the haven she had built for her little girl.

Even if it meant staying alone for the rest of her life.

There was a book she had read once. Novels had become a mainstay of her nightly routine.

Climb into bed with a good story, read until she could finally give in to sleep. A while back, she read about a woman vacationing on a Caribbean island who, after a solitary dinner, agreed to go on a moonlit walk with a man she had met in a bar. Midway through the walk, the woman had declared, "I positively ache for a man."

Stella had thrown the book across the bedroom. Who was this woman to speak like that to somebody she had just met? Were there really people out there who were so utterly able to disconnect from their normal lives and do whatever they pleased?

Well, not her.

Then she noticed something new. A group of mothers often congregated by the three benches that lined the school's front walk. They chattered like gay little birds. Stella had joined them a few times, but never connected, so now she waited in her car. Today, the women kept glancing over at the massive oak that shaded the principal's parking space. One of them said something, the others laughed. And they kept looking.

When the school bell rang, Daniel stepped out of the tree's shadows.

Despite all the reasons she had to feel the opposite, Stella definitely agreed with the ladies. That was one strikingly handsome man.

She found herself filled with all the conflicting emotions of an awkward teen. Which was just

164

completely ridiculous. She had done the right thing for all the right reasons.

Still . . .

Then she saw that big golden dog of his go on full alert. Goldie barked once—and bolted. The change was so swift it caught Daniel completely by surprise, and before he could respond, the dog had pulled her leash free from Daniel's hand.

Daniel called after her and started running . . .

Toward Amber.

"Goldie!"

The shout did not come from Daniel as he chased after his dog. Instead, Amber showed her trademark unbridled joy and knelt to greet Goldie with an ecstatic hug.

Daniel felt a thousand eyes follow him across the school's front yard. He knelt on Goldie's opposite side and watched Amber pet his dog. Amber had the look of a young elf, illuminated by some ethereal force, with a stroke as gentle as a summer breeze. Goldie sat immobile, panting softly. She looked like she would be happy to stay there all day.

There was no reason from their three previous meetings for Daniel to be as fond of Amber as he was. First at the grave of his ex-fiancée, then at a dinner when Chloe blew the roof off her home, and finally when Amber's mother told him to go away. He was searching for the right thing to say when Amber spoke softly, "My mommy needs a friend."

Daniel found himself shoved into a seated position. Not because of what Amber said. Rather, because of the thought that came to him.

He knew exactly what Amber was saying.

Since going through what Daniel thought of as his turning, his own world had become framed by friends, including Travis and others he had come to know through the AA group, and a few people who had helped him settle into Miramar. All were aware of what he had left behind and the shadows he carried still. They had helped him meet the daily challenge of staying sober.

And now there was Nicole. She was a new friend. A true one.

But he knew what it meant to be alone, and in need of someone who offered a caring hand simply because they could.

So when Stella rushed up, Daniel rose, dusted off his trousers, and said, "I need to ask a favor."

Clearly this was the last thing she expected to hear from him. "I . . . what?"

"I understand you can't make room for romance. At least, not with me."

"Daniel . . ."

"No, please, let me finish. I'm facing two huge issues that have caught me completely unaware. One of them is named Nicole, the other . . ."

Daniel stopped talking because Amber rose to

her feet and stood on her tiptoes to hug his waist. He had absolutely no idea what to do with his hands. So he just stood there, looking down at the top of her head. Then he glanced at Stella and saw how the tears had gathered at the corners of her eyes, and the whole day just got better.

Daniel gently pried Amber free and sort of passed her over to Stella. The young girl's response was curious, a sort of dimming of the light. Which did not go unnoticed by her mother. But somehow all that only made his idea seem much better. "Look, Chloe is doing her first-ever shoot this weekend."

"Shoot . . . oh, you mean with a photographer."

"Right. Veronica is also a professional cosmetician. This afternoon and tomorrow we'll be working mostly in her studio and at my place. Headshots and some fashion stuff."

Amber's light resumed its remarkable glow. "That is so cool! Mommy, can I go watch?"

Daniel could see the effort Stella required to clamp down on her automatic refusal. She breathed. Again. Then asked, "What do you think?"

Daniel directed his question to Amber. "Can you be completely silent?"

"Totally!"

"I'm not talking about a few minutes. This will make some very long hours for everybody except—"

"I want to see!"

Daniel shrugged. "She can try it this afternoon. She'll probably get totally bored by the whole deal—"

"I won't! I promise!"

Stella stroked her daughter's head as she asked Daniel, "What was it you were going to say?"

"Right. The normal stills should be done by tomorrow. Veronica wants to find someplace where she could do some location stills."

"I have no idea what that means."

"Somewhere isolated, a location that holds a singular beauty. There's a place I went to a long time back. Tranquility Falls."

"I've never heard of it."

"It dried up in the drought. I went back . . ." Trying to remember exactly when that was brought back nothing but vague, shadowy recollections. "Years ago."

Amber's eyes went entirely round. "You mean, like, a waterfall?"

"The last time I was there, the falls and the lake both had dried up," he warned. "But with all the rain we've had the last two seasons, maybe it's come back."

"Mommy, *please,* can we go!"

Daniel finished, "The hike is about two hours from the trailhead."

"We *love* to hike!" The dog responded to her

168

excitement with a whoof of her own. "Goldie wants to go! Mommy, say *yes!*"

Daniel leaned in close enough to see a reflection of his own lonely state in Stella's gaze. He said so softly the words were for her alone, "Friends. Nothing more."

He actually saw the tension vanish, swift as smoke on a sudden breeze. "Thank you," she replied. "We would love that."

# CHAPTER 29

On Saturday morning, Daniel slipped from the house while dawn was merely a faint smudge over the eastern hills. In his sleepy state, he opened the passenger door and waited for Goldie to hop inside, then realized the dog was still camped inside Nicole's room.

Nicole's room. So many changes to his life crammed into those two small words.

He drove to the church he sometimes attended, took the stairs to the basement, walked the long corridor, and entered the largest classroom. Saturday AA meetings were always jammed.

As expected, Travis was seated in the back row, showing the world an unaccustomed scowl. Even with people standing by the rear wall, the chairs to either side of Travis remained empty. Daniel slipped into the seat to his right. They sat in silence, bonded by all that remained unspoken. Only when the class broke up and the room filled with the Saturday morning din did Travis say, "Appreciate what you did."

Daniel waved to Veronica, the photographer, then shook his head when she started over.

He told Travis, "You don't need to say that."

"Yes, I do."

"You've been there for me too many times to count. I won't say it was a pleasure, but it was good to be able to help you out."

"I needed that. Help." Travis leaned back, causing the chair to squeak in protest. He saw the photographer pretending not to watch them. "Ricki said Veronica and Chloe stopped by yesterday. They went through both mother's and daughter's closets."

Daniel nodded. "I stayed outside. They loaded my pickup with about a thousand outfits. They spent yesterday afternoon and evening at Veronica's doing posed studio shots."

"And?"

"Veronica showed me a few of the best. The camera likes Chloe. A lot."

Travis sighed. "What's happening now?"

"Today we're shooting at my place. Tomorrow I'm taking them into the hills. Veronica wants to do some outdoor shots for the portfolio. She says activity wear is the new big thing, at least for models who can pull it off."

Travis disliked that intensely. "My daughter the bikini model."

"It's a lot more than that, and you know it."

"Knowing and accepting are two different things."

Daniel saw no need to respond to that.

171

Travis lumbered to his feet. "I guess I better go tell Veronica thanks."

"She knows what you and Ricki are going through," Daniel replied, hurting for his friend. "Do you want to come along on Sunday?"

The big man worked through a hurricane of emotions. All he said was, "Better not."

Daniel watched him move away, as light on his feet as a ballerina. He had asked because he had to. But Travis was right. This hike was about a lot more than Chloe getting her picture taken.

Saturday passed in a state of perpetual motion for everyone except Daniel. Veronica was a real pro, taking time between each shot to study the subject and the setting, rearranging much of his house in the process, then setting up the lights and using Nicole and Amber to hold the reflectors. Veronica did her own makeup, a throwback to the era when she was still trying to break in. Back then, she photographed the lesser models and did PR photography on studio sets. Throughout the long day, Nicole and Amber remained fascinated by what to Daniel was an extremely boring process.

Chloe was so excited she kept leaking tears, which meant Veronica repeatedly had to stop and redo her makeup.

No one complained.

That evening Chloe called her parents because Daniel insisted, then retreated to her bedroom as soon as she finished dinner. Nicole found a dusty chessboard in her closet and ignored his protests that it had probably belonged to his almost in-laws and he hadn't played in years. She beat him soundly three games straight, but neither of them cared much. Certainly not Daniel.

Daniel slept very little that night. Finally, around five he knocked on the girls' doors, expecting moans and draggy expressions and complaints over leaving while it was still dark. But the only objection to the hour came from Goldie, who drifted sleepily around, bumping against his legs and generally making her displeasure known as he fixed breakfast and called the photographer and Stella.

When they left the house, dawn was as lovely a greeting as Daniel could have hoped for, cool and windless and not a cloud in the sky. Even so, the baggage he had unpacked during the night remained a heavy burden. Not even the two girls and their sleepy cheerfulness could erase the fact that he had, at some deep level, taken another step beyond his boundaries.

An hour before she needed to rise, Stella gave up on the quarrel she was having with her bed. She dressed for the day, which meant layers. She put out clothes for Amber. She entered the kitchen and made coffee. She drank it staring at her reflection in the dark window, wishing she had the good sense to nip this in the bud. For once and for all.

And she tried as hard as she could to ignore the yearning pleasure she felt over spending the day in that man's company.

She carried the dirty-clothes basket to the garage, put a load in the washer, and returned to the kitchen to find Amber pouring cereal in a bowl. "I was just about to come wake you."

"And now you don't need to." As cool and matter-of-fact as a teen in a polite sulk.

"Do I get a kiss?"

Amber managed to slip over, kiss her cheek, and return to her stool, all without actually making eye contact. Which hurt a great deal. But Stella could not find a way to bridge the divide. So she remained silent and busied her hands making sandwiches. Amber finished her bowl and joined her, filling six baggies with apple slices and grapes. "Darling, there's only five of us."

Amber paused long enough to give her mother the sort of look perfected by young teens every-where. "There are six, Mommy. Veronica's coming too, remember?"

Stella was about to ask who Veronica was when Amber went from cool and silent to as excited as an eleven-year-old could possibly be. "They're *here!*"

She stepped into the foyer and watched Amber

fling open the front door, race down the walk, hug the shaggy blond dog, and say, "Hi, Daniel. Mommy made lunch for an army."

"Then I better go give her a hand."

Hastily, Stella finished packing their lunch, her actions sped up by the sound of Daniel's boots on the front walk. She had no idea why it seemed so important that Daniel not enter their home. She snagged Amber's forgotten case, scurried across the foyer, and slammed the front door just as he started up the steps. "Good morning."

"Hi." His smile seemed slightly canted, as if some unseen weight tugged down one side of his face. "Can I give you a hand with that?"

"Sure." She followed him to the truck, where she discovered the three girls crammed into the rear seat, with Goldie by their feet. She watched Daniel stow the two packs in the rear hold and close the hinged top, then opened her door and climbed inside. "Thank you again for inviting us."

"I just hope there's actually something for us to see when we get there."

They left Miramar by the main highway, turned north, and followed the seaside boundary of the central hills. Twenty miles later, Daniel took a county road that ran along a dry river gorge. Dawn shadows streaked the lowlands, while the rising sun rimmed the eastern hills. Stella rolled down her window and breathed the crisp spring air, redolent of sage and creosote and coming heat.

The girls chattered gaily in the back seat, their words a constant happy rush, as strong as the wind. Every time Stella glanced back, Amber was stroking the dog and glowing with that singular light. If she even noticed Stella's looks, she gave no sign.

Daniel, on the other hand, remained cloaked in shadows strong enough to defy the growing daylight. Stella moved in closer and softly asked, "Is something the matter?"

He made no attempt to deny it. "This place and I have a history."

"Terrible thing, histories," she said.

He was quiet long enough for her to assume he was not going to say anything more. Then he surprised Stella by rolling down his own window. Speaking so softly that his words were almost lost to the rushing wind, he said, "My ex-fiancée brought me here the first time I came to Miramar. It all seemed so simple then. So full of promise. I had just started my regular television gig, she was a mid-level producer with CBS, everything was going our way."

She recalled meeting Daniel at the woman's grave and could think of nothing to say except, "I'm sorry."

"We came back twice more, but the drought had dried up the lake." He turned off the county road onto a smaller lane ribbed by ancient repairs. "The falls were nothing but a stain on the high rocks."

"Daniel, why are you bringing us here?"

"With all the rain we've had, I thought maybe the falls had returned."

"That's not what I asked, and you know it."

The grip he had on the wheel bunched his shoulders. "I thought . . . to tell the truth, I don't know what I thought."

But she could read the answer on his face. Handsome, tanned, lean, and troubled. "You thought maybe it was time to lay the old ghosts to rest."

He tried for a smile, and failed. "It won't be the first time I've gotten things terribly wrong."

# CHAPTER 30

Stella was still trying to come up with a response when they pulled into a graveled parking area. The rocks were almost covered in places by weeds, and the sign pointing to the trailhead was rusted through. A late-model Nissan SUV was the only other vehicle. As Daniel cut the motor, a slender Hispanic woman in her late fifties got out of the SUV. Chloe waved out her window and said, "That's Veronica. She did runways and even did covers for *Vanity Fair* and *Cosmo* and everybody."

Veronica greeted Daniel with, "Glad I made it to the correct middle of nowhere."

"I hope I haven't brought everybody out here for nothing."

Veronica smiled at Chloe. "I'm sure we can get a few good shots, waterfall or not. Right, dear?"

"Count me in."

"That's my girl." Veronica was tall, with a delicate build and a well-lined face. Stella suspected there was a core of latent strength hidden behind those knowing dark eyes.

"I'm Stella, Amber's mother."

"Your daughter is the second-best unpaid assistant I've ever had." Veronica waved at Nicole. "Ready for another long day?"

"You bet."

Daniel opened the rear hold's door. "How long have you been waiting?"

"Not long." She turned her attention back to Amber. "I've been thinking. How would you feel about having me shoot some pictures of you as well?"

"Oh no," Stella cried, then clamped a hand to her mouth. "Sorry. That just slipped out."

Amber replied, "It'd be okay, I guess."

"Well, just okay doesn't cut it. Not in this business." She turned to Stella. "Let me know if that changes. I see potential."

"What does that mean, Mommy?"

Stella was still searching for a decent reply when Veronica indicated Chloe and said, "You have to want it as much as this young lady." She pulled a case from the rear seat and slung it over her shoulder. "The camera always knows."

Veronica Hernandez organized the group like a general marshaling troops. She was a consummate professional, speaking in the quiet tones of someone who expected everyone to obey without question. Chloe jumped rabbit-like every time Veronica addressed her. Veronica started to hand Amber a reflector, then asked Stella, "I should ask if it's okay, your daughter helping out like this."

"It's fine." She was loving the fresh excitement on her daughter's face.

"Now that you're here," Daniel said to Amber's mom, "I want to ask permission to pay her."

"That's not necessary."

He hefted a case holding battery packs and cables. "Nicole's making minimum wage. Seems only fair. But it's your call."

Stella pretended not to notice how Amber's light faded at the prospect of her mother saying no. Again. She forced a smile and said, "I suppose it's okay."

As they started off, Veronica asked Daniel, "Where exactly are we?"

"All this used to be Chumash tribal territory." He pointed north. "San Simeon is about thirty miles that way. The gorges around here were formed by prehistoric rivers. Until this recent storm season, most of the rivers and creeks have been dry for years. Pico Creek is up north, Santa Rosa Creek to the south."

The trail remained empty as they followed the arroyo through a series of snakelike bends. The hills closed in on either side until the shadows locked them down tight. Every now and then, Veronica noticed an interesting outcrop or crevice or interplay of light and shadow. She took her time adjusting the two reflectors and positioning Chloe for a shot. The third time this happened, Stella leaned against the nearside cliff, resting the weight of her pack on a ledge. She lifted her face to watch an eagle pierce the deep blue sky directly overhead. When Daniel stepped over beside her, she said, "I used to hike. Back before everything. I forgot how beautiful it could be."

He dropped his case, pulled a bottle from his pack, and poured some into his hand for Goldie to drink. "It wasn't so nice the last time I came up here. It hadn't rained in a couple of years. We got caught in a dry storm. The wind shot dust through this gorge like bullets in a funnel. Lightning blasted the ridge. We ran back under a hail of falling rocks."

She studied him, the dust streaking his features like Indian warpaint. "Why does that make you so sad?"

"It was about six months before the accident." Daniel stroked the dog's head, then slowly straightened. "We argued about something, no idea what. All I remember is, the fight was really about our lives being totally out of control. I guess we thought . . ."

Stella could read the unspoken words on his features, as clear as script. "You hoped you could find something up here that would straighten you out."

Daniel kicked a rock at his feet. "Do you think

it's possible to start over? Leave the past behind and move on?"

Stella had no idea what to say. To open her mouth risked letting out a tumble of thoughts and emotions, all tangled around a desperate yearning to do just what he said.

Then Veronica helped Chloe down from the ledge where she'd been standing and called to them, "Why don't we go see what's at the end of this road?"

Daniel was huffing hard by the time the way broadened and the sun touched the dusty trail. Rocks embedded in the walls became glaring mirrors with the strength to blind him. Which was why as Daniel made the final turning, he collided with Stella. "Oh. Sorry."

She did not respond.

When Daniel's eyes adjusted, he found himself in a world transformed.

High cliffs rimmed a bowl perhaps half a mile wide. The waterfall and lake covered about a third of the total surface, over at the valley's far end. The last time Daniel had been here, the lake had been nothing more than a gray-brown patch, the muddy surface veined with forgotten moisture. The stone walls had trapped the heat, turning the place into an oven.

Today the lake was full to the brim. But that was not what had them crying aloud with wonder.

Before them stretched a riot of colors.

The rainstorms had ended, and the desert had exploded into life. Some of the seeds had lain dormant for years, perhaps decades. A living earthbound rainbow surrounded them. Every ledge and precipice dripped blossoms.

Directly ahead, the waterfall rushed and sang.

Amber squealed and ran into the high grass. She became surrounded by wildflowers of yellow and rose and lavender and sky blue. Veronica lifted her camera and photographed the young girl laughing and spinning and singing her delight.

Nicole, the silent and reserved and uncertain young woman, became infected by the same delirious joy and raced over to join her.

Chloe followed. The three of them paused long enough to weave flowers into each other's hair. Then they began dancing again.

Daniel turned to Stella and saw what he was himself feeling. A sentiment so strong it hurt to even accept it was real.

He reached for her hand and felt an energy course through his entire being. She jerked, almost pulled away, then stopped and looked down at their fingers intertwined.

Daniel asked softly, "May I have this dance?"

# CHAPTER 31

They danced.

Their audience shrieked and gamboled about, three young women and a golden-haired dog, all laughing as they circled the two of them. Their music was a soft breeze that rustled through the tall grass and the wildflowers. The waterfall formed a liquid chorus. Daniel's arms were strong, his presence warm, his face showing her a gentle smile. Stella thought it was the finest melody she had ever known, one she would carry with her for years to come.

Despite how her fears grew with each step, each breath, every passing second.

Perhaps he could see the dark message in her eyes. Or maybe for him the melody ended. She was terribly sorry when he let her go. But at least she was able to breathe again.

Daniel leaned over so Amber could set a flower behind each ear. He laughed with them and said, "Who wants to get wet?"

The five of them formed a happy line. Daniel pointed Goldie to a spot by the lake's edge and spoke sharply enough to keep her in place.

Veronica followed at a distance, hastily changing lenses and shooting constantly. Amber released Daniel's hand and pulled Stella forward, giving her mother no choice in the matter. Stella smiled as though she was pleased with the shift, which in fact she was. Daniel's hand was as warm as his embrace.

Daniel led them around the lake's southern rim, over to where the cliff reached out one stony arm. A tight ledge extended at waist height, scarcely as wide as his boot. He showed them where some early hikers had carved steps from the rock. "The ledge broadens close to the falls. But it also gets slippery. Everybody remember to get a firm handhold before taking the next step. If you fall, push away from the face. I have no idea how deep the lake is. You may be able to stand on the bottom." Daniel reached out one hand. "Stella, you want to lead off?"

He helped them climb up, one by one, then followed. Midway around the lake, the path broadened to where they could walk straight ahead. Daniel loudly reminded them to keep a hold on the rock face. Up ahead, the water fell and sang. It was not much as waterfalls went, a slender veil that split and opened. Mist drifted in the hot air. Stella reached the falls and glanced back. Daniel gave her a thumbs-up. "Step through!"

She raised one hand to shield her head, took a step, and vanished.

The girls squealed and followed.

Behind the falls was a shallow indent, scarcely large enough to hold the five of them. The rock formed a baffle that made the falling water thunderous. They huddled together and shouted words no one could understand.

Chloe stepped forward, lifted her arms, and stood in the falls. The water played over her in a teasing rush, the light silver and golden and forming an aura around her. Then Amber joined the older girl, shrieking with an unbridled joy that was all her own. Nicole followed.

Then it was just the two of them, sheltered in their shallow cave. And it seemed as though the notion came to the two of them at the very same instant.

Daniel thought he had never known anything quite so fine as that kiss, electric and cold and molten, all at the same time.

# CHAPTER 32

They returned to Miramar. The same pickup, the same road, the same day. Only now everything was different. The light held a unique sparkle. Everyone was infected by an uncommon merriment, or so it seemed to Daniel. The three girls talked about things that made no sense to him and laughed in odd places. Amber sang half a song about being happy, and the other two joined in, then Goldie refused to be left out and added her own soft bark. Stella pointed out a flitting shadow alongside the road and asked if it was a deer, and the question required a touch to his hand. She invited him to dinner, of course with Nicole and Chloe, and the invitation meant she needed to touch him again. Not actually hold him. Just the same, their connectedness remained long after she turned back to the road.

Daniel wanted to tell her how beautiful she was when she allowed herself to be happy. How the day meant everything to him. How he had not felt this complete in a very long time, perhaps forever. He was still busy making his mental list when he turned down the road leading to Stella's home.

Which was when everything fell apart.

"Mommy, what are all these police doing here?"

The good times ended with an almost audible snap. Daniel slammed on the brakes and pulled to the curb, well away from the flashing lights.

"Mommy, what—"

"Just a minute, Amber." Daniel put his hand on the back of Stella's seat. "Look at me."

Stella's face was bone white. "It's happening, isn't it."

"Probably. Look at me, Stella."

She showed him eyes drenched with fear. "What am I going to do?"

"This is very important. Pay careful attention." He spaced each word out, trying to drive the message home. "I will handle the outside things. Do you hear what I'm saying?"

"I don't know how—"

"Your job is to stay intact and go through whatever process they require."

She turned back to the cops gathered on her front lawn. Two officials in suits stood in her doorway. "Why is my front door open?"

"They probably have a search warrant. Listen to me, Stella. They are going to make you feel powerless."

"I already feel that."

"I know. But you need to remember one thing. What is that?" When she simply stared at the horror unfolding at her home, he said, "I will take care of everything outside the process itself."

"Mommy, what does he mean? What process?"

Daniel turned in his seat and confronted three pairs of utterly round eyes. "Your mother is probably going to be arrested for something she did not do."

Stella whispered, "What do I do about Amber?"

"She will come stay with me." Daniel kept his gaze on the terrified young girl. "Is that okay with you?"

"Why do they want to arrest Mommy?"

"They are trying to protect someone who's done a bad thing. But they're not going to succeed." Daniel turned back to Stella. "Because I'm not going to let them."

"*We're* not," Nicole said.

Daniel wished there was some way he could hit the pause button, just long enough to reassure Stella's daughter and hug his niece. "Thank you, Nicole."

Stella whispered, "I don't even know any lawyers."

"I do." He patted a rock-hard shoulder. "Just remember what I'm telling you. You're not alone."

The arrest and house search were both pre-dictably awful. The chief of Miramar's police was a bearish man named Porter Wright with a voice to match his build, deep and rugged. Daniel thought he detected a distinct note of compassion to the man and his actions. He had experienced more than his share of run-ins with local law enforcement. Many officers involved in nonviolent seizures either showed cold ambivalence or dark humor. Porter was different. He allowed a terrified Amber to clutch at her mother. He asked no questions that sought to trap Stella in an incriminating response. When the time came, he gently turned the child away from her mother and did not use the hand-cuffs until Amber was well removed from the scene.

As soon as Porter led Stella away, Daniel pulled Chloe to one side and said, "One of us needs to call your mother. It really should be you."

Chloe was too shaken up by events to object. "I'll do it."

"Keep it calm and to the point. Tell her not to rush. I'll stay here through the process and follow them to the jail."

"Mom will want to take Amber."

"That's for the child to decide. Tell Ricki that. We need to let Amber feel like we're all respecting her voice and her desires." He stepped over to where Nicole remained by the pickup. "You okay?"

"It's just like on television." She kept a tight,

two-armed grip on her middle. "Only a lot more awful."

"I know."

"Everything was so wonderful—you know, before."

Daniel had no response to that, so he looked up the number of Sol Feinnes, an attorney based in San Luis Obispo, the nearest town to Miramar of any size. Daniel had used him both on the purchase of their home and in wrapping up his ex-fiancée's affairs. The secretary remembered him and put him straight through. When Feinnes came on the line, Daniel asked, "Do you handle white-collar crime?"

"We're your typical small-town practice. We take on pretty much everything that comes our way."

Daniel gave a quick summary of events. He tried to keep it calm, straight, to the point. But by the time he finished, he was boiling mad. "I want you to get her out of jail, and then I want you to defend me when I go to city hall and tear some heads off."

"It would be inappropriate for me to advise you on any felony you might be considering," Feinnes replied. "But if what you have implied is true . . ."

"I didn't imply. The figures speak for themselves, Sol. Loud and clear."

"Well, in that case, we should have no trouble

freeing our defendant." He hesitated, then said, "Forgive me for addressing the mundane matter of fees . . ."

"I'll cover them."

"Do I need to lay out the firm's fee structure?"

Daniel watched the police chief settle Stella into the rear seat, behind the wire-mesh caging. Amber's tear-streaked face reflected the late-afternoon light. "Later."

"Very well. Hold on just one moment; let me check on something."

As he waited, Daniel glanced at Nicole. She wiped tears from her own face and told him, "This is so awful."

Daniel reached for her hand just as Ricki's car raced around the corner and pulled up behind his pickup. She sprang out, hugged her daughter, then rushed over to where Amber reached out empty arms. Ricki clasped the girl as tight as she could manage. Together they watched as Stella was driven away in the chief's car.

Then Sol came back on the line, his tone brisk. "I have a mediation this evening. One of my associates will represent Ms. Dalton today. I'll take over the case starting at tomorrow's hearing. My associate's name is Megan Pierce. She's leaving now."

Despite the circumstances surrounding their first encounter, Daniel liked Megan Pierce on the spot.

She was an athletic, raven-haired beauty in her early thirties and carried herself with air of brisk competence. She could not stop the process, but she made sure everything proceeded as smoothly as possible.

While Stella was being processed, Megan asked if Daniel wanted to step away from the others. "I thought now might be a good time for us to review the information you gave Sol."

"I agree." He remained where he was, seated on the Miramar police station's hard front-office bench. Nicole was seated to one side, Ricki and Amber on the other. Chloe had gone with her father to pick up a takeaway meal that no one particularly wanted. "They are all a part of this."

Megan appeared ready to argue but, in the end, walked over to the officer on reception duty. They spoke softly, then Megan stepped to an empty desk and drew over an office chair. "Okay. Let's hear it."

"You want an overview, or all the nuts and bolts?"

"Start with the short version," Megan replied. "We can unpack this back at the office."

In response, Daniel turned to Ricki. "How long ago did Stella begin to get worried?"

"Three months, maybe a little longer."

Megan asked, "You're involved in this too?"

Ricki nodded. "I used to serve on the town

council. And I'm Stella's friend. I'm the only one she told before Daniel got involved."

Amber asked, "Are they going to arrest you too?"

Ricki strengthened her hold on the young girl. "One step at a time, okay?"

Megan nodded to Daniel. Go on.

"Ricki asked if I would take a look at Miramar's accounts."

"And she did this because . . ."

"I trained as a forensic accountant. This was back before . . ." Daniel struggled with how to abbreviate the journey that had brought him here.

Nicole finished for him, "Before he got famous."

Megan nodded. "I knew I had seen you before. MSNBC, right?"

"Yes."

"Okay. So you inspected the city's accounts. Which I assume are confidential. Which means anything you might have uncovered is not evidence we can use in court."

Daniel nodded. He had been thinking the same thing. "On the surface, everything follows a careful pattern that skirts the boundary of legality."

"And beneath that?"

"Someone, or some group, has been siphoning off funds from the town's emergency funds and the employee pension funds."

"You think or you know?"

"Call it ninety-nine-point-nine percent certain."

"And Stella's role in this is what, exactly?"

Ricki said, "She's the town bookkeeper."

"Who does she answer to?"

"The mayor. Catherine Lundberg."

Megan leaned back and stared at the empty space above Daniel's head. "Okay. Ms. Dalton will be arraigned tomorrow in San Luis Obispo. Because missing funds are involved, we can expect the prosecution to ask the judge to deny bail."

Amber cried, "Mommy will have to stay in jail?"

"I said they will ask. Our job is to make sure they don't get what they want."

Daniel liked how she addressed the child. Straight, to the point, and full of the determined strength of a courtroom warrior. "I will take care of bail."

"The judge will probably set it on the high side," Megan warned. "We're talking upward of a million."

Daniel swallowed. "I'll cover it."

"I will stay here until she's settled in for the night. Once they finish the processing, I'll have my first chance to speak with her directly."

Amber said, "I want to see Mommy!"

"Tomorrow." The way she spoke that word, calm and yet utterly firm, silenced the young girl. Megan rose to her feet. "Why don't you all go get some rest?"

# CHAPTER 33

Daniel spent most of the night fighting old wars.

He dreamed of waking up strapped to the gurney, being rolled into the back of the ambulance. And there on the asphalt beside his demolished car was a black plastic bag, lumpish and still, just large enough to hold his fiancée.

He dreamed of lying in the hospital bed, trying to answer questions about the accident he didn't remember. All the while, two detectives stared at him with eyes that said he was the one who should have been laid out in that body bag.

Just as dawn began streaking the eastern horizon, Daniel dressed in running clothes and carried his shoes down the silent hall. When Amber had begged to stay with him, Chloe had made no objection to going home. The battles with Chloe's parents were not erased, just temporarily suspended. As he passed Amber's door, he heard a faint scratching. Daniel hesitated, then cracked open the door just wide enough for Goldie to slip out. She snuffled his hand and stretched and yawned, then lapped water from her bowl and padded to the front door. Like nothing had happened. Like she had not pretty much ignored him for the past few days.

As he stretched in his front yard, he wondered if some unknown dog sense made Goldie aware of what he hid from the rest of the world. The wounds that kept opening up again. The scars that refused to fully heal. His need for the company that morning of a big-hearted dog.

He fastened Goldie to her leash and set off down the silent road. His every action threatened the safe little existence he had built for himself. Stella and Chloe and Nicole and Amber and . . . The list grew in a steady and relentless pattern. He was stretching out in every conceivable direction, linking himself to all these lives, making them rely on him when his past kept shouting at him to step back. Remove all these reasons to fall down. Erase the mess he would undoubtedly make of all these trusting people.

When running the coastal route, his normal turnaround point was the headland above Miramar's main oceanfront parking lot. He often spent a few moments in the open-fronted chapel facing the Pacific. There was little difference from the view from his own backyard. But Daniel had always liked the chapel's sheltered peace. It was a good place to sit and reflect and perhaps pray. But today Daniel kept wondering if others could sense the fault lines running through his life. If they worried that the weight of new mistakes might become too great and he might fracture again. Just like before.

Daniel was still debating his next steps when he jogged down his road and saw Travis's Escalade parked in his drive. A black retro BMW that Daniel did not recognize was pulled in behind Travis. As Daniel paused to stretch, Travis opened his front door and said, "Leave that for later. You need to have a word with the fellow waiting inside."

When he walked inside, he found a wide-eyed Nicole seated at his kitchen counter next to the film star Connor Larkin. Travis said, "You two know each other?"

"We've met," Nicole said. "At the restaurant."

Travis winced, creasing his features from forehead to collar. "Oh. Right."

Goldie lapped from her water bowl, then padded down the hall and sat in front of Amber's door. She looked back at Daniel, then at the door. Waiting.

Daniel asked, "Amber's still asleep?"

"As far as I know," Nicole replied. "I haven't heard a peep."

Daniel walked down, listened, then cracked the door wide enough for Goldie to enter.

When he returned to the kitchen, Connor pointed to the coffeemaker. "Any chance I could sample your goods?"

Travis said, "Nicole, honey, why don't you give us a minute?"

Daniel stepped around the counter. "Nicole is welcome to stay or go, but it is absolutely her decision."

"I'm absolutely staying," Nicole said.

Travis sighed his way onto the corner stool. "Chloe always claimed I have a natural gift for saying the wrong thing for all the right reasons."

Daniel took his time preparing four cappuccinos. When everyone was served, he remained where he was, the counter between him and whatever came next.

Connor said, "Ricki and Sylvie are friends."

"That being Sylvie Cassick, who owns Castaways," Travis offered.

Connor went on, "Ricki told Sylvie about what happened last night."

Travis said, "He means with Stella."

"Travis," Daniel said.

"What."

"Let the man speak."

"Hey. It's not every day I get a call from a real-live movie star who says, drive me to your pal's so I can lay . . ." When Connor turned and added his gaze to Daniel's, Travis raised two massive palms and backed up. "This is me, shutting my trap."

Connor said, "A while back, Sylvie got into this huge fight with a local mover and shaker. You ever heard the name Phil Hammond?"

"Doesn't ring a bell."

"He owns a couple of the oceanfront hotels. Made a run for Castaways. And some other stuff." Connor waved it aside. "Ancient history. Mind if I ask you something?"

"You're in my kitchen, drinking my coffee. Ask away."

"Ricki says she and Stella suspect the mayor might be behind the missing town funds and is using Stella as her scapegoat."

"Somebody certainly is. The evidence I've seen suggests it has to be an individual with enough power . . ." Daniel stopped, halted in his verbal tracks by a sudden thought.

Connor asked, "You were saying?"

Daniel shook his head. Not to the actor. To the impression behind the thought. That it was too late. There was no returning to his safe little existence. He was already committed. All he had to do was look across the counter, to where Nicole tracked his every word with absolute intensity. There was no going back. Daniel shivered.

Travis said, "You need to go shower?"

"I'm good." Daniel's voice sounded weak to his ears.

"This is excellent brew." Connor sipped from his cup. "Where was I?"

Nicole offered, "The mayor is a crook, and Stella has been set up."

"Right. When Sylvie faced her own assault, I

got hooked up with a guy." Connor rattled his cup. "Any chance of a second round?"

Daniel busied himself at the machine. "What kind of guy?"

"He makes his living hunting down hidden online evidence," Connor said. "The kind of hunt, and evidence, that you won't ever be able to use in a court of law."

Daniel said, "You're talking about a hacker."

"Right down to his Ukrainian accent."

Nicole said, "This is so totally cool."

Daniel started steaming the milk. "You want to introduce me to a Russian hacker."

"He claims to be in Alabama. I never bothered to check."

Daniel tamped down the milk pitcher. He took the cup from the machine, layered in the foam, handed it over, and asked, "Anyone else?"

"I wouldn't say no," Travis said.

Nicole pushed her cup across the counter. "Count me in."

Daniel took his time, making himself a fresh cup as well. Thinking. Because the fact was, Connor's offer dovetailed with remarkable precision with the thought that was still hammering away at his brain.

When he handed over the new brews, he said, "This sounds like somebody I need to meet."

Committed.

# CHAPTER 34

A half hour after Travis and Connor left, Sol Feinnes called to say the arraignment had been set for three that afternoon. They could meet at the courthouse a half hour earlier, and Sol would arrange for Amber to spend some time with her mother. Daniel agreed to stop by Stella's home and pick up clothes suitable for the courtroom.

About twenty minutes later, Amber emerged from her bedroom, tousled and cranky. She moaned that her back hurt from the lumpy mattress. She complained that Goldie kept waking her up and licking her face. She stated that her room was too bright and demanded to know why Daniel didn't have decent curtains. She wanted to go see her mother, and she didn't want to wait until the afternoon.

Daniel made her a bowl of cereal, which she ate with her face almost in the milk. The spoon traveled a distance of maybe an inch and a half with each bite. When she was done, she did a boneless slide off the counter stool and started back down the hallway. Goldie walked alongside her, nudging Amber with her nose. Amber kept pushing at her, telling the dog to go away. Goldie remained right where she was. Amber entered the room, yelled for Goldie to leave, then shut the door with the dog still inside.

Daniel asked Nicole, "Was it something I said?"

"She's scared. She's angry with the world. She wants to be home with her mom." Nicole shrugged. "I'd say Amber has every reason to be in a mood."

Daniel looked at her. "When did you grow up to be a very wise thirty-five?"

Nicole did not smile, but he could see she was pleased. "What are you going to do about it?"

"I assume we're no longer talking about Amber."

"Of course not. You got an idea when Connor was talking. I saw it happen."

Daniel gave that the silence it deserved. "You are quite possibly the most observant person of any age that I have ever met."

Nicole liked that even more. "Will you tell me?"

"I'll do more than that. I'll ask for your help. But only if you want."

"Why do you think I'm sitting here?" She bounced in her chair. An excited young girl once more. "Tell me!"

"I don't have a lot worked out. But here goes." Daniel sliced banana into two bowls, then added blueberries and yogurt and topped it with a sprinkling of granola. He set one in front of Nicole and stood on the counter's other side, not eating. The words came slowly, but not because he needed to think things through. The first step was fairly clear now. What impacted him far more deeply was what this move represented.

By the time he'd finished outlining the day's plan, Nicole had stopped eating as well. "This is amazing."

"It's hardly even half an idea at this point," he warned. "But I think it can work."

"I know it will." She lifted the spoon and took a single blueberry and a smidgen of yogurt. "About what you plan for this afternoon. Have you ever done that before?"

He nodded. "Back before. Several times."

"Is it legal?"

"It's not illegal. Officially we should ask the court's permission."

"But that would mean letting the bad lady know we're onto her."

"We don't know for certain the mayor is actually the real criminal. Not yet, anyway. But at least I think we're moving toward finding that out." He picked up his spoon. "Why aren't you eating? You don't like your breakfast?"

Nicole revealed her mother's dimples. "I like how you say that. *We're* moving."

"You have a beautiful smile," Daniel said. "You should try using it more often."

# CHAPTER 35

Daniel spent the next hour on the phone. The longest conversation was with Veronica. The photographer did not object to his plan. But she was cautious, insisting he walk her through the planned events twice. When he was done the second time, she stayed silent so long Daniel feared she was looking for the exit. But, in the end, she merely asked for his credit-card details and hung up.

Nicole volunteered to wake Amber and explain what they were planning. Daniel waited until he could hear the two girls talking softly in the back room, then carried the phone outside and seated himself by the vacant firepit. The Pacific was a burnished, golden-blue mirror, stretching out to where it joined with the pale horizon. A feather-like wind streaked the surface, as if the waters shivered in nervous anticipation of what Daniel intended.

He took Connor's slip of paper from his pocket, fed the number into his phone's speed-dial memory, then called. The actor came on with, "I thought it would take you longer than this to get in trouble."

"I'm not there yet," Daniel replied. "But I may be before the day is out."

He swiftly sketched out what he hoped to put in place. As he spoke, all Daniel could see were the holes in his logic. But when he was done, Connor replied, "You were right to call."

"You think?"

"This is absolutely the sort of thing my Ukrainian boy in Alabama could help with. Let me make a call."

Daniel thanked him, cut the connection, then sat cradling the phone between his hands. Finally, he reached the point where he did not feel so much ready as tired of putting off the inevitable. He dialed the number from memory.

Midway through the first ring, an all-too-familiar voice demanded, "Is it really you?"

"In the flesh," Daniel replied. "Sort of."

"You bad boy. Making me wait all this time, worrying me worse than my youngest child. Shame on you."

In a world known for careers that came and went in months, Kirsten Wright was a world-class exception. She had been head of NBC News on the West Coast for two decades. The network had twice urged her to relocate to New York and take over the entire news division. But her daughter was an anesthesiologist at Cedars-

Sinai, her eldest son worked in film, and her youngest was barely hanging on to sobriety. She loved being close to her grandchildren and trying to keep her son on the straight and narrow. She had considered Daniel an adopted basket case and treated him with the same stern affection she showed her own wayward child.

Daniel said, "It's good to hear your voice again."

Kirsten asked, "How are you?"

"Staying sober."

"Really and truly?"

"Four years and counting."

She sighed. "You should come down and give my son some advice."

"Trouble?"

"Now and then. But I don't want to cloud our first conversation in too long with such tales of woe. Are you ready to come back?"

There it was. The question he had both hungered to hear—and dreaded ever since knowing he had to take this step. The draw and the repulsion were equally strong. "Not yet, and maybe never," he replied. "But I think I may have a story."


As they left the house, Nicole slipped into the role of diplomat.

Through his open window he heard Goldie's howls. Normally the dog was pretty easygoing about life. Not today.

Amber remained embedded in her dark space. Nicole either did not care or pretended not to see it at all. "Do you know your mother's clothes?"

"Duh. We've only been living together my whole life."

"I mean, do you know what she would want to wear today?"

Amber was silent. Then, "I don't want to go in there alone."

"I'll go with you."

"What does somebody wear in jail?"

"This isn't for jail. This is for court."

"Oh." Another silence. "It's awful. Isn't it? Jail."

"I have no idea. But I doubt she had an easy night."

"I need to be happy for her."

"Not unless it's genuine. Seeing you in any mood will be enough."

Amber was seated by the passenger window, with Nicole leaning forward, inserting herself into the space between Daniel and the girl. Amber worked one finger between the glass and the frame. "Goldie wasn't happy about being left behind."

Daniel nodded to the road ahead. The dog's radar was certainly working overtime this morning.

The pickup remained silent until they pulled into Stella's drive. Amber said, "Mommy always picks out my clothes."

Nicole took hold of her hand. "I'll help."

Amber remained where she was. A tear gentled its way down her cheek. "I'm so scared."

"We're here for you."

"What if they lock her up forever?"

Daniel spoke for the first time since ordering Goldie to stay. "My job is to make sure that doesn't happen."

# CHAPTER 36

The San Luis Obispo city and county governments were housed in Spanish-style buildings encircling a tree-lined square. A bored police officer on duty at the courthouse entrance directed them around the left-hand side to a smaller door of reinforced-glass with a police emblem at its center. This duty guard was very alert. He led them through the scanner one at a time. Amber was cowed and snuffling by the time they were registered and seated in the jail's waiting area. None of the officers paid the miserable little girl any mind. She was far from the only frightened and distraught individual in the windowless chamber. Nicole held her hand for a while, then slipped her arm around Amber and drew her closer still.

Fifteen minutes after they arrived, Ricki rushed in with Chloe. "Have you seen her?"

"Not yet, but soon." He rose to his feet, hugged them both, then spotted Veronica through the front portal. "Excuse me a minute."

Veronica slipped past the guard and entered the waiting area. "Sorry, sorry."

"I was getting worried."

"Loading the software and synching five Bluetooth devices to my laptop took forever. Hi, Nicole. Amber, that's such a lovely dress; don't wipe your nose with your sleeve." Veronica seated herself on Ricki's other side and opened a purse the size of a carry-on. "Here. Never go anywhere without Kleenex. That's my motto."

Amber blew her nose. "How can you be so happy?"

"It's nerves. Sort of." Veronica glanced around. "I never thought I'd look forward to walking back in here."

Nicole asked, "You were arrested?"

"Bunch of times. Hi, Nicole, dear."

"That's for another day," Daniel said. "Did you bring them?"

"You bet. And they're all working perfectly. We're ready to rock and roll." Another dive into her purse brought out five spectacles cases. She opened them, inspected the contents, then handed one to Amber, Nicole, Ricki, Chloe, and finally Daniel. "Try them on."

The lids were embossed with the word CANON. Veronica said, "My tech guy has a wicked sense of humor."

Amber frowned at the contents. "I don't get it."

Nicole spelled the name. "Canon makes cameras. Veronica's guy makes secret weapons shaped like spectacles. I think it's cool."

Veronica said, "You and my guy would get along just fine."

Amber said, "I'm not talking about the *name*." She pulled out a pair of gold-rimmed spectacles with octagonal lenses. "I don't need glasses."

"You do today," Daniel said. He took them from her and pointed to a little aperture above the right corner. "Inside there is a tiny little camera. And here on the left side is a miniature microphone."

"Be a good girl and don't drop them," Veronica said. "They cost four thousand dollars a pop."

Amber slipped them on. "They're heavy."

"They're as light as he can make them," Veronica replied. "Think you can manage?"

"I guess." She mashed them tight to her nose. "Mom is going to freak."

Daniel handed her a note he had prepared while the girls had been inside choosing clothes. "As soon as you can, give her this. It will explain things."

Nicole said, "Don't tell her what we're doing when anybody else might hear."

"Well, duh."

Nicole's glasses were a rich brown with white streaks in the lens frames. She settled them in place and asked, "How do I look?"

"Like an incredibly intelligent and perceptive and beautiful young woman," Daniel said. "Who is great to be around."

212

Amber pointed to Veronica. "How come she doesn't have any?"

"I'm going to be in the hallway outside the courtroom," Veronica said. "Recording and monitoring and generally staying out of trouble."

Nicole said, "It's okay to be afraid."

"I'm not scared," Amber snapped. "I'm *mad.*"

"Angry is good," Daniel said. "But for your mom you need to be the little girl she wants to come home to. Think you can do that?"

Amber's chin trembled, but not for very long. "Piece of cake. Did I say that right?"

Daniel gave her a one-armed hug, then spotted the attorney coming through the main doors. "Game faces, everyone. It's showtime."

The smell took Daniel straight back.

Jails all around the globe carried a certain stench, one that no amount of disinfectant could ever erase. The result of hopelessness and tension and rage and fear and too many bodies in too small a space, all cooked in a series of tight little cages. Back in the bad old days, in those horrid hours between regaining consciousness and getting his release, Daniel had wondered if the guards even noticed the smell anymore. Or if that was part of why they all wore the same blank expression and hid behind those deeply uncaring eyes. So they wouldn't have to endure the smell.

When the first wave of stench reached her,

213

Nicole was stopped cold. Daniel said, "You can wait out front."

She jammed her glasses up tight. "Not on your life."

Daniel had worn spy spectacles on any number of televised investigations. Even now, four years since his last assignment, he found himself resuming his old role. The glasses gave him a sort of dual vision, as if they granted him a partial separation from reality. He saw the scene as the audience might.

He held back as Sol Feinnes led Amber toward the guard on reception duty. Amber's walk was uncertain, like she was trying to keep her footing in rough seas. Sol steadied her with a hand on her shoulder.

Daniel focused on Amber and watched her jerk in shock at the loud buzzer alarm. The electronic door leading to the women's wing slid open, and Sol led her inside. Daniel touched Nicole's arm and said, "Only two at a time."

Nicole asked, "Why are you standing that way?"

He gave their names to the guard, lifted the hanger holding Stella's courtroom clothes, and explained that they were serving as Amber's surrogate family. Once the guard buzzed them through, Daniel replied, "You need to frame your actions for the hidden camera. Focus on what you think the audience would find most interesting.

Hold your position long enough for the image to become clearly imprinted. Move your head as slowly as possible. Keep your head steady when you walk."

Nicole thought on that. "Why didn't you tell Amber?"

"Because she doesn't need to know. All we need from Amber's viewpoint is one close-up shot of Stella. The rest is up to us."

As she followed him and the guard down the hall, she whispered, "What's the matter?"

Daniel shook his head. The answer was, the farther he moved along the windowless corridor, the angrier he became. He had not known such rage in, well, forever. But to have a good woman locked up in here because other people thought she made a perfect fall guy left him so furious he was shaking.

Nicole did not speak again until they were standing outside the visitation room. Because Stella's attorney was present, they were given access to a small private chamber off the main visitors' area. Their escort gave Daniel a careful inspection but did not comment. No doubt rage was a familiar part of his daily life. He unlocked the steel door and pulled it open. "Knock when you're done."

Stella was seated at the metal table, her arms wrapped around her child. Sol was seated on a plastic stool anchored to the concrete floor across from them. Daniel drew Nicole into the corner, as far from the table as possible.

Sol said, "We only have a few minutes."

Stella nodded and loosened her hold on Amber. She stroked the child's face. "Are you okay?"

She sniffed, nodded, and streaked the tears on her face. "Daniel's taking care of me."

Stella glanced over. "Thank you."

"We're here for you both," Daniel said. The only reason he managed to keep his voice steady was that he felt Nicole slip her hand into his. "For as long as it takes."

# CHAPTER 37

Stella was seventh in the line of jailhouse inmates waiting for their turn in court. One of the cons farther down the line cursed her fate, the judge, her rotten lawyer, the world in general, until finally the guard offered to tell the court she was indisposed and hold her over for another day. Two held their heads and groaned softly. One man asked the next in line if he remembered what they had done to wind up here. The second man shook his head and moaned at the pain caused by his motion. The other men and women were mostly silent.

*When you need them most, men leave.*

The words formed a motto that had been driven deep into Stella's psyche. They rattled around her exhausted brain as she waited her turn before the judge. One by one, names were called, and they were drawn from their respective cages, walked down a corridor, and pointed onto a bench. Down and to her right was a door leading to the courtroom. Three guards patrolled the hall and maintained absolute silence.

*When you need them most, men leave.*

When her name was called, Stella rose and followed the guard into the courtroom.

Daniel was seated in the third row behind the prosecutor's table. Amber was seated to his left. Her daughter lifted one hand and offered a tiny wave as Stella was led to her seat at the defense table. Stella then spotted Nicole seated in the corner closest to the door she had just come through. Nicole's attention remained intently focused on the lawyers. Sol was standing in the space between the prosecutor and defense tables. He was accompanied by his associate, Megan Pierce. They talked intently with the two attorneys from the other table. Sol and Megan both looked very grim, like they were unable to accept what they were hearing.

The judge rapped her gavel. "Anytime, ladies and gentlemen. We've got a full docket today."

"Sorry, your honor." Sol and Megan returned to their positions, and the arraignment began.

Stella tried very hard to focus on what was going on. Her life and her freedom and her daughter's future all hung in the balance. But time and again, she found herself caught by the clear and simple fact that . . .

She was wrong about Daniel.

Sol began a lengthy argument with the prosecutor over what it would take to have Stella released until her trial date. The DA wanted her denied bail and held over for trial. Perry Sanchez was a singularly unattractive man with an angry, aggressive air and a voice that reminded Stella of a dentist's drill. Sanchez claimed Stella was in possession of six and a half million dollars of the city's money. Which meant she was a terrible flight risk. Sol angrily replied that Stella was innocent until proven guilty, had never been arrested, all evidence was circumstantial, and . . .

At that point, the judge rapped her gavel and set bail at one million dollars.

Stella would have laughed out loud. The sum was so far beyond her means, they might as well have asked for the moon.

Which was when Daniel stepped forward and said he had arranged a lien on his home and would post a bond for Stella's release.

She stared at this man, a stranger she had done her best to push away, and felt all her defenses fade like a dawn mist burned off the Pacific.

Over the next few days, Stella felt as though she was watching her life's storm from the safety of a bunker. People arrived in a steady stream. Ricki came morning and night, bringing food, checking on Amber, passing along best wishes and support from any number of people, filling her home with food and chatter. Chloe and Nicole became firmly attached to Amber's orbit.

Daniel was a part of their world now. Stella had no idea how she felt about that. She had very little sense of feeling anything at all. The prospect of being convicted in a court of law and being wrenched from her little girl was a constant, living nightmare. And everybody understood. And everybody cared. And everybody helped her cope. Amber, Ricki, Travis, Chloe, Nicole . . .

Daniel.

He came by every day. Sometimes twice. Never staying very long. Never imposing himself. He would refuse her offer of coffee, sit wherever she directed him, and explain what was happening next. Stella listened carefully, but the words and plans fell on her like rain. Then he left, and afterward all she could remember was his look. His strength. And the lie he made of her years-long motto. Because one thing became increasingly certain as the days passed. This was one man who had no intention of leaving. Unless she made him.

Amber went through her own transition. Gone was the elfin sprite, the sense of boundless joy. Gone also the petulant child. Instead, Amber became quiet and soft-spoken and gentle in the way she treated her mother. As though she was taking instructions from the people who surrounded them both.

Early on Wednesday, a week after her arraignment, she prepared for a trip to Los Angeles. Stella had heard the reasons any number of times, and the steps that needed to be followed while they were down there. She knew the journey was important. She knew it had to happen now. But, if asked, she could have given none of the reasons. Only that her best chance of remaining free depended upon this trip.

She dressed in one of her better pantsuits, a dark gray pinstripe with a pale, chalk-blue stripe and matching blouse, and alligator pumps she had bought for herself on a distant birthday. Her only pieces of jewelry were matching collar and lapel pins. Stella caught herself in the act of fastening on the watch her ex had given her for their first anniversary. She took it off and put it back in her jewelry box. If she needed to know the time, she would ask.

She stopped by Amber's room, only to find the door opened and one of her daughter's best outfits laid out on the bed. Shoes and all. Stella stared at the clothes for a long moment, wondering when her daughter had decided to grow up.

When she came downstairs, Amber was seated in the living room playing an electronic game on the television. Which was new. Amber rarely paid e-games much attention. "Good morning, darling."

"Hi, Mom." She glanced over. "You look nice."

"Thank you, dear. Do you want breakfast?"

"I ate already." The television gave off a blast of noise, a buzzer sounded, and Amber tossed the controls aside. "I'll never get this right."

Stella walked around the couch and stood in front of the television. She started to ask what was the matter, then realized how utterly lame that sounded, even in her head. "Sweetheart, would you rather stay here?"

"What?" Amber looked at her mother like she'd just grown a new head. "Why would I do that?"

"I don't know, you look . . ."

"Scared." She picked up the controls again and shifted over so she could watch the screen around her mother. "I am."

"Turn that off, please. I'm trying to have a conversation." When the room went silent, Stella said, "It's perfectly natural to be frightened by—"

"I'm worried about Daniel."

The words caught Stella so off-guard, she had the sudden image of some old cartoon where the characters struck each other and they vibrated from the blow. "Daniel . . ."

"He tries not to show it. But he's scared too." She picked up the controls again and traced little one-finger designs around the buttons. "Nicole says he's been having bad dreams all week."

Stella had no idea what to say. A thousand responses swept through her brain, but none of them sounded at all right. She did the only thing that seemed proper, which was to seat herself and take her daughter's hand.

Only then did she realize Amber was trying hard not to cry.

"He's doing so much. Nicole says he's been working crazy hours, trying to put things together. But he's scared too. So scared." The words tumbled out on top of each other. "He hasn't been back to Los Angeles since the bad times. He thought he'd never go back. And now he is going. Nicole tried to tell him to handle this on the phone. But Daniel won't listen. He says it has to be done in person to have any chance of working. And he needs to make sure Chloe is safe."

Stella nodded as though she understood a smidgen of what she was hearing. "Chloe . . ."

"Daniel won't let Travis or Ricki go with them. He says it's going to be hard enough for Chloe to get this right. They kind of agreed, but they argued with him anyway." Amber swiped her face with the sleeve of her free arm. "Nicole says Daniel was a grouch all day yesterday after they fought. And he had the worst nightmares ever last night. She saw him working in the office after midnight. And this morning he went for a run before it was even light outside."

The mantel clock read half past seven. "You've already talked to Nicole?"

Amber pointed to her phone on the sofa. "She texted me. Three times."

Her daughter's state forced Stella to choose her words very carefully. "I'm sure Daniel is doing what he thinks is best. But . . ."

Amber looked at her. "Promise you'll be nice to him."

"Darling, I try to be nice all the time—"

"You know what I mean. He likes you a lot, Mommy. And I like him. Really, really a lot." The tears spilled. "He's scared. But he's doing all this for you. For Chloe too. But all this work he's doing, it's mostly for you." The words became constricted now, by the fear and the sorrow and the tension in that young face. "So you need to be nice. Promise me, Mommy. It's really, really, really important that you promise."

Below Carpinteria, the coastal hills muscled in tightly to the shoreline. There was scarcely room for the highway and a thin strip of beachfront houses and trailer parks. Daniel had not spoken a word since leaving Miramar an hour and a half earlier. Everyone in the pickup had become infected by his tension. As they passed Mussel Shoals, a marine layer rose from the Pacific and blanketed the coastal route. The haze soon became so thick that all Stella could see were the taillights directly ahead of them. The light was diffused, striking from every direction. To Stella, it seemed like the fog was a perfect overlay to her state. Every option seemed wrapped in confusion.

They crawled at less than thirty miles an hour. Now and then a vague shadow roared past, unseen trucks barreling at absurd speeds. Daniel squinted through the windscreen and kept a fierce hold on the wheel. Moving forward, despite all his worries and uncertainties.

Stella breathed softly, in and out. She said, "Why don't we take a break?"

Daniel nodded. "Stopping sounds like a good idea to me. Girls?"

Nicole was already busy on her phone. "There's a Starbucks by the first Ventura exit. That's . . . three miles ahead."

By the time they resumed their journey south, the haze had cleared, and the freeway was moving. Stella had still not spoken. She could feel the words building up inside. But the will to release them, take the turning, make the step that led her into a new future . . .

It was so very, very hard.

She kept glancing over at Daniel as they left the freeway and headed into Universal City. It was almost as hard as what he was doing. For her.

Daniel pulled into the entrance to the Universal City Hotel. As the valet started over, Chloe said, "I thought you told us we had to go to where you used to work."

Daniel pointed up the hill. "KNBC is on City Plaza, in the middle of the Walk."

"Get out."

Amber said, "What's that?"

Chloe stared. "Girl, you've lived in California all your life and you don't know CityWalk?"

Nicole said, "It's this huge outdoor shopping mall."

"Not to mention all the super-cool theme stuff. Potter World, House of Horrors, you name it." Chloe stared up the sunlit hill. "I've begged them to take me there since forever."

"I've booked us three rooms. My treat." Daniel opened his door and handed the valet his keys. "You ladies go get settled in. The shuttle leaves every twenty minutes to take you to Valhalla."

Amber said, "Where?"

Nicole replied, "He's kidding."

Stella touched his arm. "Daniel, wait."

He waved the valet away and settled back. "Yes?"

"Do you want to go up there alone?"

"Not really. But I thought . . ."

"Let me come." She could see he was ready to deny her request. "You're doing all this for me. Let me be there for you."

Nicole said, "Count me in."

"Ladies, really, it's nice, but . . ."

"Daniel, please."

"I second that," Chloe said.

Stella tried for a smile. "Sounds like you've got yourself a posse."

226

# CHAPTER 38

Daniel had booked them three rooms on the fourteenth floor. He pretended to go deaf when Stella pleaded to let her pay. She and Amber could look out and watch the afternoon throngs collide with the first line of CityWalk attractions. She could hear Chloe and Nicole chatter excitedly in the room next door. Daniel was two doors farther along. It felt somehow comforting, this odd collection of friends, as if they could actually shelter her from the storm that tracked her every move.

They rode the hotel's tram up to the CityWalk entrance. Nicole play-acted the happy guide, while Amber and Chloe squealed over their first tour of LA's packaged delights. Daniel sat in the row ahead of her and Amber, isolated in his own bubble of tension. Stella felt a sudden urge to reach out, stroke the point where his neck met his hairline. She could feel his need, sense how easy it would be to join that with her own. Because she did need him. More than she was able to express. Even to herself.

*Men don't stay.*

The mantra that she'd carried ever since her husband had walked out on them, at the lowest and hardest point of her life, seemed so hollow now, seated in the row behind Daniel as he grimly watched his past rise up before him. He was there because of her.

The marine layer had burned off completely by the time they arrived. They turned away from the crowds pushing toward the CityWalk entrance and stared out over Universal City. The freeway ribbons flowed to their left and directly below where they stood. Sunlight glistened off a million bright surfaces. Far in the distance rose a line of brown, jagged peaks.

Amber whispered, "Isn't it beautiful?"

Stella nodded. Despite everything, this day held a remarkable quality of promise.

Amber moved in closer. "Everything's going to be okay, Mommy. I just know it."

Stella held Amber's hand as they wandered along the main thoroughfare, just another mother and daughter enjoying a free day, without a care in the world. Chloe and Nicole walked ahead of them, laughing and chattering like the teens they were. Daniel held to his grim solitude, at least until Stella reached out with her free hand. "Hey."

He jerked, "What?"

She said to Amber, "Tell him what you told me."

Amber almost sang the words. "Everything's going to be fine. I just know it."

Daniel almost managed a smile. "Hard to argue with that."

The three of them moved in synch through the crowds, passing the biggest Johnny Rocket on the planet, until Amber cried, "Mommy, *look.*"

Above the multiplex entrance stretched a building-sized poster from *Titanic*. Stella explained, "This is Amber's all-time favorite movie."

She was almost dancing in place. "It's the flying scene!"

Above them, Rose stood on the bow rail, supported by Jack, facing the vast unbroken seas. She raised her arms to the ocean and the golden light, and put her faith and trust in a man who had won his passage in a card game. Stella stared at the poster and felt as though she had never actually seen it before, the way Rose achieved a new understanding of hope by defying everything that had brought her to that point and trusting the right man.

She looked at Daniel and said the only words that made sense to her at that moment. "Let's go kill some ghosts."

Daniel felt as though Stella's words carried him through the tidal surge of people and noise. But as they approached the KNBC entrance, his strength faltered—just for a moment, but long enough for Nicole to notice. She took his hand and said, "We got your back, Jack."

Chloe snorted. "You did not just say that."

"Hey. I thought it was pretty cool."

"Cool is right," Stella said.

Daniel let the ladies move him forward. The crowd parted, and they passed through the electronic doors and entered the building, easy as you please.

Four years was a lifetime for the young LA crowd that supplied an endless stream of front-office staffers and production assistants. Daniel did not recognize anyone. The foyer had been remodeled, which helped as well. He gave his name to the receptionist, and the young man responded with a professional smile and the news that Kirsten Wright was expecting him.

Chloe led Nicole and Amber on a guided tour of the front room's posters. She knew the shows, she knew the stars. Just loving this moment. Here. In LA.

Daniel started to ask Nicole if she didn't want to join the others when his phone rang. He checked the screen and said, "I have to take this."

"So who's stopping you?"

"No, I mean, we all need to hear." He led them over to a sofa in the far corner, seated himself with a lady to either side, and hit the phone's SPEAKER button. "Go ahead."

The Ukrainian from Alabama said, "I find nothing." He ended the word with a soft clunk. *Nothink.* "I am suspecting, there is nothing to find."

Daniel watched Stella frown at the phone. He replied, "Walk me through what you've learned."

"This mayor, she drives the same lousy Nissan for three years and seven months. Her husband makes a peanut salary doing peanut work for the power company. They have two credit cards, they have debt, they pay when they get checks. End of story."

"Offshore accounts, maybe?"

"For what they are saving? In September, they travel to Montana; they stay in same hotel three years in a row. This hotel, it is lucky to have three stars. Please, next time give me someone interesting to spy on. This mayor puts me to sleep."

"We're missing something."

The man snorted. "Of course. We are missing a hunt for the real thief, chasing this lady mayor."

Stella leaned back. Shook her head. Said softly, "It's her. I know it."

"Who is this speaking?"

"The lady who's been falsely charged."

The man was silent, then, "I am not liking to be heard by others."

The line went dead.

Daniel pocketed the phone and sat there,

giving Stella a chance to digest and respond. Nicole twisted around so she was almost facing him. The two other girls kept chattering away, Chloe saying some show was on the way out, only the cast didn't know it yet. Stella stared out the foyer's front door, frowning at the happy throngs streaming past. To his left, the security doors swung back, and Kirsten Wright entered the reception area. The head of West Coast news spotted him and started over.

Stella said again, "It's Catherine. She's the one. I don't know why I'm sure. But I am."

Daniel held up his hand, halting Kirsten before she could speak. He said, "Let's assume for the moment that you're right."

She showed him emotions so strong they turned her eyes into rain-washed emeralds. "You believe me."

Daniel saw no need to reply that it would be truer to say he had no better culprit in mind. "We need to take a different course. Following the money hasn't brought us the intel we need to move forward. You know the woman. What could possibly be driving her to steal? That question is the key to this entire mystery." He gave that a beat, then rose to his feet. "Kirsten Wright, Stella Dalton. My niece, Nicole. Stella's daughter, Amber. And Chloe Donovan."

"The model."

Chloe replied. "Someday. I hope."

"How old are you?"

"Sixteen," she replied. Then more softly, "Any day now."

Kirsten Wright was tall, slender, elegant, and utterly humorless. She was in her late fifties, preferred timeless fashion, and used far too much hairspray in her graying auburn locks. Normally, Kirsten kept her ruthlessness sheathed in a no-nonsense politeness, mostly because she could. Everyone who spent any time around the news director knew the dagger was there and would be unleashed the instant anyone on her staff gave less than one hundred and ten percent.

"Come along, everyone." She waved to the receptionist. As they passed through the security portal, Kirsten told Daniel, "We have a situation."

# CHAPTER 39

Kirsten led them to the executive offices, which were spread in a semicircle around a central reception area holding desks for four staffers. She stopped by one office, stuck her head inside the open door, and asked someone to join them. A dumpy guy in a rayon tie and glasses perched on his wispy comb-over stepped out. Kirsten introduced him as Ray, her new head of legal. She then asked two staffers to join them. They entered a conference room, and Kirsten directed them to the side facing the interior windows. The staffers took seats by the wall behind their boss. Kirsten watched Amber and Nicole and Chloe troop in but did not object. Once they were seated, she said simply, "Okay, Daniel. You're on."

Stella thought he did a remarkably good job summarizing the situation. He kept his sentences short and punched one word every now and then, like he was already talking to the camera. His voice faltered twice in the process, and he stopped to sip from his water bottle, then continued. A total pro, even after being away from the gig for so long, even though the strain was clear on his features. She checked the wall clock when he went silent. Four minutes, start to finish.

Kirsten made a couple of notes while he spoke. When he was done, she turned to the man seated beside her. "Ray?"

"You've got a theft of city, county, and possibly state funds. Plus a conspiracy to defraud a federally run pension fund."

"Not to mention setting up an innocent woman to take the fall," Daniel added.

Ray shrugged. "This is LA. Some of the jokers in this place consider that part of their job description."

Kirsten said to her legal chief, "You're telling me it's marginal."

"If it lands in our lap, sure, I'd say run with it. But to invest dollars from our news budget?" He shrugged. "Your call."

Daniel said, "What if the conspiracy is not limited to one town?"

Both people opposite them went on full alert. "Explain."

"Something has bothered me since the first time I looked at the city's accounts. This is a very sophisticated theft."

"Six and a half million dollars make for a lot of reasons to get it right," Kirsten said.

Daniel turned to Stella and asked, "The mayor has no background in accounting, correct?"

She shook her head. "Catherine was employed as a florist. She's basically been in local politics since high school."

Daniel turned back. "Which means she's working with co-conspirators. The accounts suggest this theft was spread over three years. Say it was just five people. One point one million apiece breaks down to two hundred and twenty thousand a year. And all that time, they run the very real risk of being discovered. Loss of everything. Jail time."

The pair facing them were silent now. Watchful.

Daniel's forehead had developed a sheen from the effort of selling his concept. "I think it is highly possible, even probable, that some outside group with the necessary expertise has developed a system. They find local willing partners and milk the city funds."

"They hold themselves to smaller communities," Ray said. Into it now. "Stay under the radar. Work their way through half a dozen municipalities undetected."

Kirsten's gaze switched from one to the other. "You think?"

Ray responded by asking Daniel, "You have anything concrete?"

"Give me half an hour," he replied. "I'll walk you through the books. You tell me."

Kirsten asked Daniel, "What do you need?"

He was ready for that. "A camera team to cover

Ms. Dalton's trial. A researcher and producer to start the hunt immediately."

"You're talking real money."

"Time is crucial." Daniel did not back down. "We risk them learning that we're sniffing around."

"There's always that risk."

"Not with an innocent woman's freedom hanging in the balance."

She glanced at Stella, then away. "I'll give it serious consideration."

"Kirsten, I need a yes."

"Would you be willing to serve as your own producer?"

"At least until we know whether or not we have a story, sure." He wiped his forehead. "Deal?"

"I said, I'll consider it." She motioned toward the door. "Thank you, everyone. That will be all. Ray and Daniel, please stay. Everybody else, give us a minute."

Stella started to rise with the others when Daniel shot her a look. She suspected it was an involuntary gesture, the glance a drowning man might make at a safety line that was just out of reach. She dropped instantly back into the chair. "I think I'll stay."

"This is a confidential issue that does not pertain to your case, Ms. Dalton."

"I'm here because Daniel said it was important that I observe you at work," she replied. "If Daniel asks me to leave, I'll go."

"Stay," Daniel said quietly. "Please."

Kirsten Wright did not like it. But she did not speak. Stella met the woman's agate-hard gaze and waited her out.

When the door clicked shut, she asked her legal adviser, "Any word on Grant?"

"Arraignment's set for tomorrow."

"I thought you said your people would move things forward."

"I said they'd try. They did." Ray shrugged. "Tomorrow's the best they can do."

"Be sure and thank them for me." She looked across the table. "You remember Grant."

Daniel's forehead creased. "From the New York operation by way of Philly, right?"

"Correct. Grant is currently my one and only on-air business specialist. He's gotten himself arrested in Las Vegas."

"How is that even possible?"

Her lips decompressed enough to offer a tight smile. "How can we be down to one business anchor, or how can Grant get into trouble in Vegas?"

He wiped his forehead. "Both, I guess."

"We have a young but fairly adequate anchor-in-training. Only she's honeymooning in Tierra del Fuego. Intentionally out of phone and Internet reach. As for Grant, well, I assume he's done something suitably awful. Again."

Ray added, "I seriously doubt the Vegas judicial system even bothers to give out parking tickets for misdemeanors."

Daniel's hands made damp track marks on the table. "So use your regular new anchor."

"Come on, Daniel. You and I both know the business community smells a talking head a mile off. And that's all either of them are."

Ray said, "Steal their hairspray and they'd shatter into a billion pieces."

"Kirsten . . ."

"I want you to anchor *Market Roundup*. You want my help, that's the deal." She rose from the table and lifted her legal adviser with a jerk of her chin. "Up or down, Daniel. I need your answer now."

# CHAPTER 40

Stella saw how Daniel remained planted in his chair, the perspiration shining on his forehead, the tight way he studied the empty seat across from him. And she knew exactly what needed doing.

She caught up with Kirsten just outside the conference room. "I need to speak with you." When the news chief looked ready to fob her off, Stella added, "Ninety seconds."

"Ninety seconds I have." She waved the attorney on. "Go."

Stella pointed back through the open door. "You see how hard this is on Daniel."

Kirsten started to glance at where Daniel remained seated at the empty table, then caught herself. "Daniel's a pro. He'll make it work."

Stella didn't argue. "I think I can help him get through this. I know I can."

The news chief crossed her arms. "What do you need?"

"When does he go on?"

"In . . ." She glanced at the wall clock. "The East Coast markets close in twenty minutes.

He'll do his first wrap-up ten minutes later."

"Can you arrange for sandwiches for the girls? We missed a meal."

"Done." She waved over the nearest intern, fired off instructions, then, "Next?"

"We need someplace where we can help him refocus. Alone if possible."

"Who is this we?"

"Me and the girls."

Kirsten cocked her head. "For real?"

Stella nodded. "It needs to be all of us."

Another thoughtful glance at the clock, then, "He needs to go straight to makeup. The researcher responsible for prepping him will have pages of script ready for his approval."

"Let me handle the makeup."

"Can you?"

"Yes. Well, not me personally." Stella turned to where a wide-eyed Chloe tracked their every word. "But you can, right?"

She nodded vigorously. "Veronica's been explaining everything, you know, so I'll be able to copy her work when she's not around."

Kirsten asked, "Veronica?"

Stella explained, "A professional photographer who's helped put together Chloe's portfolio."

Kirsten gave that a moment's deliberation, then turned and called through the open door, "Daniel, time to get started."

• • •

Kirsten personally escorted them down the production hall. They passed a sound stage filled with bright lights and two people seated on a mock stage, while another woman made hand gestures in front of a blank green wall and described the weather. The man seated at the stage was checking his hair in a hand mirror, while the woman next to him reviewed pages of script. Kirsten let them hover in the doorway for a moment, long enough for a man with earphones standing behind the central camera to say, "Twenty seconds."

The woman set her pages below her desk, and the man closed his compact. Kirsten said quietly, "Let's go."

Nicole whispered, "This is so totally awesome."

Where the hallway took a sharp left turn, Kirsten stopped by a door on the right, knocked once, and entered. Stella saw a long narrow room with an adjoining bathroom at the back. The entire left-hand wall held a mirror rimmed by lights. A woman was seated in a high-backed office chair, the collar of her dress shirt protected with a long strip of paper towels. She texted on her phone while a cosmetician worked on her hair. Kirsten snapped her fingers. "Everyone out."

The woman did not look up. "She's not done, and I'm on set in—"

"Now. You too, Doris. No, leave your kit."

The woman ripped the towels from her collar and gave Kirsten a dark look as she passed. When the room was empty, Kirsten ushered them inside. "You, Chloe, get to work. I'll go see to those sandwiches. Daniel, nineteen minutes."

He spoke for the first time since leaving the conference room. "I don't have any clothes."

"Forty-four long, right? We're seeing to that. Okay, everyone. The clock is counting down."

When the door closed behind her, Nicole said again, "Awesome."

# CHAPTER 41

S tella leaned against the shelf running beneath
the wall-sized mirror and watched Chloe work
on Daniel's face. She felt intensely calm. Perhaps
she had carried this with her all day, she couldn't
remember. Only now her internal state was
contrasted against the studio's frenetic energy. A
television mounted in the upper corner showed
the two anchors smiling at the camera, then the
scene cut to a drug ad. A voice from somewhere
down the hall called, "Ninety seconds!"

In response, a woman shrieked, "The monitor's
still down! Where are the pages for my next
segment!"

In response, Daniel shivered.

People came and went in a steady stream. The
cosmetician named Doris brought a navy jacket
and shirt and tie in plastic wraps. Stella thanked
her and draped them over the chair back next
to Daniel. Doris inspected Chloe's work on
Daniel's face and nodded approval. She departed
just as Kirsten arrived. She asked, "How's our
star?"

"He'll be fine," Stella replied.

The news chief checked on Chloe and allowed, "Very nice work."

"Thanks."

Kirsten said, "You never know how someone will respond to pressure."

Chloe replied, "Hey. I was made for this."

Kirsten studied her a moment, then said to Daniel, "Our top business analyst is also our best writer. She's still working on your intro and first segment. Something about a last-minute announcement from Treasury. The pages will be here soon, or somebody will be looking for a new job."

Daniel did not show any interest in responding, so Stella said, "Daniel will be ready."

"I'm counting on that." Kirsten crossed the room, opened the door, then turned back. "The writer's name is Radley. She's young, she's eager, and she's smarter than all my anchors put together. I want you to be nice to her. There toward the end I lost too many good people to your tantrums. I don't want that happening with her, understand?"

After Kirsten left, Stella touched Chloe's arm and motioned for her to join the other two girls by the back wall. Daniel continued to glare at his reflection, the stone mask firmly in place. Closing himself off from everything. Emotions, people, the place, what was about to come. Shielding himself from what he never wanted to endure again.

Stella studied him and saw a male version of her own attitude for seven long years.

Outside their little dressing room, people raced up and down the hall. Voices shouted. A woman laughed, her voice strident, one notch off a full-throated shriek. In contrast, Stella found herself thinking of the lake in front of Tranquility Falls. Standing there by the blooming meadow, watching the girls dance. Wanting desperately to join them.

She knew whatever she said would be inadequate. Just the same, it had to be said. "You're going to be great."

Daniel continued to stare sightlessly at his own reflection.

"You're not that Daniel anymore. That man is not you."

Daniel did not respond.

There were a hundred things she wanted to tell him. Starting with how, for the first time since the death of her child, she thought hope might be real. For her. She could actually taste it. The flavor rested on her tongue like a spice from younger, headier days. But now wasn't the time for such confessions. This wasn't about her at all. Now Daniel needed to hear her say, "It's not the cameras or the lights that scare you. You're a pro. You don't lose that."

Nicole said softly, "Like riding a bike."

Stella nodded. "What scares you is who you

were. What you did. And you're afraid you'll do it all again. Fall down and never get up."

He looked at her, really looked. Revealing the shadows and the fear.

Stella shifted around so she stood by his right shoulder and lowered her face so that it was in line with his. She pointed at the three girls standing by the rear wall. "That's how I know, Daniel. These four people whose lives are better because of who you've become."

Daniel tasted the air, but the words did not emerge.

She gripped his shoulders in as fierce an embrace as she could manage, crouched down like that. "You're a good man, and you're getting better."

# CHAPTER 42

A woman in her early twenties rushed into the room. Her dark, shoulder-length hair held alternating pink and purple streaks. "Mr. Riffkin, I'm Radley, your writer-analyst." She offered a sheaf of pages. "I've got your intro and the first story you'll be covering."

"Thanks."

Stella could not say whose hand trembled more. She retreated to the doorway and waited. Radley wore a black sweater over a white shirt with dangling cuffs and shirttails, and black trousers. Her dark eyes were covered by dark, round glasses. The absence of color magnified her hair's highlights. As Daniel read, she shifted back and forth from one foot to the other, adjusted her glasses, then said, "I guess I better get back—"

"Give me another minute."

It seemed to Stella that Daniel steadied as he read. He finished the final page, tapped them together on his leg, then asked, "You wrote this?"

She swallowed. "Yes."

"It's very good."

Her voice rose a full two octaves. "Really?"

"Actually, it's better than that." He pointed to the pages. "Treasury just made this decision public?"

"Fifteen minutes ago. That's why I'm late."

"You're not late. You're right on time." Daniel looked at his reflection. Thinking. "What's the second segment?"

"The original headliner. Three blue-chips announced earnings well below market expectations."

"You'll tie this to what Treasury has?"

"Sure, that is, if you think . . ."

"After-market trading will go nuts. You know that, right?" When she nodded, he went on, "Give them both barrels. Anyone who's exposed is going to get scalded. They need to dump."

"I'm on it." She opened the door, then turned back and said, "I grew up watching you, Mr. Riffkin. It's an honor. Really."

When the door closed, Nicole said, "That's my uncle she's talking about."

"They're about to start singing your tune." Stella hugged him a second time. "Go get dressed for the dance."


Back toward the end of his time in LA, Daniel had started seeing the television studio in a totally different way. Before, it was like standing in the middle of a whirlwind. The people swarmed, the lights gleamed, everyone was

249

massed and ready for him to step onto the stage and perform. Precision equipment, the glassed-in balcony housing the production staff gleaming with all the flashing screens, the crew making him beautiful for the audience. The thrill was incredible, the high so intense it was the easiest thing in the world to step off the stage and enter into whatever high was next on offer that night.

But during the last couple of months before the accident that killed his fiancée, when he entered the soundstage, what he saw were the shadows.

All the light and energy and equipment were focused upon the set piece where he would sit and speak. Beyond the lights' reach loomed a dark realm. Out there, shadows gathered and waited for the chance to devour him whole.

Daniel walked the long hall leading to the soundstage and felt as though the only thing holding him in place was Stella's grip on his hand. The soundstage was a massive cave, a cube fifty feet to a side. Steel girders and dolly systems ran overhead like man-made stalactites. Sounds echoed back from the rushing technicians. The cameras squeaked and whispered as they shifted on their rubber wheels. Technicians readjusted the lights by whacking them with rubber hammers. Stella walked him up to where the technician held his mike and battery pack. He let himself be wired and thought he heard the shadows laugh at him once more.

But when he was seated, and the final count-down began, and his heart was beating frantically to escape the cage of his chest, he saw them. The four figures who defied the shadows. Stella's words came back to him, more clearly than when she had spoken.

He was not the same man.

Then the evening anchor turned to him and said, "Today, we have a special guest to walk us through a roundup of the markets. Hello, Daniel, it's good to have you back."

Daniel was able to reply, "It's good to be here."

And he almost meant it.

# CHAPTER 43

Thursday was Chloe's chance to shine.

A little before five, Daniel and Stella managed a few quiet minutes over coffee in the lobby. She was headed back to Miramar, hoping to arrive in time for Amber's school day.

He accompanied Stella as she booked a car at the Hertz counter in the lobby. She tried to argue when he insisted on paying, but it was a polite public quarrel between two friends. Daniel finished the discussion by leaning in close and telling her how much he was making for his session in front of the camera. She gave him a look of suitable astonishment and let the Hertz lady take his credit card.

On the way back to her room, they shared a few words, mostly just reassuring one another that the previous day had been real. Amber was still fast asleep. Stella carried their cases while Daniel held the child. He loved the feel of her feathery hair on his cheek, loved the sleepy fragrance. The valet had Stella's ride out front. The air was chilly and smelled of eucalyptus. Daniel settled Amber into the rear seat, then stepped back so

Stella could tuck a blanket around her and fasten the belt. They spoke a few more words, shared a final embrace and kiss, then he stood and watched as she drove into the gray light of dawn.

Daniel had agreed to return for that afternoon's *Market Roundup*, basically because Kirsten had given him no choice. He bought another coffee from the lobby café, returned to his room, and began a process that had once been routine. Radley had set him up with a password to the station's news feed. He studied the alerts that had come in during the night. He read the midnight previews, the newest quarterly reports, the standard stream of data that had formed his morning hours for years. As he completed the tasks, an e-mail popped in from Kirsten announcing that their regular business anchor was still tied up in the Vegas courts, and they had not been able to reach the South American honeymooner. Which meant Daniel would be needed for a third day. Kirsten did not ask, nor did she threaten. There was no need for either.

When Nicole and Chloe phoned to say they were headed downstairs for breakfast, he was writing a memo to Radley, outlining the points he thought they should cover in that day's feed. By the time he finished and arrived downstairs, the girls were waiting in the lobby. Both looked nervous to the point of becoming physically sick. As they waited for the valet to bring his pickup around, Daniel started to reassure them. But, in the end, he decided silence was a more honest approach to what lay ahead.

Veronica had sent Chloe's portfolio to three agencies where she still had senior-level contacts. All three had agreed to meet her. The agencies were based in the Beverly Hills–West Hollywood area, all in swank buildings with polished interiors, all filled with beautiful people. The receptionists showed Chloe the sort of mild contempt that Daniel knew all too well. Chloe sat between Daniel and Nicole until it was her turn to go inside. Afterward, Daniel held her hand as they walked back to the car. Her fingers were like ice.

Chloe kept it together until after the third meeting. It was approaching the lunch hour by then, so Daniel stopped for smoothies. Chloe only drank when Daniel urged her to put something in her stomach. She managed a couple of sips, then asked softly, "Why are they like that?"

Nicole said, "Anyone as young and beautiful as you is a threat."

"If they can make you feel small and unwanted, so much the better," Daniel agreed.

Another sip, then, "The women in the offices were nice. Two of them, anyway. But the look in their eyes scares me."

Daniel started the car and pulled away from the curb. "Your time here is just beginning.

I think you have a good chance of making it."

"Really?"

"Absolutely," Nicole said. She was seated in the back seat, directly behind Chloe. "Daniel wouldn't say it if it wasn't so."

He went on, "You need to fashion a response to the people who would rather see you fail. Something that protects you and doesn't give them a reason to snipe."

Chloe drank more of her smoothie. Thinking. "You just defined high school."

"There you go." Daniel glanced in the rearview mirror. "Back to the hotel?"

Nicole's face pinched up tighter than Chloe's. "No."

"You sure?"

Nicole's only response was to fasten her attention on the world beyond her side window.

Daniel took Beverly Glen up past the LA Country Club. The route grew increasingly steep as it entered Holmby Hills, the narrow development that formed the boundary between Beverly Hills and Bel Air. So many things were exactly as he remembered, the same perfectly manicured lawns, the same glitzy cars, the same gardeners making things perfect for the rich and famous. As he took a left on St. Pierre and entered Bel Air, he glanced back at Nicole. She had withdrawn into a tight little shell by the side window.

Their home on Nimes Road had originally been built in the sixties, then expanded and renovated any number of times. Daniel had always considered it a beautiful place, with Italianate columns curving out from the large front door like a pair of welcoming arms. The front garden held a number of blooming cherry trees. Daniel parked down the road, beneath the shade of a massive magnolia.

He cut the motor, settled back, and waited.

Chloe finally said, "For the past two years, I kept her *Vanity Fair* cover taped to my bedroom mirror." She looked at Daniel. "She really said she'd help me?"

"At this point, Lisa is only willing to meet you." Daniel chose his words very carefully. "You need to understand, my sister can be very difficult."

"Mom's had two protégés," Nicole said. She addressed her words to the side window. "She called them interns. They get coffee, they carry cases, they fetch dry cleaning, they drive her car, they shop for groceries. They stand around all day holding outfits and fielding calls. When Mom's on a shoot, the whole crew uses her interns as unpaid runners. One left after a year and is back home somewhere—Des Moines, I think. She hates Mom."

Chloe continued to inspect the silent house. "The other?"

"She models with Anne Ford. Mom's agency. She hates Mom too. But politely."

"After this morning . . . do I have any choice?"

"Absolutely," Daniel said. "Go home. Finish school. Take lessons. Come back."

"I can't hold my breath that long."

Nicole said, "There's an upside to interning with Mom. Now or later, she'll tell you about what happened on her second shoot. The head of the magazine invited her to dinner at his hotel cabana. She shows up, he's in a robe. Nothing else. He's sixty-something, Mom's just turned fifteen."

When Nicole went silent, Chloe pressed, "What happened?"

"No idea. I only know that much because I was sneaking around and heard her tell the story to both interns. She promised it would never happen to them."

Chloe leaned forward and squinted at the house. Thinking. She glanced at Daniel, showing real fear. "What do you think I should do?"

He had been waiting for that. "Talk to Lisa. See if there's a chemistry. We'll go back to the hotel, and you can sleep on it tonight. Tomorrow, I'll put you on the train back to Miramar."

"I just told you . . ."

He halted her with an upraised hand. "Go home," he repeated. "Talk it through with your parents. Try and make peace. If you succeed, give them the chance to drive you down. Let them be part of this."

Chloe's chin quivered. But she clenched down tight and regained control. "If they won't come around?"

"I'll bring you back to LA myself. But at least this way you know you gave it your best shot."

She remained like that, locked down tight, for a very long moment. Then she rammed open her door, almost leapt out, and started up toward the house.

As Chloe approached the front walk, the door opened, and Daniel's sister appeared. She stared at the truck for a long moment, then ushered Chloe inside and shut the door.

Daniel breathed in and out, forcing air around the lancing pain caused by seeing his sister again.

Nicole's voice held the same distress Daniel felt. "I need to go talk to her. Don't I?"

"When you're ready, and not before."

A hand reached out and touched his arm. "I really, really like how you talk. *With* me. Not *at* me."

Daniel had no idea how to respond. Silence gathered. He opened the truck's four windows to the air and the birdsong. A car passed. From somewhere in the distance came the shriek of a band saw. Then silence.

Nicole surprised him by asking, "What was the mayor's name again?"

Daniel turned in his seat. "Excuse me?"

"The bad lady you can't get a handle on."

"Lundberg. Catherine Lundberg."

"Right. Her." She traced the rim of her open window. "I've been thinking. What if Stella is right."

Daniel swung around as far as he could go. "This Alabama Ukrainian is supposed to be really good at his job. And he couldn't find anything that even suggested the mayor is on the take."

"Sure. Okay. But what if it's like you said back at the station?" Nicole turned from the window. "What if this isn't about money at all? What if it's something else?"

"Like what?"

"I don't know. Maybe . . ." She shrugged. "Something you said when we were with the ice lady."

"Kirsten."

"Right. You've been bothered since the beginning at how sophisticated this is. You think it might be a bigger deal going down than them stealing from just one town."

"So?"

"So what if the bad lady isn't bad?" Her face was scrunched up again, only now there was an absence of the old pain. She was concentrating. Struggling to put this idea of hers into words. "What if she's being forced? What if somebody else is robbing the city?"

Daniel felt as if the script was being written in the trees and street and lawn and silent house. "This is excellent. Only . . ."

"What?"

He drew the phone from his pocket. "Let's see what our hacker friend has to say."

# CHAPTER 44

Stella made it to Long Beach before the freeway traffic slowed with rush hour. The Chevy only had seventeen thousand miles and drove well. Amber woke and climbed into the front seat, something she had insisted on doing since the day she turned ten. Stella wished her daughter a good morning and asked if she wanted to stop for food or a restroom break. When Amber did not respond, Stella glanced over and saw her daughter had her feet sticking straight out, like a little girl inspecting the toes of a new pair of shoes. "Is everything all right?"

Amber hummed a little note but did not speak.

"It's not like you to be so quiet."

"I've been remembering."

"About what?"

"Daddy."

Stella experienced the same uncertainty she had known ever since the previous week's argument. Amber continued to break all their unspoken rules. Stella's life was at least partly defined by how her daughter never became angry. She never raised her voice. She never lost her cheerful ability to lift Stella's spirits. She never . . .

Amber never spoke about her father.

The man who had abandoned them and rarely visited and then left for Georgia. And remarried. And sent cards and called his own daughter maybe three or four times a year. Never, never, never.

Stella settled in behind a lawn-maintenance truck. It allowed her to focus on what was happening inside the car. It felt like her world was being canted sharply onto some new course. One she could neither identify nor even see clearly. Her little girl was changing, growing up, and becoming a stranger.

Amber broke into her thoughts with, "Do you remember, after he left? When things were so hard?"

Stella nodded her head. Unable to speak. She remembered.

"You cried a lot back then. I hurt too, Mommy. I cried with you sometimes, but it didn't get any better. I didn't know what to do. My sister was gone, and Daddy, and you . . . It felt like you were leaving me too."

Stella unclenched the wheel long enough to clear her eyes. The truck in front of them remained somewhat blurry, but her vision was better now. Unlike her heart, which had shattered so completely it hurt to breathe.

"Then one night I heard you crying. I crawled into bed with you. I said I wanted to make things better." Amber's voice held to that same new tone, utterly calm and matter-of-fact, even though she was now using both hands to clear her own cheeks. "You said that we were going to get through this. You promised me. But you said you needed my help. Remember, Mommy?"

Stella managed a whispered, "No."

"It's true. I didn't dream this. You said you needed me to be your little angel. I had to be there and sing for you and be happy for you, so you could find strength in me." Amber was quiet for several miles, then said, "It was so hard."

Stella wanted to find an exit and pull over. But it was tough enough just to keep a clear eye on the truck and the cars to either side.

"But I did it, Mommy. And you got better."

She said, "You have been my angel."

"But I'm tired, Mommy. I feel like I've had all these tears inside me. And I couldn't let them out because you needed me to be happy."

"Oh, darling, I never—"

"When I met Daniel, I thought he might be able to help me. And be the strong one. For you. And for me. Only you won't let him." She wiped her face again. "Now I don't know what to do."

# CHAPTER 45

B ut their hacker did not answer.
The third time Daniel speed-dialed the Alabama number, Nicole said, "Here comes Chloe."

Daniel cut the connection. The young girl looked more than beautiful, standing there on the home's front step. The early-afternoon light angled between the trees and caught her in a golden spotlight. She positively glowed. Daniel could feel her magnetic draw and wished her parents were here for this moment. Chloe laughed at something Lisa said, then turned and started down toward them.

Daniel asked Nicole, "Do you want to go speak with Lisa?"

Her voice had shrunk to little-girl size. "Tomorrow. Maybe."

It was the answer he had expected. "I think it would be a good idea if I went up." Daniel took her silence as assent and opened his door. He approached Chloe and said, "Looks like things went well."

"She'll take me on. Her third and last intern."

"And?"

"It all came together when I was inside." She hugged herself. "You're right. I need to let Mom and Dad be a part of this. If they want to."

"You're entering a huge change," Daniel agreed. "Your life is taking a new direction. They love you. Let's hope that's enough to change them too."

"And if it isn't . . ."

"I'll bring you back. Whenever you say."

The grip she had on her middle tightened further. "Okay."

He pointed up to where Lisa stood in the doorway, watching them. "Let me go have a word with my sister."

The distance from Daniel's pickup to where Lisa stood in her front door was not far. Call it a hundred yards. But it was long enough for the old tension to take hold. The vise was tight and somewhat pleasurable. All the desires and flavors of his former life flooded in, inviting him to release the hunger, enjoy the forbidden pleasures. Just this once.

Daniel looked back to where the pickup rested in the tree's shade. The two girls were not visible. He breathed in and out. Again. Feeling himself becoming anchored to the man they needed him to be.

Lisa broke into his thoughts with, "Is she there?"

Daniel turned around. "She is. Yes." When Lisa merely continued to stare at the truck, Daniel said, "You need to make peace with your daughter."

His sister responded by walking back inside. Leaving the door open. The message was clear. Come or go, it was his decision. But he needed to leave that portion of the conversation outside.

As he entered the foyer, Lisa said, "Chloe has promise."

"I'm glad you think so." Daniel shut the door. "She assumed getting here and having a chance would change everything. She's just now learning it's only shifted things up a notch."

"She's young," Lisa said. "The question is, can she learn."

"You did."

"We both know I learned the hardest lessons before that woman ever stepped through her patio doors."

That woman. The producer's wife. The person responsible for giving Lisa her chance in life. Daniel said, "Chloe is sharp."

"And quite attractive."

"And intelligent. And the camera loves her. She'll manage."

Lisa made a vague gesture toward the kitchen. "You want something? I can fix you a drink."

"I'm good."

Lisa stood in the middle of the domed foyer,

where the chandelier cast her in an ethereal glow. She always had a star's ability to capture the spotlight.

"Don't you want to know about your daughter?"

"Marvin said she was settling in."

"That's not the issue, and you know it."

She looked out over the living room, past the sliding glass doors that vanished into the side walls, out to where her gardener trimmed an already perfect shrub. "I saw you on the news yesterday."

Daniel knew there was nothing to be gained from pressing his sister.

"You said you'd never go on air again. Or come back to LA." When he remained silent, she pressed, "That's what you said. Or shouted."

"I wasn't the one yelling, and you know it." He headed for the door. "Good-bye, Lisa."

"Where are you going?"

"Our hotel. This conversation is going nowhere, and I'm tired."

"Daniel, wait." She showed him a little girl's uncertainty. "What do I say to her?"

He kept his hand on the doorknob. "That you love her. You understand why she did what—"

"I *don't* understand. I'll *never*—"

"Do you want to hear what I think or not?"

The flatness of his voice, the hard edge, halted her tirade before she could really begin. That and the fact that he opened the door, showing her how close he was to walking out of her life.

"Go on, then."

"Tell Nicole you understand she had reasons of her own to look for the truth. And that is what she found, Lisa. Despite years of your lying to her. And yourself. It happened, Nicole was right, and that's why you're angry. Because she found you out." He hadn't planned on being that tough, but her haughty attitude had always bored under his skin. "You're the one who should be asking forgiveness. For the lies, for how you treated your own—"

"Stop. Just stop."

"Your own daughter. You've spent years trying to mold her into someone she isn't. Nicole is completely different from you. She is also a truly beautiful young lady. Perceptive, funny, incredibly intelligent. Someone who deserves a great deal better than you've ever given her. It's time you accept her for who she is."

"You're making me cry."

He was tempted to go to her. Offer the comfort she clearly wanted. But Daniel couldn't tell whether it was an act or not. Lisa had always been a marvel at manipulating the moment. So he opened the door and said, "Last chance, sis. I'll bring her by tomorrow."

# Chapter 46

A storm swept in off the Pacific that evening. Daniel was awake and seated by the window, watching the lightning cut silhouettes from the city skyline, when his phone rang. Nicole said in her little-girl voice that she and Chloe were scared.

Daniel found the two girls wrapped in blankets and seated on the fold-out sofa, not watching a black-and-white movie. They cut off the television as he took the room's only chair. Rain lashed the window so hard the world disappeared, just washed away in the downpour.

The longer he sat there, the more irritated he became. He only half listened as the girls whined over the coming day. Chloe fretted about her parents and Lisa and the agencies. Nicole worried about whether she should actually meet her mom. They wanted more from him. Comfort, assurance, another something in the nonstop list of needs.

Finally, he rose, told them to get some rest, and returned to his room. Daniel stood by his bed until he lost the argument with himself. Then he grabbed his jacket and money and set out again.

He did not take his truck, in case the tide broke wrong and he was consumed. Instead, he returned to the habits of long ago. He walked to the concierge and asked for a limo. A taxi would not do. Not for where he was going. This time of night, arriving by taxi meant the occupant was either a tourist or a lowlife who guarded his wallet. A limo was Daniel's pass to all the city's midnight doors.

Daniel's internal cauldron was spiced now by four years of unvanquished hunger. He was back. He had come to the wrong place for all the right reasons. The girls' confidence in him only added to his conflicted emotions. Internal discord like this did not require a target, or a reason.

LA showed a secret face after midnight, one splashed with sparkling mascara and candy-pink lipstick. The smiles were electric, the crowds drawn not to the lights but rather the stars. Daniel had once been counted among the beautiful people. Not a top-tier name, of course. But he was a man on the rise, and the people who guarded the late-night doors had known it. The VIP tables were his, the hip young artists all knew him, or knew someone who made sure Daniel was included. Being included was everything.

He ordered the driver to head west and spent the ride trying to decide which place to hit. His favorite late-night club had been the Argyle, with a bi-level bar, sixties-era décor, a quiet alcove with a fireplace, and a two-story VIP table that had once been his to claim.

But as the limo descended into the city's vibrant late-night crawl, Daniel knew there was only one place that suited the hour and his state of mind. He leaned forward and told the driver to take him to the Chateau Marmont.

Armed security stood at the entrance, which meant some major star was in residence. Daniel lowered his window, allowed the guard to take a good look, and was waved up the drive. All part of the show.

Chateau Marmont stood at the top of a rise overlooking Sunset Boulevard. Its white edifice had been completed just before Black Monday and the stock market crash of 1929. The hotel's reputation had been going downhill ever since.

Sharon Tate and her bad-boy husband, Roman Polanski, had lived there. Jim Morrison had some of his most epic revelries on the hotel's second floor. John Belushi died of a drug overdose in Bungalow 3. The hotel's legacy was more sordid than the legends, because most of the truly bad stuff was kept hidden by the tight-lipped staff.

The Marmont bar had recently undergone a complete renovation, which meant its century-old décor sparkled and beckoned. Daniel took his customary place just around the curve, where he could survey both the bar's clientele and all the beautiful people passing through the entrance. He vaguely recognized the older of the two bartenders, which was something, because for Daniel the Marmont had always been his last stop. When the night would not let go and his penthouse apartment had been just another place to pass out. That particular bartender had often arranged a room for Daniel, and he had always left a C-note with the concierge as a tip. The bartender had never thanked him, because as far as the outside world was concerned, the event had never happened. That was service, Marmont-style.

"Good evening, Mr. Riffkin. Nice to see you again."

The name popped into Daniel's brain at just the right moment. "Stephen."

"Your usual?"

"Why not."

It said a lot about the bar's clientele that the house champagne, the bottle that was always kept open and ready, was vintage Cristal. The bartender placed the slender-stemmed glass down on a napkin, uncorked the bottle, and filled it to the brim. Another glass was set beside the first, this one to receive a finger of twenty-year-old vintage malt. These were Daniel's late-hour drinks of choice—room-temperature whisky that seared its way down, soothed by golden bubbles one degree off ice.

Why not indeed.

"Enjoy, sir." The bartender moved away.

Daniel sat there, staring at the two glasses.

Daniel was filled with the old exultation, a hunger as strong as fresh rage, the bitter triumph of playing king. He had known all along that his status was nothing more than a lie others accepted because it suited them. This station at the bar had been a mythical throne, a place to sit and bask for his very own mythical hour. The truth had been there in the eyes that watched him, the smiles cast his way, the laughter, the invitations. No matter how much he drank or stuffed up his nose, he had always known.

He ran a finger down the sweating champagne goblet and shivered. The blues were made for a time like this.

The bartender drifted back down his way. "Everything all right here, Mr. Riffkin?"

Daniel heard the raw edge to his own voice. "Can people change, Stephen?"

When the bartender did not come back with an immediate response, Daniel looked up, just in time to see the empty grave within the man's gaze. All the dark hours, all the ghosts who wandered in and out of the man's place of business, they haunted the bartender's dark eyes.

Then Stephen gave his traditional smile, gentle

and forgiving. "What's the point of that, sir? A lot of struggle and trouble, and nothing to show for it in the end."

Daniel did not respond.

Stephen reached for a bottle and poured another shot of whisky into the glass Daniel had not yet touched. "Change isn't worth the effort, if you ask me."

Daniel waited until the bartender moved down the bar to rise from his stool. He dropped two hundred-dollar notes on the surface and headed for the exit.

# CHAPTER 47

To his utter astonishment, though he had only slept a couple of hours, Daniel woke refreshed. He lay there a moment, reflecting back on other mornings after a session at the Marmont. The sweat-stained sheets, his own foul odor, the uncertainty of where he was or what he had done. Instead, Daniel rose and dressed and stretched and went for a dawn run.

As he left the hotel, Daniel thought about what Nicole had said their first day together. The joy she had known when he took her to the zoo. Daniel had no idea what zoo she was talking about. It was entirely possible he had driven her down to San Diego, in a state that had endangered them both. He had often been told by friends about trips he had taken, driving himself and others, journeys that he could not recall. Being straight only heightened the burn of guilt and regret over such past events. Daniel used the next several drumbeats of breath and steps to stamp down hard on both the emotions and the thoughts. Now was not the time.

The storm had left a crystalline freshness on the light and the air. He needed to set a number of things in motion, and running helped. The steady beat of his track shoes on the sidewalk aligned the torrent of thoughts into a single, unified stream. Forty-five minutes later, he returned to the hotel and stretched at poolside.

He felt . . . clean.

As he took the elevator up to his floor, he decided that *clean* didn't go far enough.

He felt ready.

For what, he had no idea. And for that one sweet moment, he decided it really didn't matter.

Daniel showered, dressed, and found the two young ladies downstairs in the breakfast room. Chloe sat beside a silent Nicole, eating oatmeal and fresh fruit. Nicole played with her food, but Daniel did not see the spoon actually reach her mouth. He prepared a bowl of yogurt and berries and granola. The coffee was awful, so he ordered tea. He would stop somewhere on the road later for an espresso.

Nicole broke the table's silence with, "You look better this morning."

He saw no reason to disagree. "I had a lot on my mind last night."

Chloe huffed a humorless laugh. "Join the crowd."

Nicole asked, "What's the matter?" When he

stayed quiet, she pressed, "We showed you ours. Now it's your turn."

"It's about the station," Daniel began. "I've known Kirsten for years."

Chloe asked, "The ice lady?"

Daniel thought the tea tasted almost as bad as the coffee, but drank anyway. "She's probably going to ask me to come back. Permanently."

"Back to LA?"

He nodded. "She and the station attorney stayed in the production booth through yesterday's broadcast. Afterward I spotted her watching the tape with a couple of suits. I recognized one of them from before. He's on the West Coast board of advisers. At least, he was."

Chloe shook her head. "Imagine that. A ticket to the big time. How awful for you." When Nicole gave her a long look, Chloe said, "What?"

Nicole asked Daniel, "If you don't want it, just say no."

Chloe snorted.

"That's just it," Daniel replied. "I don't know whether I want it or not."

Nicole gave him the same sort of look she had given Chloe. "You mean, you want it, but you don't know if you can do it and stay straight."

"That's it, exactly," Daniel said.

"You liked being back," Nicole said. Not asking. Saying.

"You were great," Chloe said. "I believed

277

everything you said. I *enjoyed* it. And I don't know a thing about business."

"It was so exciting, watching you perform," Nicole agreed.

"I never thought of it that way before," Chloe said. "Not just reading the news. Performing."

"You were living it, and so was I." Nicole tasted a microscopic spoonful of her meal. "I like what Stella told you before that first broadcast."

"That was private."

"Then she shouldn't have said it when we were all crammed together in that little room," Chloe said.

Nicole went on, "You're not the same person."

"You don't know that," Daniel said. "You can't. Not after what, two weeks?"

Nicole did not give him an inch. "I know you're not the man who was so stoned he doesn't remember the last time he hugged me."

"Wait," Chloe said. "What?"

"I know the words you say and the smile you show me are real. I know you're there for me." And all of a sudden, she was struggling not to cry. "I know you didn't judge me after I wrecked my parents' marriage. I know you looked beneath the surface and saw why I did what I did, even when I couldn't put it into words. I know you *care*."

Daniel had no idea what to say.

Chloe said, "She's right. You know she is."

He tasted the air, managed, "Helping people doesn't mean I'm strong enough to go back."

"It might," Chloe said. "You'll never know unless you try."

Daniel started to reply that he wasn't even sure he wanted to. Try.

Nicole must have read the thought on his features, for she said, "You want it. You'll do it. And you'll be great."

Chloe asked, "What would it be like if you didn't try?" Her features became as crimped as Nicole's. "What if you stayed in your safe little world? What would it be like when it's over, and they don't want you anymore? What if you never had the chance to see if you could make it work for real?"

Daniel thought that made for a fairly good moment to say, "We should get started."

Daniel drove to the LA train station, bought Chloe a ticket to San Luis Obispo, and carried her bag to the platform. As they watched the train pull in, Chloe asked, "What if my folks won't let me come back?"

Daniel crowded in close enough to fill her field of vision. "That's not going to happen and you know it."

Chloe tried to move away, far enough to see beyond the train's open door. "I'm here. Maybe I should just stay."

Daniel closed the distance a second time. "Chloe, look at me. You're doing the right thing."

"I'm so scared."

"I know you are, and it's okay to feel that way. You are going home for all the right reasons. And you have friends who are going to see you through this." He moved closer still. "This is just another step in your dream come true."

"Will you call them and say what's happening?"

"I've already spoken to them twice." Daniel had told her all this before. "They're both coming into San Lu to meet the train. They understand this is temporary. They have agreed to drive you back down and get you settled at Lisa's."

She wrapped her arms around his chest. Strong. "When my prince charming shows up, I hope he's at least a little like you."

Daniel and Nicole made the drive to Bel Air in utter silence. He parked in the same place as the previous day, just down from the driveway, sheltered by the blooming magnolia. The plate-size blossoms filled the car with their scent, a promise of better times. Daniel cut the motor and turned to his niece. "Do you want to do this?"

"It all seemed so clear and simple, you know, before we drove to LA."

"Chloe will be moving in later this week. It will give you the perfect reason to wait—"

"If I don't go now, it will haunt me."

He nodded. He thought so too. "I'll come if you want."

"No." Quiet but certain. "Mom always said two people make an audience."

"I remember that."

"If you're there, she won't . . ."

"React to you honestly. I agree. You have me on speed dial?"

Nicole held up her phone.

Daniel opened his door, walked around, waited for her to stand, then held her tightly. Wishing there was some way to fill her with his own strength, he said, "You are the bravest person I know."

She turned and walked up the drive. Shoulders hunched. Alone.

Twice during the forty-five minutes he sat there, Daniel started to make the call. The pressure on him to get the ball rolling was intense. Stella's look of caring trust branded him now. Sitting on his hands, watching the pickup's digital clock count down her hours of freedom, were very hard indeed.

But when Nicole emerged from the house and walked back to the truck, he knew he had been right to wait.

She opened her door and slid into her seat and just sat there, wearing the same miserable, broken expression as that first day, outside the Miramar church. Daniel fought down a surge of rage over the young woman's pain. He could not insert himself into the situation any further. He could not do what he wanted, which was to march up the drive and give his sister a dose of his fury. He could not tell his niece that everything would be okay.

But he could say, "I know this is a hard moment for you. But Stella's freedom is on the line."

"I . . . what?"

"We need to contact the Ukrainian," Daniel said.

"Now?"

He nodded. "I tried from my room. He said to call back." Actually, what had happened was, Daniel had called and asked if they could talk later. But still. He tapped the radio-clock. "Every minute counts."

"Daniel . . ."

"It's your idea, Nicole. You don't need to speak. But you do need to hear this. Just in case you can come up with the next step." He waited for her to object, then added, "I really need your help. And so does Stella."

She snuffled, wiped her face, said, "Okay."

"Thanks." He instantly hit redial.

The Ukrainian in Alabama answered with, "Are you alone this time?"

"I'm with the lady who came up with what I think is a great idea."

"Good, great, awful, is all the same. I deal with just one person." When Daniel remained silent, he went on, "I should charge you triple, all these people in our very private conversation."

Further argument would get them nowhere, so Daniel launched straight into the concept. When he was done, the phone stayed silent.

Daniel said, "Hello?"

"This is the sound of me thinking." Another couple of minutes, then, "So explain precisely what you want."

Daniel looked at Nicole. Willing her to emerge from everything she'd just been through and *see*.

Nicole sniffed, wiped her face, and said, "There is no precise."

"Explain this."

"What if there are other small towns," Nicole said. "Places like Miramar, with good finances, a strong . . . what do you call it?"

"Pension fund," Daniel said.

"You should tell him."

"It's your idea," he replied. "You're on a roll."

"Somebody please move into a forward gear," the Ukrainian said.

"Other towns doing okay," Nicole said.

"They need to be in solid financial positions," Daniel explained. "Otherwise the state will have watchdogs in place, monitoring their every move."

"These towns discover someone in authority has stolen funds," Nicole said.

"And when the supposedly guilty person is arrested, they claim someone else stole. They were set up. They took the fall," Daniel said.

The Ukrainian cleared his throat. "So I am looking for . . ."

"Towns that have declared their pension funds or city accounts show missing funds," Daniel replied. "You know this because there have been recent arrests."

"And all the while," Nicole said, "the real villain stays hidden."

"It would probably be good to look at other states in the region with wealthy municipalities," Daniel said.

A hint of the former Nicole emerged with the words, "Maybe check on the Miramar mayor again. See if she's hiding something."

Daniel reached over and touched her arm. "See? This is why you needed to be here."

"You like?"

"It's great." He raised his voice a notch. "Tell her it's great."

"Okay, so maybe I don't charge you triple after all," the Ukrainian replied. "But I'm telling you, I checked this woman mayor out."

Daniel said, "You checked her money trail. But what if it's not money?"

Their hacker remained silent.

"What if she's passing on everything she steals?"

"She's got a secret," Nicole said. "Something so bad she'll do anything to keep it hidden."

"Okay, enough. I have the scent." The man barked like a dog. "I will see where it takes me."

The line went dead.

# CHAPTER 48

Daniel drove to a shopping mall down from the John Wayne Airport and entered Brooks Brothers. He selected a navy gabardine, off-the-rack suit and matching shirt and tie, articles he wouldn't have been seen dead in back when such things as the labels on his clothes mattered. As his trousers were being measured for hemming, he asked Nicole if she was hungry. She seemed surprised by the question, as if food shouldn't be part of such a traumatic day. Daniel then asked the saleswoman where she would go for a fast lunch. They were directed two blocks south to a low-rent strip mall housing a taqueria between a Laundromat and a payday loan shop. The pulled chicken and homemade *salsa verde* was some of the best he had ever eaten.

Daniel picked up his new clothes, then returned to the hotel and left his pickup with the valet. He and Nicole took the tram up to CityWalk. Despite the fierce heat and the overlay of humidity from the storm, the crowds were even thicker than the previous day. The high temperature served as a vise, compressing his thoughts into a tight focus.

By the time they arrived at the station, Daniel was as ready as he would ever be.

From the moment he and Nicole entered the foyer, the situation changed. The intern on reception duty had clearly been alerted, because he positioned Daniel, took a photograph, and printed out a plasticized ID. Daniel then pointed to Nicole and said, "Issue her one as well."

"I don't have any instructions—"

"As of today, she's a salaried researcher, news division," Daniel said. "Do it."

Nicole took her place in front of the mini-camera and whispered, "For real?"

"It's time," he said. "A reward for all the good ideas you're going to have."

He watched a smile grow and felt so good about the move his chest hurt. He could still see the puffy remains of Nicole's recent tears, like they had the power to stain her features. But she was recovering now. She was looking *beyond*. Daniel took a long breath and smiled in return.

Whenever Daniel looked back upon what happened next, it seemed as like his view was filtered through drifting smoke. It was as though a massive California blaze had roared through the next valley, leaving cinders and waving heat and hazy vision. That was how close it seemed they were to utter ruin, standing in tinder-dry brush, waiting for their world to ignite.

Daniel was fairly certain the idea came to him and Nicole in the very same instant, as if they were both so exposed and vulnerable, the station's electric tension created a telepathic bond.

They had just entered the makeup room when it began. Doris was still tucking the paper towels around his collar when the door pushed open and Kirsten entered. Ray, her in-house attorney, followed. "We need to talk."

"Go ahead."

Kirsten glanced at Nicole. "Give us a minute, please."

"Nicole, stay where you are."

"Handing her a badge and a title does not . . ." She caught something in Daniel's gaze and changed course. "You sure that's how you want it?"

"Say your piece."

"Grant has actually topped your record for mayhem. He parked a stolen police motorcycle—"

"Allegedly stolen," Ray said.

"—in the middle of the Strip and proceeded to do just that. The hospital claims he had ingested a brand-new pharmaceutical developed for African game preserves."

"Which is so new it's not actually illegal," Ray added. "Yet."

"He may or may not be released this evening.

The question is, do we want him back?" She crossed her arms. "We've managed to contact our number two, and she's promised to return in time for Monday's show. But our board doesn't feel she's ready for the top slot. Which brings us to . . ."

Which was when the idea struck them. Daniel and Nicole. At the very same instant.

Daniel did not actually laugh. It was more like the bark of alarm that Goldie might make at the first rumble of thunder. Nicole drew in a sharp breath, and her eyes went totally round. Right then.

Kirsten demanded, "Just hear me out."

In response, Daniel turned to Nicole, "What you told the Ukrainian. Say you're right."

Nicole was already on her feet. "What if the mayor isn't taking what she's stealing."

"She's just the conduit."

Kirsten said, "I'm the one talking here."

Daniel went on, "It's been staring us in the face."

Nicole said, "If she's not taking the money . . ."

Daniel said, "We completely missed how Stella handed us the key."

Nicole started a tight little two-step, shifting from one foot to the other. "The mayor's not an accountant!"

Daniel leaned over in the chair to pull out his phone. "I can't believe we didn't see this before."

Kirsten started to snap, but Ray stifled her protest. The attorney gripped his boss's shoulder and squeezed. Once.

As Daniel speed-dialed Stella, he said, "And what does that make the mayor?"

"She's another fall guy!"

Daniel put the call on speaker. "It's a shell game."

Ray was with them now. "I'm thinking more like three-card monte."

"Same thing."

Stella came on the line with, "I was just getting ready to call you."

"Stella, there's something vital we need—"

"No, Daniel, *not now.*" A steadying breath, then, "Sol just contacted me. Perry Sanchez, the county DA, wants to meet us tomorrow. On a Saturday. Sanchez told Sol it's time we viewed the evidence they have against me."

Daniel watched Nicole freeze in mid-step. "They're going to offer you a pretrial deal."

Stella's breathing was tight, rasping. "The DA told Sol I was looking at serious jail time."

Ray asked quietly, "When was she arraigned?"

"Four days ago," Daniel replied.

"That's too fast," Ray said. "Something's up."

Stella demanded, "Who's that talking?"

"Ray, the station attorney. Nicole is here with me too. And Kirsten."

"Daniel, what am I going to do?" Her voice came near to breaking.

"Hold that thought. Has anybody recently quit working for the mayor's office?"

"I don't . . . what?"

Daniel repeated the question. "This could be really important. Think."

"Daniel, there's only the four of us . . ."

"What is it?"

She was silent a long moment, then, "Maddy."

He watched Nicole scramble for a pad and pen. "Who?"

"Madeline Ying. She didn't work directly . . . she was the outside auditor responsible for the city accounts."

Daniel asked, "When did she quit?"

"I can't remember exactly . . ."

"Was it around the same time you and I met in the café?"

"I'd have to check, but I think . . . maybe."

"Stay on the line." He looked at Nicole. "Step one, they target a local figure."

Nicole restarted her dance. "They insert their man."

"Woman."

"Whatever. Then they find a fall guy."

"They start robbing the city. And then they stop . . ."

Nicole clapped her hands. "They knew!"

"No. That's not . . ." Daniel lifted the hand not

291

holding the phone. "The mayor is trapped too."

Nicole breathed, "Awesome."

"The mayor was being framed. She was as trapped as Stella. She went to them with the news that I was involved. A forensic accountant. What happens but . . ."

Nicole clapped her hands. "The mayor reports seeing you with Stella because that news might be her way out!"

Stella said, "What are you talking about?"

"Timing," Daniel said. "It was right in front of us from the very beginning. Ling is the key."

Nicole said, "Ying."

"Ling, Ying, Ping, we have got to find her." Daniel turned to Kirsten. "We need to bring in a local detective."

Stella offered, "The police chief seemed nice. Even when he was arresting me. I think he's on my side."

Ray was already shaking his head. "Anything we tell the police, they are duty bound to pass on to the prosecutor's office."

Daniel said, "No cops. Hear that, Stella?"

"What do you want me to do?"

"Call Sol. Tell him what we've just said."

"I don't . . . all right."

"Ask him to call the DA. The meeting is on."

"With a camera crew," Kirsten said.

"Leave that with me," Daniel said.

A hint of something new entered Stella's voice.

Not hope, not exactly. More like a reason to calm down. "When are you coming back?"

"Tonight." Daniel said his farewells, cut the connection, then handed Nicole the phone. "Call the hacker. He's listed under 'Alabama.' "

"He won't like me calling him."

"He will when you tell him why." He looked at Ray. "About that detective . . ."

Ray was already headed for the door. "On it."

# CHAPTER 49

With Ray and Nicole off somewhere, the room went very quiet. Kirsten watched as Doris finished his hair and face, inspected him carefully, then pulled out the paper towels from his collar. She picked up her makeup kit and left as well. Ten seconds later, Radley entered. She handed Daniel a sheaf of pages and said, "Here's your opening and the first two segments. I focused on the impact of Treasury's announcement on West Coast industries, like you said."

Kirsten remained where she was, leaning against the counter, watching in silence as Daniel read through the pages. He ignored her intense inspection as best he could.

"Can I use your pen?" He made a couple of notes on wording, then handed the pages back. "This is excellent, Radley. First-rate work."

She smiled so big, her face turned incandescent. "Wow."

He nodded. Wow indeed. "I haven't checked since this morning. Markets are still holding steady?"

"Like they're frozen in place."

"This is what I want you to do." He looked at Kirsten. "I assume you're here because you want me on-air next week?"

Kirsten worked on her response for quite a while, then simply nodded.

Daniel said to Radley, "You mind doing a little extra work over the weekend?"

Radley looked from one to the other. "Is that a joke?"

"Okay, so what happens if there's an external jolt. The Brazilians renege on their next debt payment. The Chinese start playing hardball with all the dollars they're holding. The tech world is struck by a massive Europe-wide tax bill, and their stocks sink by half."

Radley's eyes had gone completely round behind her dark-rimmed spectacles. "You're describing the nightmares that keep me up nights."

"Forget trying to find what the actual issue may be. That's what all the Wall Street analysts have been doing for months." Daniel kept his voice almost toneless. "We want something different here."

She relaxed a notch, drawn back from the ledge by his calm. "Look at the aftermath."

"Everybody is in agreement," Daniel said. "The risk of a jolt is very high."

"Forget what form it takes," Radley said.

"Tell me what you think comes next."

She now held to the same quiet tone as Daniel. "Boom."

He nodded. "The Treasury and the Fed have both run out of bullets. They've been trying to re-arm since the Great Recession. Another couple of years, and they might be ready. But right now, they're not."

"It's happening, isn't it."

"Again, that's not the issue. The question we need to pose for our viewers is this. Are they ready *in case* the markets tank. Because the risk is real. Nobody can say for certain one way or the other. But the threat of a huge downshift is growing by the day."

"Which is making everybody nervous. Including me."

"But that's not enough. If things go south, with the e-traders now holding such power, the downward spiral will be set in motion before the markets even open. So what do we tell them?"

"Be ready. Now. In advance. Just in case."

"It's a risk, our telling them this," Daniel said, patiently spelling out their new direction. Wanting Kirsten to fully understand. "We could be totally wrong. If so, we'll be labeled Chicken Little of the airwaves."

"But we're not," Radley said. "Wrong."

"The percentages are on our side. The risk is real. So our aim is to set up a series of steps they can take."

"Should take," Radley corrected.

"But first we need to explain why we think it's important they change course. Forget the momentary profit taking. Yes, the markets are moving in the right direction. Today. Think about tomorrow. And here's what you need to do to shield yourselves."

Kirsten spoke for the first time. "You're not just talking to the major West Coast players."

"Of course not. Our message needs to be designed for our entire audience."

Kirsten said to Radley, "Go ahead and get started. Tell Ray I said you have the green light for the overtime."

Radley replied, "Wow again."

"Step one," Daniel said. "This first week, all we do is lay out the risks."

"I don't need extra hours for that. I could write that in my sleep." She realized what she had said, and added, "Oops."

"I didn't hear that," Kirsten said and pointed to the door. "Go get started."

# Chapter 50

"Wait," Daniel said. "Stay here a while longer."

"You and I need to talk," Kirsten said.

"And Radley needs to be a part of this," Daniel replied. "Please."

The room became a stationary tableau. Daniel seated in his chair, Kirsten leaning against the shelf with arms crossed, Radley poised wide-eyed by the exit, her hand on the doorknob.

Kirsten said, "I don't recall you ever using that word before."

"My bad."

Kirsten continued to inspect him. "I take it you think you know what I'm going to say."

Daniel nodded. "Your business anchor is more trouble than he's worth. You agree with the board that your number two isn't ready."

"And she may never be. Go on."

"You want me to come back." He could scarcely believe how calm he sounded. As if he were discussing the weather, and not breaking every rule he had set for himself and lived by.

For four years.

"Right so far," Kirsten said.

"The key days are Thursday and Friday. Summarize the week, and prep for what's ahead."

"Two days is three less than I want."

Daniel did not respond.

She sighed. "You're on a roll. Go on."

He could feel his heart hammering against his rib cage. But his voice remained as steady as it had through the hardest of the on-camera moments. "I'll do one more day each week. You can vary that according to what's happening. But I want to do that one from my home studio."

"Your home."

"In Miramar."

Her features tightened, but she did not speak. Which he took as a very good sign indeed. Daniel went on, "Next week I'll come in Wednesday, Thursday, and Friday because you're in a bind. After that, the third on-air day doesn't start until we complete this current investigation. And I'd like Radley to be assigned as my producer-writer for the duration."

Kirsten inspected the wide-eyed young woman still clutching the doorknob. "Anything else?"

"I've been using a professional photographer based in Miramar. Veronica Hernandez. She's done several cover shots for *Vogue* and is experienced as a videographer. She's able to shoot with natural lighting when necessary. She also can insert herself and remain relatively unnoticed. I'd like to use her for this new project's on-site work and also for the *Market Roundups* I shoot from home."

Kirsten's gaze remained laser tight. "Radley, give us a minute."

"Sure thing." She opened the door, then leaned around the news chief and offered Daniel a silent *Thank you so much.*

When the door clicked shut, Kirsten demanded, "Where is this headed?"

He didn't understand the question and assumed she was referring to the investigation. "If we're right, the mayor is as trapped as Stella, but in a different way. Behind her is a group, totally hidden. They hunt out towns with strong cash reserves. They find somebody who is vulnerable, who becomes their cutout. They plant their over-seer, Ying, the only person who is even partly visible. She handles the cash, while the unseen group handles the cutout. The cutout's job is to find a patsy and set them up."

He waited, expecting her to come back with all the potential holes in his case. How they didn't know anything for certain. How there were a hundred other possible ways this could go, starting with how Kirsten wasn't sure that Stella wasn't actually playing him for a patsy. How—

Instead, she said, "That's not what I'm talking about, and you know it."

Daniel leaned back. "Actually, I don't."

"The last year or so you anchored was a night-mare for everyone on the news staff. We kept you on because you were the best there was at your job. Despite the tantrums and the drugs and the . . ." She sighed. "You left. Ratings sank by almost half. We've clawed back some of what we had. Not all. I don't know how many times I started to track you down. But, in the end, I decided you were too much trouble. Which, given your ratings, was saying a lot."

Daniel had no idea how to respond. Her words burned his chest like a branding iron. Silence came easy.

Kirsten leaned in closer, as if searching for something she could not find. "What happened to you?"

He managed, "I changed."

"If one of my staff came in and told me that, I'd fire them for drinking on the job." Her eyes were glacial bullets. "You're actually sober?"

"Four years."

"But it's more than that, isn't it?"

"Yes."

"What?"

He breathed around the ache. Searched for some way to describe it. And finally settled on, "It feels good to be needed."

She found an element of bitter mirth in his words. "Better than living stoned?"

"I can't . . ." He breathed again. "Being there

for them is the hardest thing I've ever tried. It wouldn't be possible to do this any other way than full on."

In response, Kirsten straightened and pushed herself off the ledge. She walked to the door, opened it, started through, then said, "Okay, I'm sold." She glanced at the wall clock above his head. "You're on in five."

# CHAPTER 51

When Daniel came off-air, there were a multitude of pressing issues that required immediate action. The station was as good a place to work as any. And the surrounding intensity seemed to lift Nicole out of herself and the morning's traumas.

They formed three workstations in Radley's cramped office. The LA group did not have any free space, as they now fed regional shows to eleven stations in three states. As a result, the group had managed to pare down advertising costs, and were thriving in a highly competitive market. All this Radley explained as they worked in her windowless office.

He and Radley decided to call their new project "Risk Aversion." Daniel assumed the advertisers would probably dream up something far catchier. They sketched out two lead-in segments for the following Wednesday and Thursday. Radley taped a long strip of program paper to the wall behind her desk and started sketching out the coming weeks.

Daniel paused now and then to discuss tactics

with Nicole. There was no answer on Maddy Ying's home phone. All her accounting firm would say was that Ms. Ying had taken an extended leave. Nicole then spoke with Stella, giving her the briefest of updates, urging her not to try and find out anything herself. There was too much chance the mayor might learn of their efforts. Daniel yearned to speak with Stella himself, but now wasn't the time. He kept his phone by his right hand, refusing to accept that the Alabama hacker would leave them hanging.

When they exited the studio's parking garage, the freeway overhead was a blocked artery. The entry ramp was jammed all the way down to the street. Daniel turned away from the highway and headed farther into the Valley.

Half a mile later, he pulled into an upscale strip mall and parked by a food van painted every rainbow color and then some. Nicole leaned out of her open window and said, "That smells like heaven."

"You're hungry?"

"Starving."

"Why didn't you say something?"

"Because I didn't want to eat another Johnny Rocket burger. And I hate smoothies."

LA street fare was the great social leveler. Places like this, with years of positive reviews backing their tiny kitchens, were one of the city's few places where every stratum of society mingled. The food truck's long rush-hour line contained people in rumpled business clothes, teens busy texting on their phones, moms with strollers, and day laborers talking in the soft manner of men exhausted by long hours in the heat and dust.

She stood beside him, her thumbs a pair of blurs as she continued researching the accounting firm's list of clients. They had still not discussed what Lisa had told her daughter. Given Nicole's state when she had returned to the pickup, Daniel had to assume his sister had been at her acerbic worst. Which meant Nicole would be staying at his place for the duration. He probably should not have felt so delighted at the prospect. But there it was. Nicole was part of his world now. His life. And he was the better for it.

The van's specialty was called by many names in Cuba. In LA it was known as chicken mojo, a slow-cooker delicacy. Deboned chicken was marinated for two days in freshly squeezed orange and lime juice spiced with garlic, oregano, and cumin. Daniel had come here at least once a week back in the day. They recognized him now, after all this time. The family crowded into the open window to say hello, ask where he'd been, meet Nicole. The elder daughter, she of the flashing eyes and overwide smile, shyly introduced her new husband. Then the father leaned through the open window and cleared away a trio of Cuban ladies who he claimed would occupy one of his six tables until dawn. The women scolded everyone within reach but departed. Daniel sent Nicole over to claim the rickety table, then arrived bearing plates of chicken and dirty rice and an extra portion of Cuban-style beans.

As they were finishing the meal, Sol Feinnes called. "Stella and I were hoping you might have something to report by now."

Daniel rose to his feet and waited while Nicole carried their debris to the waste bin. "So did I. But it hasn't panned out."

The lawyer sighed. "The DA sent over the police case file. Normally that's something I have to do battle to receive. You understand what I'm saying?"

"They want you to see the case they have against Stella."

"It doesn't look good," Sol said. "The evidence is crushing."

"It should be," Daniel said. "The unseen enemy has spent months preparing for this moment. Years."

"Proof," Sol said. "We can't make claims like that without substantiation."

"I'm trying." When Sol did not respond, Daniel went on, "I'll bring a videographer. You can tell them we're building a public record of the pretrial actions. Maybe that will tone down their hardball tactics."

"Don't count on it."

He could feel Nicole's eyes on him and wished he could hide his bitter disappointment. "Stella must be terrified."

"That makes two of us," Sol said. "The meeting's set for nine."

# CHAPTER 52

The traffic eased as they entered the hills beyond Calabasas. Daniel watched the road open up ahead of him and wished for something, anything, that might make the way clear. The conversation with Sol had only heightened the helpless sense of watching a good woman be dragged down by deceit. Beside him, Nicole sighed so loud it bordered on a groan. He asked, "You okay?"

"Tired. Upset."

"You want to tell me about what happened with your mom?"

"Do I have to?"

"No, Nicole. Just know I'm here whenever."

"I probably should. And I will. In maybe a couple of centuries." The descending sun cast a pale glow on her features. "Why won't you speak with Stella?"

"I don't want her to know I've struck out. Not yet. I'm afraid . . ."

"She might hear it in your voice," Nicole said. "How worried you are."

Daniel kneaded the wheel. "Try the hacker again."

But Nicole had no success. Daniel tightened his grip on the wheel, released, did it again, wishing there was some way to apply that pressure to a Ukrainian's neck. Show him just how important it was to move their case forward.

Then he crested the rise outside Thousand Oaks, and they faced that rarest of central California events.

An empty highway.

Seven lanes descended, and another seven climbed. And theirs was the only vehicle.

Nicole said, "Oh. Wow."

Daniel nodded. For a brief instant, he was able to set aside the aching worry. His truck was captured by a sunset glow that turned the freeway into a golden waterfall. He slowed, wanting to draw out their descent. Beyond the ridge, the plains opened like a sunlit sea.

Nicole murmured. "Maybe it's a sign."

He opened all four windows. The air rushed in, as warm and soft as the dusk. Up ahead, the weary flatland city glimmered, like a thousand flickering gemstones, a million mirrors.

There came a gap in the western hills, and the light strengthened to where the world ahead was swallowed by the afternoon luminosity. Daniel felt as if he had suddenly become poised inside a perfect now. For just one moment. An open road ahead, the past lost to the golden radiance.

Then the road met the plains. The city's first

exit came up, and a stream of vehicles crowded in. Daniel rolled the windows back up and sighed.

Nicole said, "A sign of something good. Please."

It was well into the night, and Stella knew she should be asleep. She was tired in a way she hadn't known since the early days after her little girl died. Back then, sleep had become a stranger, so foreign she could not have named it, much less invited it into her dark hours. That was how she felt now.

Stella waited until she was certain Amber was fast asleep, then entered her daughter's bedroom and stretched out next to her. Goldie lifted her head, snuffed softly, then settled. They had picked up the dog from Ricki because Amber had begged. After Amber's confession on the highway north, there was basically nothing Stella would have denied her child.

Stella lay there, fully clothed, on top of the covers, knowing she would not sleep, simply wanting to be close enough to this amazing little girl to feel her comforting heat. Smell the clean fragrance, know the incredible intensity of her own love.

She knew everyone was worried. Sol had not said anything about what was going to take place in the morning, beyond the fact that the DA would probably offer her a deal. Years in a cage, locked away from her child, for a crime someone else had committed. Some deal.

Stella was no longer sure that Sol actually believed she was innocent. But that bothered her less than perhaps it should. Because she was surrounded by other people who knew with absolute certainty that she had been set up. More than that. They put their lives on hold to help her.

Ricki and Travis had come by with food she couldn't eat. They had waited until Amber was lost in the television to say that they were there for her and would do whatever was required—meaning take in the child if or when that became necessary. Both of those strong fine people were rendered almost mute with sorrow. And furious over what was going down.

The instant she heard the car's approach, she was up and moving. Long before it pulled into the drive, she was rushing down the stairs, out the front door, there to see Daniel step wearily from his pickup. She flew along the front walk and gripped him.

Daniel simply stood there, not even lifting his arms. Stella had the impression he needed her embrace so much he could not even respond.

Finally, he whispered, "I'm so sorry."

The words were precisely what she needed to hear. Which was ridiculous, having him admit defeat. Stella gripped his hand with both of hers and pulled him down the walk, through the front door and into the living room, and down onto the sofa. She was not content simply to sit next to him. She curled up like a cat, half beside him and half in his lap. "Hold me."

Strong arms pulled her closer still. "I wish I knew what to do."

"You're doing it."

"I mean about tomorrow. I was so sure we could come up with the evidence we need to make this shift our way."

"What *we* need," Stella whispered. "To go *our* way."

She was not certain he even heard her. "But we've come up with nothing useful. I don't even know what to say, except that I'm sorry. I've let you down in a big way."

The words simply rose inside her and spilled out. She heard herself talk about what was hidden, and do so with neither pain nor regret. He needed to hear, she needed to tell. This dark hour was made for releasing her secret shadows.

She told him about the days that followed the burial of her child. Of her husband shattering the last tiny fragment of hope by leaving them. Of finding a bit of strength each morning in the sound of Amber's voice, in the needs of her one remaining daughter, in the light Amber brought into every room, every hour.

It seemed almost natural that in the midst of her telling, she felt another warm body come and nestle into Daniel's other side. Amber did not speak. Daniel released one arm from holding Stella so he could draw the child closer. The three of them sat there, and Stella talked. She described what it meant to heal through her daughter. She would never have thought it might be possible to love again. The word slipped out with all the others, a simple admission of what she knew was real. Love a man who was there for her in yet another impossible hour. A man she could trust not to leave her nor turn away. A man who gave and gave and gave, and then apologized because he could not give her enough to make the dark hour vanish. As if that was his job, to erase the hardship.

The words simply ended. There was so much else she wanted to say. But just then the words were gone.

She pried herself away from him, just far enough to see his face gleaming in the moonlight. She kissed the damp skin below his left eye. His neck. It was a gentle act, all she would reveal with her daughter snuggled up to Daniel's other side. A brush of lips, and it was over.

For the moment.

She settled back, warmed by the thought of what she knew was coming. The certainty was strong enough to push away the fears, at least for a time.

Finally, Daniel whispered, "Amber is fast asleep."

She took that as her signal that it was time to release her hold and rise to her feet. She watched Daniel slip his arms around the child and lift her to his shoulder. Amber moaned softly, then went quiet. Stella directed him up the stairs and into her daughter's bedroom. Goldie's eyes tracked them from her place on the bed, but the dog did not move. Stella stood in the doorway and watched him settle the child, tuck in her covers, then stroke the hair from her face. His touch as tender as, well, as a father's.

Stella kissed him then in the bedroom's doorway. Again by the front door. A final time by his truck. Then she returned to Amber's room and stretched out beside her daughter.

She slept and did not dream.

# CHAPTER 53

Daniel carried the warm, heart-level glow back home. Stella remained so close she might as well have been in the pickup with him.

His mind drifted back to concepts that he seldom thought of anymore. During his first year in Miramar, seven elements had basically framed his existence. But nowadays the only time he laid them out in concrete terms was when he was helping a newcomer struggle with those first awful days of recovery.

In dealing with the opioid epidemic, the medical world broke down addiction into seven stages.

The first was called Gateway. The body naturally produced its own natural version of opioids, called endorphins. They served as the reward circuits of a healthy brain, making a person feel good after positive actions. Many drugs, including alcohol for some people, circumvented this process. They created a tidal wave of reward-centered pleasure. When the high wore off, its impact on the brain lingered. For some people, this developed into a biological lure with uncontrollable force that drew them back to their drug of choice, over and over and over.

The second stage was Tolerance. The user chased that first experience. But a thousand more doses, double and triple the initial amount, never brought back that first high. The reason was simple. The brain's production of endorphins was automatically controlled. When external sources were brought into the process, the brain's own production system shut down.

Gradually, the brain's circuitry became rewired. These chemical changes only increased the desire to repeat the experience. The urge was magnified until it blinded the user, until their actions and the impact they had on other people went completely unnoticed. Nothing else in life offered any real satisfaction. The more they took, the more the brain adapted to the drug, and it demanded still more.

Daniel pulled into his drive and sat there. Images of what those words had meant to his own life flooded in. All of them ended with the sound of the crash he had not actually heard and the sight of that body bag being zipped shut.

The third stage was Withdrawal. Only at this point did the user realize how ferocious the trap held them. Crippling pain, vomiting, insomnia, spasms—on and on the struggle grew. Few people actually died from withdrawal. But at some point during the withdrawal process, most users wished they could.

The fourth stage, Relapse One, had been a repetitive action for Daniel. He had tried to stop four times that he could actually recall. But his brain had always screamed for more. After few days staying clean, a week at most, he dove back in.

The medical profession called the fifth stage Transition. But Daniel knew it by different words. For him, it was called Rock Bottom.

Stage six was the one he had managed to avoid for the past four years. But anybody who had become truly hooked knew with utter certainty that Relapse Two was always there. Waiting for the weak and terrible moment to strike. And draw him back down again.

The seventh stage was the one he had been working on for the past four years and counting. Recovery was a singular process. It had the beauty and the pain present in any significant work of art. Each day of sobriety created another brushstroke on the canvas of life.

But as Daniel sat in his drive and stared at Nicole's bedroom window, feeling Stella's arms, remembering the joy of her kiss, he wondered if he might actually be entering an eighth stage.

He could not even name it yet. But it was there, as clear and powerful as the shadows he had run from for so very long.

# CHAPTER 54

Daniel woke just before six. He had slept less than four hours and felt grainy with banked-up fatigue. But he was too pressured by the coming day to worry about being tired.

He checked Nicole's door as he passed but could not hear any sound from inside. As he prepared the day's first coffee, Daniel wished there was some way he could trade places with Stella. The lady deserved happiness. She deserved a life filled with good things. She deserved the chance to watch her daughter grow into a fine young woman. Daniel washed out his cup, started another coffee, then called Veronica.

She sounded as if she had been up for hours. "Any news?"

"Nothing good."

She sighed. "So we're going with plan A."

He nodded to the window. "Don't have much choice. Did Sol call you?"

"Only to say he had insisted I be granted permission to film." She paused, then added, "I had the distinct impression that he's going in with an empty gun."

"Where are you now?"

"Headed into church. But I could skip this morning, if you think . . ."

"No, there's no need. Do me a favor: Say a prayer for me. And Stella."

"Brother, I haven't stopped."

Nicole entered the kitchen as he cut the connection. She must have read the absence of hope in his expression, because all she said was, "Nothing?"

"Sorry."

"You don't have a thing to apologize for."

"I just wish . . ."

Daniel stopped because his phone rang.

Afterward, whenever he thought back to that moment, the first thing he recalled was how much it meant to have Nicole standing there beside him. Dressed in cutoffs and an oversized T-shirt, hair a tousled mess, face still creased from sleep. See her eyes go completely round when he showed her the readout and said, "It's him."

"Every time we talk, I am thinking of reasons to charge you more."

Daniel had put the call on speaker and placed the phone on the counter. He handed Nicole the coffee he'd just made. She needed it far more than he did. Daniel's heart was already approaching redline. "You have something?"

"I have more than that." The heavily accented voice sounded grainy. Exhausted. "I have the smoking gun."

"Tell me."

The Ukrainian proceeded to do just that.

# CHAPTER 55

Stella was late getting started the next morning. She could have pushed Amber to move faster. But the day was too full of more important issues, and she didn't want to say good-bye to her little girl after an argument. She let Amber move at her slow pace and pretended not to watch the clock count down the minutes. Her stress had nothing to do with Amber, and everything to do with the trip she was about to take. And the meeting that awaited her.

Despite everything, the nighttime visit with Daniel still lingered, such that twice Amber asked why she was smiling. The second time, Stella replied, "You were right about Daniel."

Amber dropped her spoon into the bowl, splashing milk all over the counter. "Really?"

"He's a very good man. And I . . ."

"Tell me, Mommy."

"I'm scared to say it." She took a long breath. "It feels good to need him. Trust him. And come to love him. Maybe. Someday."

Amber smiled around a wreath of milk. "Someday like today, maybe?"

"Your face is a mess."

"Is that a yes?"

She used the dish towel to clean her daughter's face. "You even have cereal in your hair."

Amber sang around her mouth being rubbed a little too hard. "My mommy's in love."

Stella had just pulled in front of Amber's school when Daniel phoned. "We might have something."

Amber had already missed school that week. Stella had twice spoken with the principal's office, once before they left and another time from LA. There were a dozen reasons why she should have ordered her daughter to hurry inside. Especially as the school bell chose that moment to ring, warning them both that Amber was now officially late for her Saturday dance class.

Instead, Stella turned to where Amber stood frozen, half in and half out of the car, and said, "Get in."

Daniel said, "Excuse me?"

"Wait just a second, Daniel." She motioned for Amber to refasten her seat belt, then drove away from the narrow kiss-and-ride slot before one of the carpool cops could swoop down. Stella pulled into a space half a block farther down the road and said, "Define might."

"Sol doesn't think we have enough. But he agrees we've taken a step in the right direction."

Stella reached across the divide. Amber responded by gripping her hand with both of hers, so tight her fingers cramped. Stella did not mind in the least. "Tell me everything."

# Chapter 56

Stella had always liked San Luis Obispo. The city was a way station for the entire central coast, from Santa Barbara to the southern reaches of Silicon Valley. Early settlers had traveled here for markets, dry goods, doctors, a night out, a good meal. The historic district was one of the most beautiful in California. Which made Perry Sanchez's office even more of a shock.

Palm Street bordered two parks and a dozen lovely Spanish-mission structures. By contrast, the prosecutor's building rose like a glass-and-steel wart. The seventies-era structure had three stories, a flat roof, and oversized city shields adorning both front doors. Perhaps a sand-bagged gun turret and a barbed-wire perimeter fence would have made it less inviting, but Stella wasn't sure. As she entered, she hoped desperately that whatever awaited her inside would not permanently stain her affection for the city.

They passed through security and were directed to the DA's office on the second floor. Stella walked the corridor a few paces behind Sol and Daniel. Nicole was more or less alongside her, but the young woman was focused intently upon her phone. She typed furiously, using just her thumbs. Daniel called back, "Anything?"

Nicole did not look up. "When I know, you know."

Sol directed Daniel and Stella onto a hard, wooden bench. "I'll tell them we're here." He swiftly returned to announce, "They're running late."

"Good," Daniel replied. "That gives me time to convince you I'm right."

Sol motioned for Stella to slip over and seated himself between them. Nicole leaned against the wall to Stella's left, still working her phone. Sol said, "Let's review things from the DA's perspective."

"We've been through that," Daniel replied.

"Just humor me." He ticked points off the fingers of one hand. "The DA himself is handling this case. I've been up against him four times and still carry the scars. Perry Sanchez is known among the local defense community as the Piranha, and for good reason. Perry has lost only a couple of cases since coming into office."

"Which is why he won't want to take this forward."

"Hear me out." Stella thought Sol looked both worried and thoughtful, as if he was certain of his stance and yet open to being convinced otherwise. "We're here because Perry is absolutely certain the evidence against my client is overwhelming. He wants to pull this dump truck up to the conference table and unload so much weight we'll have no choice but accept their terms. He and his team have spent the past week preparing their case."

"Which is bogus."

Sol lifted his hand. "I'm not suggesting you're wrong. I'm simply saying it's not time yet to go on the offensive."

"The longer we wait, the more entrenched they become."

Sol's hand remained poised in midair. "If we reveal what we know and they go away unconvinced, they will simply prepare a counter-argument. Which means all we've done is given them a chance to prepare more ammunition."

Daniel did not respond.

"Say we hold off. We walk in, just Stella and I. They've allowed me to video the conference because I insisted. For the moment, you remain officially out of the picture. The prosecutors will spend however much time they need laying out their case. They will conclude by offering terms. Which will include jail time."

"No," Daniel said. "No."

"Whatever they offer, we respond that we need time to decide. Perry will insist upon our replying now. That's why we're here. On a Saturday. Because the DA intends this to be a 'take it or leave it' offer, conditional upon Stella making up her mind before she leaves the table. He then shows up Monday bright and early and informs the judge the bow has been tied around his case."

"That's not happening."

"This is one of Perry's favorite tactics. Stressing the situation. But the weekend meeting actually works in our favor. Whatever he says, however much he pressures us, we insist on forty-eight hours to decide. He may withdraw his offer and say we're going to trial."

"Everything you've laid out just means more stress for Stella," Daniel said.

"That's where you're wrong." Sol leaned in closer. "When we leave here, *we know their case.* We can prepare a response to every issue they raise. A trial date will be set, probably a month or so from now. You continue your hunt for evidence to support my client's position. Once we have all the bases covered, we ask for another meeting. Perry will assume it's to counter. He'll come in prepared to blow our case out of the water. Instead, we do it to him."

Daniel spoke to the opposite wall. "And all the while, we've forced Stella to live another month in fear for her freedom."

Sol looked at her. "Do you have anything you'd like to say?"

"Just that I love how you two are talking," she replied. "As if we're facing this together."

"There's no 'as if,'" Daniel replied, still focused on a point where the cracked linoleum floor met the peeling paint. "We're with you. And it's staying this way."

She was trying to find some way to tell them how much that meant when Nicole said, "I think I've found something."

# CHAPTER 57

Nicole was still walking them through the information on her phone when the elevator pinged open and Veronica appeared. "There's a man downstairs asking for Daniel."

Stella watched his gray eyes turn electric, like lightning flashed down deep. "The station brought in a detective. Carl Dellacourt."

"That's the guy. He says he's not sure you will want him to join us."

Sol asked, "Meaning what, exactly?"

"All he told me was, if the DA sees him, they might guess he's come up with the goods."

"Wow," Nicole said.

"Wow works for me," Daniel said.

Veronica smiled a greeting as she settled in beside Stella. "How are you holding up, honey?"

"Better and better," Stella said. She rose to her feet and told Daniel, "You stay and plan. I'll go bring him up."

Carl Dellacourt was a Cuban fireplug with wide, stubby legs. When Stella approached him, he said, "As I live and breathe. The lady herself."

Stella liked him immediately. "You must be the man who's bringing the life preserver."

"That's my job." Dellacourt followed her back to the elevator. "Where's Riffkin?"

"Upstairs with my attorney, trying to keep me out of jail."

"Works for me." When the elevator doors slid shut, he asked, "You managing to keep things together?"

"There are bad times," she replied. "But less than I might have expected. At least I'm not alone."

Dellacourt grunted. "Good thing to have around, friends."

"You were a police officer?"

"Gold shield." He must have detected confusion, because he added, "Senior detective. Burglary, then white collar. I always hated shoddy investigations. Almost as much as I hated prosecutors looking for the easy way out. This is both."

"I didn't do what they said. Steal the town's money."

"I know that." He offered her reflection an angry smile. "And before we're done here, they will too."

When they stepped out, both Sol and Daniel were there to greet them. The three men entered a swift huddle right there in front of the elevator. Stella returned to the bench. She had little interest in hearing what was being said. It was enough to watch the electric light spread from Daniel's gaze to his face. He motioned for Nicole to join them. Thirty seconds later, the young woman started a tight little two-step.

When they finally started down the corridor toward them, Sol told Daniel, "Looks to me like you were right all along."

"Correction. We've been handed what we needed to turn things around."

"Maybe," Sol corrected.

"Maybe works for me." Daniel turned to where Veronica relaxed on the bench. "Where is your gear?"

"In the car, waiting for you to give me the word."

As if in response, the prosecutor's door opened, and a woman searched the hall for Sol. "They're ready for you."

"Stay here. This could take a while." As Sol passed Veronica, he said, "Go prep. If we get the green light, we'll need to move fast so they don't have time to change their tiny minds."

# CHAPTER 58

During the next hour, Sol returned twice to the corridor. Supposedly, it was to convey the DA's dire threats. In truth, it was to discuss strategy. Things were shifting rapidly now. The prosecutor was understandably irate that Sol refused their offer of a deal. Perry Sanchez had started this day thinking his case was so powerful nobody in their right mind would take it to court. His entire strategy was centered upon crushing any hope Stella might have of getting off. Sol's polite rejection of any pretrial deal left the DA threatening to go for the maximum sentence. Ten to twenty years with no chance of parole.

The second time Sol reseated himself in the corridor, he said, "We may need to come back another day."

Daniel stopped scrolling through Nicole's phone to say, "Works for me."

"Stella?"

"I am absolutely happy to leave this in your hands."

Sol showed them all a rare smile. "And here I thought this day would be a trial."

"Bad choice of metaphor," Daniel said.

Then the court stenographer opened the door to announce, "Mr. Sanchez asks how much longer you will be."

Sol rose to his feet. "Looks like it's my turn to offer an ultimatum."

Fifteen minutes later, Stella entered the conference room alone.

Perry Sanchez was a ferret-faced man, all nose and forehead and attitude. The assistant prosecutor was Daphne Lane. She and the court recorder were both big, solid women. Stella wondered if they needed the extra bulk to shield them from their boss's ire. Which was now directed at Sol. "How much more of our valuable time do you intend to waste here?"

Sol gave no response. Water off a duck's back, Stella thought, as he escorted her around the table and seated her directly opposite the prosecutor. Her heart hammered, being this close to the man who wanted to send her to prison. Strip away her freedom. Tear her from her daughter's life.

Sol walked back around the table. He waited as Veronica wired up Stella's collar mike, then seated himself two chairs down from the prosecutor.

Veronica returned to the small table set in the room's far corner and said, "Let me hear your voice, please."

"Test, test."

"Fine." She checked the laptop's screen. "Sol, shift your chair to your right a few inches; you're partly out of view."

"Oh, for Pete's sake," the prosecutor said.

Veronica gave Sol a thumbs-up.

Sol began, "As I explained earlier, this will not be a full deposition. But do feel free to ask any questions you feel are pertinent to our moving forward."

"Point of order," the DA snapped. "Where do you get off, assuming you know my intentions?"

Sol waited through a full thirty seconds of silence. Finally, Sanchez told the court reporter. "Swear her in."

Then Sol began with, "Please state your name for the record."

"How long have you served on the city's payroll?"

"Nine years. First as part-time bookkeeper. When the auditor retired, I took over his position."

"You earned your CPA degree during that period, correct?"

"Yes. At night school here in San Luis Obispo."

"When did you first notice the missing funds?"

"Three months and two weeks ago. The third of March. But the evidence I discovered went back much further."

The DA snorted softly but did not speak.

Sol asked, "When did the thefts actually begin?"

Stella focused on Sol and did her best to ignore the glowering DA, his number two, the court stenographer, Veronica, the cameras, the omnidirectional mike stationed before the prosecution team. "At that point, I wasn't sure there had been any theft at all."

Gently, Sol guided her through that horrible first day. Night, really, as she had labored for eighteen hours before she finally accepted that the nightmare was real. A steady depletion of funds had been taking place. From the city maintenance and fire and rescue departments, and the largest theft of all from the employee pension fund. Supposed bad investments and sky-high fees that, when glimpsed in fragments, appeared to simply be a series of wrong choices. Added to this were charges for new equipment that did not exist and services that had never been rendered. Taken together, it all added up to only one conclusion.

Sol surprised her then. He leaned back, tapped his pen on the legal pad, then said, "Your witness, counselor."

Perry Sanchez was clearly taken aback. "That's it?"

"For the moment."

He glared at Sol. "So we're clear, *counselor,* she is not a *witness.* She is the *accused.*"

Sol studied the notes on his legal pad and did not respond.

Sanchez glared across the table. "Back to his question. How long ago did you begin stealing from the city's funds?"

Stella remained silent.

Sol offered a tight smile. "Perhaps you'd care to rephrase that question?"

Sanchez snapped, "Don't presume to teach me *my* business in *my* office."

Stella continued to watch Sol. Only when he rolled one finger did she reply, "I never stole a dime."

"The evidence says differently. It shows clearly that you began siphoning off funds the same month you took over as auditor."

Stella nodded slowly. This realization had kept her up far too many nights.

Sol held to his calm monotone. "If you'll grant me just a few more minutes, I think you may be glad you didn't continue in this vein."

Sanchez did a lizard thing, slowly wheeling around, ready to pounce. But Daphne Lane reached over and touched his arm. A subtle gesture. Stella saw it, though. And so did Sol.

Sanchez glanced at the assistant DA. Daphne Lane shared his hard gaze but held to a look of caution. Or so Stella thought.

Sol went on, "My aim is to lay out our case. Three more witnesses. Afterward, you are welcome to bring Ms. Dalton back in and continue. If you want."

Sanchez chewed on that for a long moment, then said, "Get on with it."

# CHAPTER 59

But as Stella started to rise, Sol said, "Just one more question." When she seated herself, Sol continued, "Ms. Dalton, how would you respond to the mayor's claim that she discovered the theft?"

The shock punched her back in her chair. "Catherine said that?"

The DA snapped, "You're wasting our time."

Sol said, "Ms. Dalton?"

"She couldn't have. It's not possible."

"What makes you say that?"

Only then did Stella realize Sol had planned this. He had intended for the DA to see her astonishment. Sanchez's dark gaze continued to smolder. But there was something else now—a curiosity, perhaps even caution. She replied, "Catherine is hopeless with numbers."

"Hearsay," Sanchez said.

"What do you mean hopeless?"

"She can't add. Numbers terrify her. She has trouble working a calculator."

Sol tapped his pen again. "Say we were in court, and I wrote a series of numbers on a whiteboard, then asked her to add them up."

"She couldn't do it. Catherine was a florist before she became mayor. She used to say the nicest thing about her new job was, she didn't have to worry about billing customers. She was always getting the numbers wrong."

Sanchez gestured to his second chair. Daphne Lane began writing furiously. Sanchez said, "So the mayor was informed of the theft by someone else. So what?"

"Don't you find it of interest, counselor, that I'm revealing gaps in your case now? Before trial? While you still have time to correct?"

"I stopped worrying about defense attorneys and their shoddy tactics a long time ago."

Sol smiled at her. "Thank you, Ms. Dalton. That will be all."

Stella asked to stay. When Sanchez looked ready to argue, Sol pointed out that it was customary in court for witnesses to be granted leave to remain. The DA muttered something that Stella did not bother to hear. Sol then directed her to a chair in the corner beside Veronica. Veronica greeted her with a tight squeeze of her hand.

It began to rain as Nicole was brought into the conference room. Stella had not even noticed the clouds gathering. The rain fell in rushing sheets, beating the windows. Stella felt as though she was seeing Nicole for the very first time. The fifteen-year-old was certainly no child. Stella had the impression that at some level beyond logic or reason, Nicole had become an adult out of necessity. She had weathered her mother's strange views on life and things of value by growing up far too early.

Nicole's face was pale and her features tight. But she did not hesitate as she crossed the room and settled into the chair Sol held. Perry Sanchez studied her with a squinted gaze. "Is this a joke?"

Sol resumed his seat, then said to the court reporter, "Please swear her in."

As Stella watched the young woman go through the formalities, she had the sudden impression that this was how Nicole had confronted her mother. Frightened and weary both. Yet resolute. Possessing an iron-hard determination and an intelligence to match. Stella wished she could rush over, embrace the woman-child, and tell Nicole just how amazing she was.

Sunlight broke through the clouds as Sol asked Nicole to state her name for the record. Droplets streaking the windows were transformed into liquid gemstones. The refracted colors painted the room in shades of hope and promise. Stella found herself thinking of their day in Tranquility Falls, watching sunlight through the liquid curtain, hearing her daughter squeal with joy, feeling the hot-cold flavor of Daniel's lips.

Sol asked, "How old are you, Nicole?"

"Fifteen. Sixteen in September."

"You attend school, yes?"

"Marymont High in Los Angeles until . . . recently. Now I'm studying in Miramar."

"You have also recently taken on a second role, have you not?"

Sanchez broke in with, "What is this?"

"Five minutes," Sol replied. "Six at most."

"Are you actually suggesting she brings something of value to the meeting?" Sanchez gave the women to either side a look of theatrical disbelief. "Can you believe this guy?"

"Answer the question, Nicole."

"I've been hired as a researcher," she replied.

Sanchez threw up his arms. "You're telling me a high school dropout has found what professional investigators couldn't?"

"No, counselor. I'm saying they didn't look." Sol kept his gaze on the young woman seated opposite. "You were working in conjunction with a second researcher, correct?"

"Yes."

"And he cannot be here because . . ."

"He's still in Alabama."

"Doing what, exactly?"

"Finding more cities."

"This would be other towns where a similar pattern of theft has taken place, correct?"

"Right. I mean, yes."

Sanchez said, "Put a ring in her nose and lead her on a leash, why don't you."

Sol maintained his steady calm. "What is this gentleman's profession?"

"He's a hacker. His name is Sergei. At least, that's what he says. I don't know what his last name is."

"This is low, even for a defense attorney." Sanchez threw his pen on the table. "Do I actually need to remind you that anything these two have found is inadmissible in a court of law?"

"But we're not in court," Sol replied. "Are we?"

Sanchez's response was cut off by his assistant prosecutor speaking for the first time. "We're missing something."

The DA turned to the woman. "Excuse me?"

Daphne Lane used her chin to point at each person in turn. Nicole, Stella, Veronica, and finally Sol. "Look at them."

Sanchez glanced over. "So?"

"Do they look worried to you? I mean, even the least little bit?"

Sanchez took a longer look. He opened his mouth, but no sound emerged.

Daphne leaned forward and asked Sol, "Where are you going with this?"

In reply, Sol asked Nicole, "How many cities have you identified?"

"Sergei found two. I just uncovered another. I think."

"You think."

"Right. Sergei's been looking for the same pattern of stolen funds with a . . . I forgot the word."

"Plaintiff."

"Right. Somebody the court found guilty of stealing, and they've always claimed they were set up. Sergei found one town in Southern California and another in Nevada."

"These were cities where the municipal funds were stolen, then an innocent person was assigned the blame?"

"That's what we think."

"And your city?"

"Montecito."

"The town in the next county south of here."

Nicole nodded. "I read an article online. When they started rebuilding after the mudslides, they discovered the city's accounts were missing almost forty million dollars. So I accessed the city records. They show the same kind of steady—what's the word?—attrition."

Sol glanced at the DA. "This information comes from the public record and thus is available to any police investigation, correct?"

"Yes. But the city's records aren't complete. A lot of them were destroyed."

"Or so they claim," Sol added.

Nicole did not respond.

Sanchez spoke his objection to Daphne. "No

judge is going to allow something she's found to be entered into these proceedings. Everything is tainted by the hacker's involvement."

When Daphne Lane did not reply, Sol rose to his feet and said, "With your permission, I'll call my next witness."

# CHAPTER 60

The conference room was utterly silent as the private investigator entered. To Stella it felt as though even the chamber held its breath, not just the people. The room and the law and the pending verdict—all were rendered silent as Veronica fastened the mike to Carl Dellacourt's collar. The quiet was so intense, Stella thought she could hear a faint buzzing, a frequency normally beyond human range. The sound of energy rising to a frantic pitch. A note of building pressure, strong enough to change the course of someone's future.

When Veronica resumed her seat and did the sound check, the court reporter swore Dellacourt in, then Sol asked him to give his name for the record.

The prosecutor said, "I remember you."

The detective responded with a cop's flat-eyed glance. "Yeah? Well, that makes two of us."

"When did you cross over to the dark side, detective?"

"When the cops on San Lu's payroll stopped doing their job."

"I'll be sure to pass that on to the detective in charge of this case."

"You do that. Give him a message from me. Tell him I said, Blind leading the blind."

Sanchez shoved back his chair. "Okay, that's it. I'm out of here." When his assistant did not move, he said, "You coming?"

"Boss, I think you should stay."

"For what, more of this charade?"

"I've been up against Sol Feinnes twice. My only two losses in seven years." Daphne gave that a beat, then added, "Feinnes doesn't make rookie mistakes."

"So he's making up for lost time."

She turned to where Sol stood by the front window. "How much longer?"

"Three minutes with this gentleman, one further witness, and we're done for the day."

Daphne turned back to her boss. "What's the worst that can happen? He hands you more ammo."

"I don't need any. Taking this to trial is asking for the nuclear option."

The woman did not move. "I'm staying, and I think you should too."


Carl Dellacourt was ugly in the manner of a man who treated his appearance as an unimportant detail. He occupied his chair like a lump of aging muscle. His hairline had receded to behind the crease in the top of his skull. His voice grated deep and rough. The knot of his mud-brown tie was an afterthought. In response to Sol's first question, he replied, "The fellow in the hall, he gave me two jobs. I completed the second one about an hour ago."

"Let's deal with them one at a time. What came first?"

Dellacourt opened the folder on the table in front of him and handed Sol a sheaf of photographs. "Uncovering the mayor's dirty little secret."

Sanchez sat up straight. "Wait. What?"

Sol passed out three eight-by-ten booking photographs. "Who is this gentleman?"

"His name is Christopher 'Top' Rankin. Doing ten to twenty at Rikers Island for a third count of armed robbery."

"And he is important to this investigation because . . ."

Dellacourt responded with the next trio of papers. "Before Mayor Catherine was a Lundberg, she was married to one Sam Rankin. Here's her marriage certificate."

"How can we be certain it's her?"

"This is her birth certificate, naming her as Catherine Yeats." Another trio of pages. "Same as the marriage docs. Both the first and second go."

Sanchez responded to the news with a soft whuff.

Sol asked, "How is it we were unaware of this until now?"

"Lundberg had the first marriage annulled when Rankin senior went up for assault and battery." Dellacourt offered the DA a cop's grin. "Like father, like son."

"How can a convict in the New York penal system have an impact on this investigation?"

"A buddy in the parole system had a word with Rankin. He was threatened. He begged his mother to do as she was told or he gets the knife."

"When was this?"

"The first warning came about three years ago. Long time to live in terror for his life."

"Did your friend make any promises in response for this information?"

"He was moved into solitary. First time he's slept through the night in three years, according to the convict."

Sol tapped his pad three times, a soft drumbeat to emphasize the moment, then said, "Your witness."

When Sanchez continued to study the detective in silence, his assistant said, "You stated there were two duties."

"With your permission," Sol replied, "I'll let my final witness address that issue."

Sanchez's voice reminded Stella of a long-dead fire. The final ashes smoldering, but the flames gone now. He said once again, "Get it over with."

# Chapter 61

The detective crossed the room and seated himself by the side wall. There were four of them now, Veronica behind her little wheelie-table, then Nicole and Stella, and now Carl Dellacourt. The DA kicked up a fuss about this unwelcome audience, but Stella had the impression it was mostly for show. Perry's assistant did not speak, and Sol continued to look through his notes as the court reporter opened the door and invited in the final witness. Stella thought Daphne Lane's concerns had finally infected her boss. At some deep level, Sanchez already knew the case had shifted. The events unfolding in this room were out of his control.

The court reporter stepped back, allowing Daniel to enter. The room was so quiet, Stella could hear the court reporter's gasp. Perry heard it too.

Daphne Lane said, "Oh my."

Sanchez said, "What?"

But Daphne did not respond. Perry squinted across the table as Veronica wired up Daniel and asked him to speak for the sound level. After the court reporter swore Daniel in, Sol rose to his feet and he said, "Please state your name for the record."

"Daniel Riffkin."

The assistant DA huffed softly, as if hearing Daniel's name confirmed something she was only now understanding. Perry said, "Hold it right there."

Sol asked, "Counselor?"

"I thought . . ." Perry's aide tapped his arm, then pointed with her chin at the camera aimed their way. He glared at the lens, then decided, "Never mind."

Sol walked Daniel through his previous career as MSNBC West Coast business anchor, his semi-retirement, his life in Miramar. Then, "What are you currently working on?"

"I've been contracted to put together a special report for *NBC News*."

The words punched Sanchez back in his chair. He opened his mouth, then looked at the camera again and did not speak.

When Sol was certain the DA was going to stay silent, he went on, "Your report has to do with the theft of funds from the Miramar city government, does it not?"

"Yes and no. The investigation began with Miramar's missing funds, but it has grown steadily. We are now looking at a multi-state fraud." Daniel glanced at the two attorneys seated across from him. "Which means either you alert the federal authorities or I will do it for you."

"Hold your responses to my specific questions, Mr. Riffkin." Sol took a step closer to the DA. "You're suggesting this is part of a pattern?"

"Not suggesting." Daniel kept his gaze on the DA. "I'm stating for the record."

Sol swiftly walked Daniel through his initial review of the Miramar accounts, the pattern of supposed losses, the sophistication of the entire process. Then, "Your witness, counselor."

Sanchez opened his mouth, shut it, then turned to his assistant and said, "Go ahead."

Daphne shot him a tight look of her own, hating how Sanchez had set her up for the fall, knowing she had no choice but to ask, "Are you aware, Mr. Riffkin, that you broke the law when you inspected the city's confidential accounts, and that nothing that you supposedly discovered will be permitted into court records?"

Sol remained on his feet, leaning against the wall behind the conference table, making notes on his legal pad. "But we are beyond all that, aren't we, counselor? We all know this will never see the inside of a courtroom."

The assistant DA responded with, "The city's accounts must have been extremely complex."

Daniel did not reply.

"You've described a theft of funds that stretch back over three years. You claim that you found a pattern of stolen money from three accounts. That suggests you were able to find patterns in hundreds and hundreds of pages."

Daniel remained silent.

"Do you not have anything to say, Mr. Riffkin?"

"I'm sorry. Was there a question?"

"How does a former news anchor consider himself capable of inspecting multiple complex accounts and discovering a pattern that had been missed by the city's outside auditors?"

"There are two parts to my answer."

"I'm listening, Mr. Riffkin. We all are."

Stella saw the detective seated beside her smile at the DA. The two prosecutors saw it as well. Carl's teeth were perfectly squared off, like he had spent years grinding them down to little white bricks.

Daniel replied, "Before I became a news anchor, I specialized in forensic accounting."

The two prosecutors remained utterly motionless. But Stella could see in their gazes that this news struck deep.

Daniel went on, "You'll find records of my testimony in multiple state and federal cases."

When the assistant DA did not speak, Sol asked for her, "And the second part to your answer?"

Carl Dellacourt was up and moving before Daniel replied, "We knew there had to be a third element. A hidden enemy using Catherine as their second shield. Before being elected mayor,

Catherine Lundberg was a florist. She had no experience with accounts. Which meant we had to find who was hiding behind her."

The DA and his number two remained silent as Daniel accepted the documents. Clearly the prosecutors had relinquished control of the situation. Sol asked, "What did you discover?"

"The outside auditor for Miramar's accounts was a woman named Madeline Ying. Or so she called herself in Miramar." At a gesture from Sol, Daniel handed the prosecutors a photograph. Then, "Our investigation has revealed that no such person has passed the state's CPA exams or is registered as an auditor."

This time, it was the DA himself who huffed in response to the verbal blow.

Sol asked, "Did you question Ms. Ying?"

"No. She vanished the same week Stella was arrested."

"Is there anything else you discovered that might interest the state?"

"Yes." Daniel passed out his final document. "This is a signed affidavit from the employee arrested in the Nevada case, identifying this same woman as the city accountant. Only there she was known as Carolyn Yang."

The room's only sound came from Sol softly tapping his pen on the legal pad. A quiet drumbeat of triumph.

Daniel chose that moment to turn and look

Stella's way. All the emotions she felt were there in his gaze, a shared tension and joy and excitement and realization that things were indeed changing. Not just the court and her arrest and her coming release. They were sharing something far greater. As far as Stella was concerned, Daniel Riffkin was the way all heroes should look.

"Let the record show," Sol declared. "We formally request that all charges against Stella Dalton be dismissed."

# CHAPTER 62

The resulting legal brawl lasted another three and a half weeks. The only thing that made the time bearable was that so much else filled those days.

Grant, the delinquent business anchor, was convicted on several counts, serious enough that even the somewhat lax Las Vegas criminal system required him to do time. When the number-two anchor learned she was not automatically being given the top slot, she walked out. Leaving Daniel with little option, at least as Kirsten Wright was concerned, other than to take over full-time.

Daniel would have been rendered a nervous wreck had he and Stella not remained intimately connected by phone. Daniel said as much, almost every day, and she had to accept his need as real. He moved into a furnished apartment near CityWalk, worked out in the hotel gym, swam in the hotel pool, and called her three times a day. Sometimes four.

Chloe moved into Lisa's guesthouse and endured the woman's mercurial moods. She was talking to her parents almost daily, which everyone considered the best part of a good resolution.

Midway through that first week, Stella moved into Daniel's home. He asked, and she replied, "Of course."

Daniel did not want to force Nicole to move again, and she was too young to remain on her own. Amber treated it as the start to a perfect summer, spending her weekdays with a part-time dog and sister.

A nuclear heat gripped the entire region. It was normal for the wretched Southern California summer to reach the central coast, at least for a day or so. But three weeks of unrelenting high temperatures ensued. Tempers frayed, and even locals who relied on tourists for their livelihood remained perpetually on edge. At least once each week, the region was lashed by out-of-season storms. Great thundering beasts marched off the Pacific and hammered the region with torrential rain. But the next day the winds would turn back and come from the southeast, bringing heat and humidity both. Stella thought she was the only person in Miramar who remained unscathed.

Sol refused to be rushed. He either phoned or met personally with Stella twice each week. There were new developments to discuss, meetings in chambers with the judge, documents to be signed and notarized. Each glimpse into the grinding process of legal gear shifting gave her fresh nightmares.

Daniel's weekends were given over to the documentary. It was a real project now, with a budget and personnel and a tentative airdate. Miramar's mayor had turned state's evidence. She resigned from office and was taken into protective custody, and her son was moved to a different prison and held under an assumed name. The missing accountant, identified as one Amelia Zhao, was the subject of a nationwide manhunt. Carl Dellacourt discovered he enjoyed growling for the cameras.

The documentary's working title was "Stella's Story," which Amber considered the coolest thing ever. NBC granted a verbal okay to air the project nationally. The FBI white-collar crime division was involved now, both in hunting down the missing accountant and in searching for the invisible ringleaders. They asked, then threatened, and finally begged NBC to postpone airing the story. Kirsten Wright repeatedly said the matter would be open for discussion only after Stella was cleared of all charges. Which meant the feds now pressured Perry Sanchez, which he hated worse than losing a case.

Kirsten Wright, NBC's head of West Coast news, was not blind. She could see the toll this dual role was taking on Daniel. Finally, at the end of week four, a young up-and-comer from the New York station arrived, and Daniel was allowed to step back from three of his weekly airtimes.

That Friday, Daniel called Stella from the

pickup just as she pulled out of his driveway. Daniel told her, "When we're done with your story, maybe they'll let me do a piece on how tired one guy can get."

Despite the sandpaper-rough edge to his voice, she loved hearing him over the car's speakers. "Where are you?"

"I'm trapped on the 101 parking lot just south of Santa Barbara. I should be home sometime next week."

"You should have stayed over."

"Not a chance. I miss my girls."

There was no reason why those words should cause her to smile. "Nicole and Goldie will be very happy to see you."

"You know exactly who I mean."

"Yes." She was talking around a grin as big as her face allowed. "I know."

The silence was comfortable now, warming.

Someone beeped behind her, and Stella realized the light had turned green. Daniel asked, "Where are you now?"

"Driving my hungry girl home."

Amber said, "Hi, Daniel. Mommy made a mess in your kitchen."

"You weren't supposed to tell him."

Which only made Amber shout, "Mommy made pea soup, you know, like the place in Solvang. It exploded. She even got green goop on the ceiling."

"That's not true."

"Mommy had to ask Ricki to come over with a ladder!"

"All Daniel needs to hear is that he has a lovely dinner waiting for him when he gets home."

Daniel replied, "The next noise you hear is my stomach growling."

Stella pulled into the driveway and just sat there, sharing this moment with her daughter. Daniel went on, "We've started moving again. Maybe I'll make it home by midnight. Which brings us to the subject of tomorrow."

"What about it?"

"I was wondering if I might interest you ladies in another hike to—"

Amber sang the words, "Tranquility Falls!"

"The flowers will probably be gone," Daniel said. "They're mostly desert blooms and won't last this long. Especially with the heat wave. But with the rains—"

"Please, Mommy, pleeese!"

Stella loved how her daughter bounced on her seat. The light in Amber's gaze was strong enough to fill her own heart. "I don't know. We had plans tomorrow, didn't we, darling?"

"No, we didn't!" Her voice a melody now. "Tell him *yes!*"

"Maybe we should wait for next week, see if the weather grows a little cooler. It's too hot for us to walk all that way—"

Amber looked ready to explode. Then she heard Daniel's chuckle and accused Stella, "You're teasing me!"

"No, darling, I was just worried you might be too hot—"

"I hate it when you tease!"

Daniel said, "What do you think, Amber. Should we make her stay in her room?"

"And stand in the corner!"

"Not all day."

"Yes! She blew up your kitchen, and now she's teasing me!"

They were all laughing now. Daniel said, "Okay, I'm almost back up to cruising speed. I'll pick you folks up at six."

Amber came bounding into Stella's bedroom just after five. "It's time, Mommy! You have to get up!"

Daylight's gray smudge disappeared when Amber switched on the ceiling lights. "Turn that off."

Amber started flicking the lights. On off, on off.

"Girl, I am warning you."

"You teased me, now I'm teasing you back!"

Stella pulled the pillow over her head. "Go turn on the coffee, and come back in an hour."

On off. On off. Amber raced over, stole the pillow, and went back to playing with the switch.

"I'm going to leave you in the closet."

Amber danced down the hall. "I'm making lunch!"

They left Miramar with the dawn. Stella insisted on driving Daniel's pickup. He looked exhausted, and she wanted him to have this chance to relax, set down his burdens, and let others do for him.

Other than occasional directions on where she needed to turn, they made the drive in silence. Amber and Nicole occupied the rear seat. Goldie panted softly between them, shifting her head toward whoever stroked her pelt. The girls showed no more interest in speaking than the adults up front. Four people and perhaps even this remarkable dog, united by the unspoken fact that they were all in the midst of massive change.

Daniel's growing love was introducing Stella to a new level of fear. She had so many broken pieces. So many half-healed wounds. So many fragments to render herself unlovable.

And yet the more Daniel came to know her, the stronger grew his love.

Unbelievable.

Stella pulled into the empty lot and cut the motor. The day was cool, with the sun barely above the horizon, but it would soon become stifling. They moved together, accepting packs containing drinks and food and two blankets. Stella applied sunscreen to the two girls' faces and arms, then herself, and finally Daniel. It felt so nice, tracing her fingers over his features, feeling the strain and tension ease somewhat under her touch. Nicole attached Goldie to the leash, and they set off. They moved in easy tandem, walking in silence, the loudest sound from doves nesting in the Coulter pines and the jangle of Goldie's leash. Easy and comfortable. Like they did this all the time.

Like a family.

The girls moved on ahead, with Goldie taking an impatient lead. As she walked hand in hand with Daniel, it occurred to Stella that she had entered a thin place. One where the distance between earth and some different realm, a haven with the strength to heal even her, was reduced to almost nothing. She walked a golden path toward a place she could not name, where the messiness of her life, the burdens she carried, could finally be set aside. Making room for something she could not even name.

When they reached the bowl, the flowers were almost all gone. But the waterfall still sang its welcome, the lake still shimmered, the grass rustled a breezy hello. She and Daniel stood holding hands and watched the girls dance with Goldie. Then the four of them walked around the ledge and gathered beneath the waterfall's chilly curtain. Daniel laughed with them but otherwise remained quiet. Stella did not mind. If any man on earth deserved the right to ponder in silence, it was him.

They spread their blankets on the sand bordering the pool and ate an early lunch. Afterward, as the girls started to return for another dance beneath the falls, Daniel asked if he might have a word.

"You need to understand," he told them. "I'm not making a declaration here. I'm asking you for advice. I want to know how you feel. Nothing more."

For an endless moment, all they heard was the falling water. As though the place itself wanted to be included in this conversation. Finally, Amber asked, "About what?"

"You three have played such a role in my . . ."

When he seemed unable to continue, Stella said, "Becoming who you are. Taking the next step."

"That's just it." He rocked slowly back and forth, nodding with his entire upper body. "Accepting that it *is* a next step. That this is a permanent shift. That I *am* this person."

He breathed in, out, in, then ventured, "I feel like I have become defined by this process."

Nicole said, "You mean, helping us out."

"Again, that is exactly the issue. Do I help you, my loved ones?" He looked from one to the other. "Or do I try to reach further?"

Stella could see where he was going now. "You mean, help more people."

"You're already doing that with the documentary," Nicole pointed out.

Daniel kept nodding, rocking back and forth, his eyes on the blanket in front of him. "I am. Yes."

Stella realized Amber was holding her hand. "You're thinking about doing something more?"

"Only if you agree." He met her gaze, and revealed a new . . . something. Light or strength or love. "You three have become the most important people in my world. Whatever comes next, I need to feel like you are a part of this. That you want it to happen."

Stella felt a shiver course through her as Amber cried, "Want *what* to happen?"

"I feel like the town needs me. When word gets out of what's been happening, a lot of people are going to be angry, hurt, and very afraid."

"Yes," Stella said. "Do it."

"Absolutely," Nicole said. "It's a great idea."

"Do *what?*" Amber looked from one person to the next. "What are you people *talking* about?"

Daniel replied, "I'm thinking of running for mayor."

# Acknowledgments

Many families and professionals shared their experiences only after I promised them anonymity. From the first day I started this research, I have been deeply moved by the willingness of experts and survivors to discuss addiction and treatment and recovery, emphasis on that last word.

So many great strides have been made in turning recovery from a distant hope into a reality shared by millions. Families and relationships and lives are being transformed as a result. That is what I wanted to focus on here: the power of recovery, and the hope of what lies beyond.

This story is dedicated to everyone who taught me so much and granted me new reasons to hope.